P9-BYO-820

Really Truly

ALSO BY HEATHER VOGEL FREDERICK

Absolutely Truly

Yours Truly

The Mother-Daughter Book Club

Much Ado About Anne

Dear Pen Pal

Pies & Prejudice

Home for the Holidays

Wish You Were Eyre

Mother-Daughter Book Camp

Once Upon a Toad

The Voyage of Patience Goodspeed

The Education of Patience Goodspeed

Spy Mice: The Black Paw

Spy Mice: For Your Paws Only

Spy Mice: Goldwhiskers

Hide and Squeak

A Little Women Christmas

Really Truly

A Pumpkin Falls Mystery

HEATHER VOGEL FREDERICK

Simon & Schuster Books for Young Readers
NEW YORK • LONDON • TORONTO • SYDNEY • NEW DELHI

SIMON & SCHUSTER BOOKS FOR YOUNG READERS
An imprint of Simon & Schuster Children's Publishing Division
1230 Avenue of the Americas, New York, New York 10020

Jacket design by Krista Vossen
Interior design by Hilary Zarycky
The text for this book was set in Fournier.
Manufactured in the United States of America
0420 BVG
First Edition
2 4 6 8 10 9 7 5 3 1
Library of Congress Cataloging-in-Publication Data
Names: Frederick, Heather Vogel, author.
Title: Really Truly / Heather Vogel Frederick.
Description: First edition. | New York : Simon & Schuster Books for Young Readers, [2020] | Series: A Pumpkin Falls mystery | Audience: Ages 10 to 14. | Audience: Grades 4-6. | Summary: "Truly Lovejoy is excited for the perfect summer in Pumpkin Falls, New Hampshire: swim practice outside, working at the bookstore, one-on-one time with her mom, and best of all, time with the dreamy R. J. Calhoun who may just like Truly back. But the idyllic falls apart when she's sent off to mermaid academy—sparkly tail and all. Luckily, a mystery is never too far behind the Pumpkin Falls Private Eyes, and this one may just encourage Truly to come out of her shell, in more ways than one"—Provided by publisher.
Identifiers: LCCN 2019041522 (print) | LCCN 2019041523 (eBook) | ISBN 9781534414372 (hardcover) | ISBN 9781534414396 (eBook)
Subjects: CYAC: Mystery and detective stories. | Camps—Fiction. | Swimming—Fiction. | Buried treasure—Fiction. | Community life—New Hampshire—Fiction. | New Hampshire—Fiction.
Classification: LCC PZ7.F87217 Re 2020 (print) | LCC PZ7.F87217 (eBook) | DDC [Fic]—dc23
LC record available at https://lccn.loc.gov/2019041522
LC eBook record available at https://lccn.loc.gov/2019041523

For Naomi

PROLOGUE

There's a mermaid tail hanging in my closet.

And it's all my cousin Mackenzie's fault.

Look, I love anything to do with water—especially swimming. I've been on a swim team since I was five years old, and my father likes to tease that H_2O is my native element. But mermaid lessons? That would never have occurred to me in a million years. Maybe a billion. Mackenzie, though, was all over the idea the minute she spotted the brochure at the library.

I should have known that a place with a name as lame as Sirena's Sea Siren Academy could only spell trouble. Which I've had my fair share of ever since we moved to Pumpkin Falls, New Hampshire, and I accidentally became a middle school private eye. This time, however, I found myself way over my head in the trouble department as I tangled with pirates onstage and off, suffered a very public wardrobe malfunction, and embarked on a near-disastrous spelunking expedition while hunting for long-lost treasure.

(I didn't know what "spelunking" meant either, until it was too late to turn back. It's a good word, well worth looking up.)

But before any of this happened, and before anything remotely resembling a mermaid tail showed up in my closet, I had one major hurdle to face: the annual Gifford Family Reunion.

CHAPTER 1

"Smile like you mean it!" My grandmother clapped her hands, trying to attract the attention of the seven adults who were lined up on the steps of the Pumpkin Falls Public Library, talking and laughing. She turned to the woman behind the tripod beside her. "Aren't they something?"

The tripod, and the camera attached to it, belonged to Janet Foster, ace reporter for the *Pumpkin Falls Patriot-Bugle*. If it were possible for a newspaper as teeny as the *Pumpkin Falls Patriot-Bugle* to actually *have* an ace reporter, that was.

"They certainly are," Janet replied, peering through her camera lens. Janet moonlighted as a professional pet photographer. I had no idea how she was with people pictures, but in a town the size of ours, you took what you could get. And my grandmother had done exactly that, hiring her to take our traditional family reunion photos.

Grandma Gifford beamed. "All my beautiful babies!"

My brother Hatcher let out a snort. Our grandmother slipped her arm around him and squeezed. "Just you wait! Someday you'll have kids of your own, and then you'll understand. Your babies are *always* your babies, no matter how old they are."

I gazed skeptically at the half dozen men and one petite woman who were being photographed. It was hard to imagine any of my big Texas uncles as babies. Or my mother, for that matter. She stood at the end of the lineup like the period at the end of a sentence. Or rather, an exclamation point. Dinah Gifford Lovejoy didn't have much to offer in the height department, but she wasn't lacking in spunk.

"So these are all your kids?" Janet asked, pulling a small notebook and pen from the back pocket of her jeans.

My heart sank as I watched her switch into reporter mode. Janet may have been hired to take our family reunion photos, but she clearly knew a story when she spotted one. Not that we were hard to miss: thirty-seven Giffords in matching T-shirts parading through Pumpkin Falls were a sight to behold, as my grandmother would say.

"You bet your sweet cowboy boots they're my kids!" Grandma G replied, her voice brimming with Texas sugar and sass. "A boy for every day of the week and a girl for Sunday."

I looked at my mother, wondering how she'd survived growing up with six brothers. Six! And I thought two was bad. Hatcher and Danny were a handful, but my mother had had to deal with Uncle Teddy, Uncle Lenny, Uncle Craig, Uncle Rooster (his real name was Richard, but no one ever called him that), Uncle Brent, and Uncle Scott.

Then again, she'd had our grandmother's example. Grandma G was petite like my mother, but she had a voice like a bullhorn and backbone to spare. There was no mistaking who was boss when my grandmother was around. She'd had to be strong to raise seven kids by herself after my grandpa died.

I'd never met my Texas grandfather, but I still felt like I knew him. He was practically a legend in our family—the penniless cowboy from West Texas who'd pulled himself up by his bootstraps, swept our grandmother off her feet, and built a ranch near Austin with his own two hands. Theodore Roosevelt Gifford. My uncle Teddy was named after him.

I didn't have a favorite uncle, not really. I loved them all. But if I *did* have a favorite, it would be my uncle Teddy. He was my cousin and best friend Mackenzie's father, and I knew him almost as well as I knew my own dad. The hardest part about leaving Texas and moving across the country to New Hampshire had been moving away from them. And I knew I wasn't the only one who felt that way. Uncle Teddy and my mother were at the tail end of the Gifford lineup, and the closest of the Gifford siblings in age, barely eleven months apart. The two of them were best friends when they were little, and they were still best friends now that they were grown up.

"How are you enjoying Pumpkin Falls so far?" Janet asked my grandmother, her pen hovering over her notebook.

"Mighty fine!" Grandma G enthused. "You've got yourself a real slice of American pie here."

I could tell by the way Janet was nodding and scribbling that she liked that quote. It was perfect headline material, and I braced myself for the fact that, thanks to my ridiculously quotable grandmother, my family was probably going to end up plastered all over the front page of the *Patriot-Bugle*.

If only we'd kept the reunion in Texas, where it belonged! The Giffords had gotten together every summer since before I could remember, but until now our reunions had always been at the ranch. That's where my mother and her brothers had all grown up, and everyone but us still lived within half a day's drive. This year, though, for the first time, we were breaking with tradition. This year, my mother had invited everyone to spend the Fourth of July with us here in Pumpkin Falls.

The town didn't know what had hit it. Giffords had started arriving yesterday morning, and they'd kept streaming in all day. My father had been put in charge of logistics for our reunions years ago, and he organized the weekends like a military operation. This was right up his alley, seeing as how he was a former lieutenant colonel in the United States Army. Everything ran like clockwork thanks to him, with rotating squads of Giffords in charge of transportation, food shopping, meal setup, cooking, cleanup, and more. This year, Mr. Military had rented a school bus, and he and my brother Danny had taken turns running shuttles to and from Logan Airport in Boston, and would now spend the holiday weekend ferrying all of us around Pumpkin Falls.

This morning, we'd all gone downtown and descended on Lou's Diner for donuts (Dad had called ahead of time to warn them that thirty-seven hungry customers were on their way, to make sure there would be enough). Afterward, we'd given everyone a tour of Lovejoy's Books, our family's bookstore, and then stopped by Mahoney's Antiques for a peek at the big silver pumpkin trophy that would be awarded later this weekend to the winning Fourth of July road race team. Finally, we'd headed to the Pumpkin Falls Library, whose front steps had been selected as the best place in town for our reunion photographs.

As I watched Grandma G looking over the shots that Janet had taken so far, Hatcher spotted the expression on my face and grinned.

"Cheer up, Drooly," he whispered, calling me by my least favorite nickname. My real name, Truly, was odd enough, but Drooly? Please. "It will all be over soon."

I shot him a look. Thirty-six more hours hardly qualified as "soon."

It's not that I didn't love our epic family reunions—I did. They were great, when they were in Texas where they belonged. We were invisible on the ranch, and safe from prying eyes. We could be as goofy and loud as we wanted, without the rest of the world looking on. Here? I glanced around. By my calculations, at this very moment fully half of Pumpkin Falls was gawking at us.

"That should do it for this group," said Janet, after she and my grandmother settled on the winning shot. "How about one with just the grandkids next, and then we'll go for—what is it you call it? The full Gifford?"

My uncles let out a collective Texas whoop. I scowled, not feeling nearly as enthusiastic. Our upstairs hallway was plastered with "the full Giffords"—group portraits that had started when my mom and her brothers were little, gradually swelling in size to include their spouses, and then us kids. Our parents and aunts and uncles had all looked ridiculously young when they were first married, hardly older than Danny and Hatcher, who dubbed the photos Hairstyles Through the Ages. Most of the men had long hair and mustaches back in the day, and a few had even sported mullets. ("Business in the front, party in the back," as Danny liked to say.) Not my dad, of course. Mr. Military's hair was even shorter back then.

The portraits had grown larger each year as more and more cousins and siblings came along. I used to love looking at baby me and toddler me, and all the rest of us as we grew over the years. Now, when he really wanted to needle me, Hatcher called the pictures "the full Truly," for the way they charted my astronomical growth. I'd been a normal-size kid for a long time, but at the beginning of sixth grade I'd started to shoot up like one of the giant sunflowers in Grandma G's garden. At six feet tall, I towered over all of my classmates and most of my immediate family, and I was happy not to be reminded of that fact.

"Hey!" said my cousin Mackenzie, slipping her arm through mine. "There's Cha Cha and Jasmine!"

Cha Cha Abramowitz and Jasmine Sanchez were my closest friends in Pumpkin Falls. They waved at us, grinning hugely. I could tell they were enjoying the Gifford reunion spectacle. Mackenzie and I waved back.

"Ooo, and there's Calhoun!" My cousin stretched up on her tiptoes to see over the crowd. Mackenzie was petite, like my mother and grandmother. Whenever I was with her, I felt like an ostrich standing next to a chickadee.

I could feel my face flush. I'd been studiously ignoring Romeo Calhoun ever since I'd spotted him at the edge of the crowd. I could only imagine what he thought of this sideshow. I slid a glance over to where he stood talking to his sister Juliet. Seriously, those were their names, Romeo and Juliet, thanks to their father, who was a huge fan of "the Bard," as he called Shakespeare.

Calhoun wasn't my boyfriend, but I liked to think that we were more than just friends. Or at least that we'd both like us to be. We weren't officially dating or anything—my father said I was much too young for that. "When you can drive, you can date, and not before," was his motto, and when Lieutenant Colonel Jericho T. Lovejoy laid down the law, us kids said "yes, sir" and fell in line. Calhoun and I hung out a lot, though. I'd taken him bird-watching a few times—my favorite hobby—and we went to the General Store for ice cream and stuff with our group of friends. But unlike Jasmine's brother Scooter, who had ambushed me on my birthday last Spring Break with a big smooch I wasn't looking for, Calhoun hadn't so much as tried to hold my hand. Mackenzie thought he just needed encouragement. I wasn't sure what to think. Despite the fact that I had two brothers, boys were still a mystery to me.

"Kids!" called my grandmother in her bullhorn voice, momentarily silencing the crowd. "Come and get your pictures made!"

As Mackenzie and I headed toward her, Aunt Angie appeared with the stroller containing our youngest cousins. Twins Bella and Blair were just six months old.

"Why don't you girls hold them for the picture?" our aunt suggested, passing a baby each to Mackenzie and me.

Mackenzie was a pro, thanks to all the babysitting she did back in Austin. Babies weren't my thing, though. In fact, they were way up on the list of things I wasn't good at. Blair must have sensed that, because the minute I took her, she started to cry.

"Jiggle her up and down, like this," said Mackenzie, bouncing Bella gently.

I tried to mimic her, but it only made my tiny cousin cry harder.

"I'm right here, peanut!" cooed Aunt Angie, waggling her fingers.

"Give her to me," said my younger sister Lauren, scooping Blair out of my arms. She made googly eyes and silly faces and bounced her expertly on her hip until Blair stopped crying and produced a toothless smile.

Aunt Angie gave my sister an admiring glance. "Don't you have the magic touch!"

Lauren turned pink with pleasure at the compliment. "Babies aren't that different from kittens."

"No, Lauren, you can't have a kitten," my mother said automatically. My sister had been angling for another pet ever since we'd arrived in Pumpkin Falls.

Lauren heaved the deep sigh of the misunderstood, then followed Mackenzie and me onto the steps to join the rest of our cousins.

"Two rows! Tallest in the back, shortest in the front!" ordered Grandma G.

"How about we try something different?" Janet suggested. "Let's put Truly in the middle, and then staircase down from there on either side."

I grimaced. I'd been hoping to hide in the back row. I knew Janet didn't mean anything by it, but Truly-in-the-Middle was my father's nickname for me, since I was the middle kid in our family. And ever since my growth spurt, it was like my family couldn't resist showing me off. My parents had put me smack-dab in the middle of our last Christmas card photo, where I towered over both of them, and over my brothers and sisters, all of us in our matching holiday sweaters my mother had knit for us. Talk about a sight to behold.

Aunt Louise, Mackenzie's mother, sorted us into place with help from Aunt True, who was a Lovejoy, not a Gifford. They went up and down the line, wiping noses and brushing stubborn cowlicks into place in an effort to make us presentable. This was Aunt True's very first Gifford reunion. If she was feeling a little overwhelmed, you'd never know it. My father's sister seemed to take everything in stride, including giving up a life of travel to move back to her old hometown and help run the family bookshop.

"I think that's as good as it gets," said Aunt Louise finally.

My aunts retreated to the sidelines as Grandma G gave Janet a thumbs-up. The camera whirred and clicked.

"Looking good!" said Janet. "How about one more, just in case? Smile, everyone!"

Just as the camera shutter clicked for the final time, my cousin Matt, who was ten and a show-off, made a face. This meant another retake, of course, and there were two more misfires after that, one because my little sister Pippa got distracted by a butterfly and another because Uncle Rooster's two youngest boys started swatting each other. Finally, Janet managed to take a picture that satisfied my grandmother. Which was a good thing, because my cheek muscles were starting to hurt from all the smiling.

"Time for the full Gifford!" Grandma G announced. She gave her lips a fresh swipe of her signature bright red lipstick as the rest of the Texas side of my family crowded forward.

"True, you get in the shot too," my mother said.

"Yes, True, come on up here and join us," said my grandmother. "And bring that long drink of water with you." She winked at Erastus Peckinpaugh, my aunt's gangly boyfriend, who taught history at Lovejoy College. Their romance—which my friends and I helped rekindle last winter—was finally out from under wraps. It was also a subject of keen interest to the residents of Pumpkin Falls, who were placing bets as to when Professor Rusty, as everybody called him, would propose.

"But we're not Giffords!" Aunt True protested.

"Neither am I," said my father, taking his place beside my mother. "But we're all still family."

"Honorary Giffords!" Aunt Louise decreed, and another big Texas whoop went up from my relatives.

Aunt True smiled and shrugged. Grabbing her boyfriend's hand, she squeezed in beside me. Suddenly I didn't feel like such a freak. Aunt True and I were the same height.

"Stand your ground, tall timber," she whispered, giving me an affectionate nudge with her shoulder.

Aunt True liked to refer to the two of us as "tall timber" and often joked that we were born to stand out in a crowd. Maybe someday I'd have her confidence. Right now, I was still getting used to my newly attained height. And my size-ten-and-a-half feet. I took a deep breath, straightened up, and smiled once again at the camera.

"And that's a wrap!" said Janet half a dozen clicks later.

My father stepped forward, thrust two fingers in his mouth, and gave a sharp whistle. "Head 'em up and move 'em out! The bus leaves in two minutes—there's just enough time before dinner for a swim over at Lake Lovejoy. Y'all know what's on the menu tonight: Teddy's famous ribs!"

This announcement brought another chorus of whoops. Uncle Teddy's barbecued ribs were always a highlight of our reunions. I could hardly wait. Pumpkin Falls didn't know the first thing about barbecue. New Englanders called it "having a cookout," and it mostly involved hamburgers and hot dogs, not brisket and ribs.

As I followed my family across the village green toward the waiting school bus, I waved to an elderly woman seated on a bench. She waved back. Thelma Farnsworth and her sister Ethel were married to a pair of brothers. Ethel and her husband Ike Farnsworth ran the General Store; Thelma and Elmer Farnsworth had a small dairy farm at the edge of town. Every summer, the Farnsworth sisters also helped out as cooks at Camp Lovejoy.

"Are you part of a circus?" Thelma asked me, puzzled, as the stream of Giffords in matching T-shirts flowed past her bench.

"We might as well be," I muttered in response.

"Did you hear that, Elmer?" Thelma shouted to her husband, who was bent over a nearby trash bin, sorting through its contents. A bag full of empty soda cans was at his feet. Elmer loved collecting junk. "One man's trash is another man's treasure" was his motto.

"ELMER!" Thelma called again, louder this time. "THE CIRCUS IS IN TOWN!"

Elmer was hard of hearing but refused to wear a hearing aid. The reason I knew this pretty much summed up my life in Pumpkin Falls. There were no secrets in a town the size of ours. Everybody knew everything about everyone else—including the fact that Elmer Farnsworth had a stubborn streak which, combined with his pride, was keeping him from admitting that he didn't hear as well as he used to. This had been a topic of lively discussion recently on the General Store's front porch, where he and his buddies liked to hang out, and where I often overheard their conversations when I was eating ice cream with my friends.

Elmer snapped upright like he'd been poked with a pin. "I LOVE THE CIRCUS!" he bellowed.

I did a mental face-palm and ran for the bus.

I loved my family and I loved our reunions, but I didn't

love being such a public spectacle. Stealth mode was more my speed, my term for flying under the radar. I didn't love people staring at us or the prospect of being front-page news, and I especially didn't love our matching T-shirts—this year's were a blinding shade of neon green with a bright orange pumpkin on the front and THE GIFFORDS GO TO PUMPKIN FALLS! splatted on the back.

I hated to admit it, but as much as I'd been looking forward to our family reunion, I was looking forward to it being over, too. Because then my perfect summer could finally begin.

CHAPTER 2

I hummed to myself as I set out paper plates and napkins on the half dozen picnic tables that stretched end to end across our backyard. My dad had tacked a note to the bulletin board at the General Store last week, asking if anyone had any extra we could borrow, and just like that, trucks had started pulling into our driveway with picnic tables. Small towns had their drawbacks, but there were definitely advantages, too. I'd always thought that Texas was friendly, but Pumpkin Falls could give it a run for its money in the neighborly department any day of the week.

I plunked down another paper plate and thought about the perfect summer that would soon be mine. It shimmered in my mind like a lane in the pool first thing in the morning, before anyone else dove into the water. Smooth as glass, not a single ripple—perfection! Well, except for the fact that Mackenzie wouldn't be here. That definitely counted as a ripple. Still, I was looking forward to long lazy days, with plenty of time for bird-watching and bike rides and hanging out with my friends. Plus swim team. Summer swim team was the best. It was much more relaxed than during the school year, and practices were going to be outside, just like in Texas, since Coach Maynard had wangled special privileges for our team at Lovejoy College's outdoor pool.

Helping out at the bookstore was near the top of my list of things to look forward to as well, which was kind of a surprise. When we'd first arrived in New Hampshire, I'd thought the bookstore was stupid. Well, not exactly stupid—I'd loved visiting it when Gramps and Lola, my Lovejoy grandparents, had been in charge—but to me, the family business represented the whole reason we'd had to move away from our home in Austin, so I'd resented it at first.

That wasn't fair, of course. It wasn't the bookstore's fault that my father had lost his right arm in a bomb explosion in Afghanistan, and that he couldn't be a pilot anymore. But it had taken me a while to understand that.

Lovejoy's Books had been in a sorry mess when we'd first arrived, teetering on the brink of closure. But my dad and Aunt True—with help from all of us, and from Belinda Winchester, the town's resident cat lady, who had unexpectedly stepped forward to invest in the business—had done what had at first seemed impossible. These days, the bookshop's future was looking a lot less rocky.

It still surprised me how much I loved spending time there. Unlike my sister Lauren, who loved books the way I loved water, I wasn't the world's biggest bookworm. But there was more to running a bookstore than just reading, as it turned out. I got to help Aunt True come up with creative displays for the windows, which I was surprisingly good at. I got to use the cash register and help set up for events, and I was Aunt True's assistant for Story Hour on Saturday mornings. And now that we'd added Cup and Chaucer, the mini café that was my aunt's latest marketing scheme, I also got to run the espresso machine and make hot beverages for our customers, which was fun.

And then there was the cherry on top of my summer sundae: Romeo Calhoun.

Calhoun loomed large in my plans for a perfect summer. Right after school had finished, he'd casually asked if maybe I'd like to go to the Lovejoy College Summer Film Festival with him. I'd tried to sound equally casual when I said yes, but inside I was jumping up and down. A whole week of movies! With Calhoun! I didn't care that his father was the one who'd suggested it, or who'd arranged free tickets for us, or that Calhoun had invited all the rest of our friends along too.

This year's film festival was featuring movies from the 1950s. Aunt True had pounced on the brochure when I showed it to her.

"Wait until you see *Rear Window*," she'd said with a

happy sigh, scanning the list of movie titles. "Grace Kelly is SO gorgeous! And so is Audrey Hepburn—you'll love her in *Sabrina*. And you'll love *Singin' in the Rain*, and *Born Yesterday*, and *Ben Hur*, and *Father of the Bride*!" She looked up at me and smiled. "What a fantastic series! I think I'll get tickets for Rusty and me too."

I wasn't sure what to say to that. Double-dating with my aunt and Professor Rusty did not exactly fit into my perfect summer plans.

"Truly!" My mother's voice snapped me out of my daydream.

"Yes?"

"Can you feed Bilbo?"

"Lauren's home for the weekend—that's her job!"

"I know, but she's busy. Rooster's organized a scavenger hunt for the younger kids."

"Can't Hatcher do it?" As usual, my brother had gone AWOL—military shorthand for "absent without leave."

"He's helping your father show Aunt Lily and Uncle Scott the Underground Railroad hiding spot," my mother replied.

Of course he was. My brother always managed to find something more interesting to do than chores. "Fine," I grumbled.

"Excuse me?"

"Fine, ma'am." My parents were sticklers for politeness. And in a military family, that meant plenty of sirs and ma'ams.

This past Spring Break, the Pumpkin Falls Private Eyes—that was what my friends and I called ourselves—had solved another mystery in town. Two, actually. One involved maple syrup rustlers, or at least what we'd thought were rustlers, and the other involved the Underground Railroad. It turned out that one of my ancestors had been involved with helping runaway slaves. She'd hidden them right here in Gramps and Lola's house. We'd discovered the secret compartment under the front stairs that had concealed the runaways and the escape tunnel that led through the cellar and under the back lawn to the cemetery. After the tunnel caved in, my parents had decided it was too dangerous to preserve, despite its historical value. Professor Rusty had begged my father not to seal it.

"It would be an irreparable loss!" he'd protested, but my father hadn't budged. My aunt's boyfriend still hadn't quite forgiven him, although he was somewhat mollified by the fact that the secret compartment under the stairs was left intact.

I pulled my cell phone from my pocket and checked the time. I was going to have to hustle to make it over to the Mitchells' and back before dinner.

The Mitchells were our neighbors. They were away for a few weeks and had offered us the use of their house for the reunion. It had six bedrooms, just like Gramps and Lola's house, and half the adults were staying there. Most of my cousins were sleeping outside in tents. Only Mackenzie and I opted to stay indoors.

"Smart girls," Grandma G had said when she'd heard this. "I like my creature comforts too."

I double-timed it around the picnic tables, slapping down the rest of the paper plates and anchoring them with silverware, then setting out rolls of paper towels. Uncle Teddy's blackberry jalapeño ribs were famously messy. The aroma wafting over from the grill was making my mouth water. Uncle Teddy was the undisputed king of barbecue in our family. "Low and slow" was his motto when it came to smoking meat, and he knew exactly how much heat to put in his signature sauce: enough so your lips tingled a little, but not so much that it made your nose run. That didn't stop half my family from adding extra hot sauce. I smiled, thinking about the surprise that would be waiting for them at dinner.

One thing about our family reunions—the food was always fantastic. Everyone contributed their favorites, from Uncle Rooster's signature lasagna to Aunt Sally's famous banana French toast to Uncle Teddy's ribs and more. On the final night, we always "splashed out," as my mother called it, and chipped in to have dinner catered. And being Texans, and being Giffords, there was no such thing as too much barbecue, so we always had the catering for that meal done by the Salt Lick, a family favorite near Austin.

This time around, though, we were in Pumpkin Falls, not Texas, and my parents had opted to host a clambake for our final meal. Not that we were anywhere near the ocean—you pretty much couldn't get any more landlocked than the Pumpkin River Valley—but clambakes were a New England tradition, and my mother was determined to send everybody home having had what she called "a genuine taste of Yankee food." And this year that meant a house call from Lobster Bob, instead of the catering team from the Salt Lick. But the clambake wasn't until tomorrow night. Tonight, there was barbecue!

I sniffed the air again greedily, then loped off across the lawn toward the neighbors' house. Lauren was the animal-lover in our family, and she was usually the one who looked after the Mitchells' pet ferret. This summer, though, my younger sisters were both away at camp, so most of the time I was the one who ended up stuck with cleaning Bilbo's litter box and giving him his meals.

Another part of my perfect summer was the fact that, with Lauren and Pippa at Camp Lovejoy, and with my brothers shortly heading off to a weeklong wresting clinic at Boston University, I would have my parents' undivided attention.

As the middle kid, it was easy to be overlooked. But this summer, for a whole week, I wouldn't be Truly-in-the-Middle, I'd be Truly-the-Only-Child! My mother had already promised to fix my favorite foods and take me to West Hartfield shopping for a new swimsuit and treat us to pedicures. She'd even mentioned driving down to Boston for the day, just the two of us. I was looking forward to being pampered and spoiled a bit. It was going to be perfect.

"Hey, Bilbo!" I called, opening the Mitchells' back door. I heard scrabbling from across the kitchen. The ferret was waiting by the door of his cage, pacing back and forth and looking at me with his bright little eyes. I wasn't wild about any animals except birds, but even I had to admit Bilbo was pretty cute. We'd almost become friends.

After I'd fed him, given him a little playtime, and made sure he was settled for the night, I headed back outside. There was no fence between my grandparents' backyard and the Mitchells', so my father had commandeered the entire expanse of twin lawns for our reunion. The picnic tables were on our side, closest to the kitchen. The fire pit and lawn chairs were just beyond, also on our side. The tents and hammocks were spread out pretty evenly across both backyards, and the far side of the Mitchells' back lawn had been arranged with separate zones for badminton, croquet, and horseshoes.

"Organized mayhem" my dad called it. He was more cheerful this weekend than I'd seen him in months. There was nothing Lieutenant Colonel Jericho T. Lovejoy liked better than bossing people around, and the reunion had given him a real boost in that department.

Just then our back door banged open, and Hatcher finally appeared. "Need any help?"

I shot him a look. "Not anymore."

He shrugged and sauntered off. I glared at his back. I'd hardly seen Hatcher all weekend. He'd vanished into the herd of older male cousins, all of whom were sharing one of the huge tents that Hatcher and Danny had set up at the far end of our lawn. It shouldn't have been that big of a deal, Hatcher spending time with his favorite cousins. I was spending time with mine, after all. But I hadn't seen a whole lot of Hatcher since summer started—and for months before that, now that I thought about it. He'd been involved with the Pumpkin Falls Private Eyes, at least for a little while over Spring Break. But other than that, he always seemed busy with wrestling and his school friends. It wasn't like it used to be. Back in Texas, Hatcher and I had always been a team—the two of us against the world. Now things were changing. I'd seen them change before, after my brother Danny started high school. He'd gotten his driver's license and a girlfriend and a part-time job, and after that he was hardly around anymore. This fall, Hatcher would be starting high school too. Would the same thing happen to him?

Does anything ever stay the same? I wondered. My gaze wandered over toward my dad. That question was easily answered. Things could and did change in the blink of an eye.

I watched as he picked up a spatula with the Terminator and started showing off for some of my uncles. The Terminator was what we called my father's fancy prosthetic arm, the one made of black titanium. He'd gotten it this past winter, after our move to Pumpkin Falls, so none of my relatives had seen it in action before. Some of the littler cousins had been afraid of it at first, just like Pippa had been, but fascination eventually won out over fear.

"Having a bunch of brothers-in-law around is good for him," said Aunt True, coming up behind me.

I turned around. "Huh?"

She nodded toward the grill. "Your father. It's good for him. All that male-bonding stuff."

She was probably right—my aunt usually was. My father did seem like he was in his element this weekend. Besides the whole I-get-to-organize-everything-and-boss-everyone-around thing, he adored my uncles, and they adored him. The seven of them had always had fun together. My father had even agreed to an arm-wrestling competition, for old times' sake. The tale of how my uncles had made my dad arm-wrestle every single one of them before they'd allow him to date their little sister—now my mother—was part of Gifford family lore.

After his injury had forced him to become a lefty, though, my father wasn't as invincible as he used to be. Last night, Uncle Lenny had finally managed to beat him—something he'd been waiting years to do.

"Time for Rooster Rover!" hollered Uncle Rooster, popping through the back door like a jack-in-the-box. The scavenger hunt was over, apparently.

A herd of younger cousins spilled out of the house behind him, squealing with excitement. I smiled. I used to squeal like that too.

Uncle Rooster had made up the game years ago. It was just like red rover, except instead of chanting "Red rover, red rover, let so-and-so come over," he'd changed it to "Red Rooster, red Rooster." And before a player could run toward the opposing team to try to break through the line of linked arms, he or she had to crow like a rooster. Of course the little kids thought this was hilarious, and everyone tried to outdo everyone else. By the end, it wasn't much of a competition, just a bunch of kids collapsed in a pile of giggles.

I watched my uncle as he led the group to the far side of the lawn. His nickname suited him perfectly. Uncle Rooster was, well, like a rooster. Big, colorful, and loud. A bit of a show-off, he definitely liked to strut. And right now, he was strutting his stuff at the head of a line of little kids who would come to dinner worn out, hungry, and happy.

I did a final sweep of the picnic tables to make sure everything was ready, then headed to where I'd stashed tonight's surprise.

"Three at every table," my mother whispered from the kitchen window, startling me so much that I almost dropped the box I'd fished out from under the back steps.

"Yes, ma'am," I whispered back.

Acting as casual as I could, I distributed the bottles on the tables. No one paid me the slightest bit of attention except Hatcher, who suddenly materialized again.

"They turned out awesome!" he gloated, picking up one of the bottles. "You're a genius, Drooly!"

"Thanks," I said, and smiled at him. It was hard to stay mad at someone who was paying you a compliment, even when he called you by your least favorite nickname.

I stood there for a moment, admiring my handiwork. I'd worked hard on the design, with a little help from Aunt True. The bottles were tall and thin, with bright red stoppers and a shiny silver label. On the label was a flexed arm that looked identical to the black titanium one my father was currently wearing. In its fist was a flag with a skull and crossbones on it, along with two words in fiery red: THE TERMINATOR.

"Ribs are ready!" Uncle Teddy called just then.

It was the announcement we'd all been waiting for. Giffords swarmed from every direction. Mackenzie and her mother and a long line of aunts and uncles appeared from the kitchen, carrying platters and bowls piled high with corn bread, coleslaw, and Grandma G's baked beans, which were almost as famous as Uncle Teddy's ribs. Everyone raced for the buffet table, where we piled food on our plates like we hadn't eaten in weeks.

"What have we here?" cried Uncle Rooster as he took a seat and spotted the Terminator bottle nearest him.

"A little something to spice up your sad, bland life, Rooster," my father teased.

"It's homemade hot sauce!" blurted my sister Lauren, unable to contain her excitement any longer. "Dad made it, and everybody gets to take a bottle home, like a party favor!"

"Is that so?" My uncle reached for the bottle nearest his seat. "'The Terminator,'" he read aloud. "I like it already."

"Fair warning," my father told him. "It packs a punch. You might want to try just a drop or two to start with."

A collective "oooh" went up around the long tables as Uncle Rooster grinned at him, then picked up a rib and defiantly shook three drops onto it.

Beside me, Mackenzie shook her head. "What is it with our uncles and hot sauce?"

"Beats me."

Our family's naturally competitive nature meant that our barbecues always ended up with a bunch of us—my uncles, mostly—trying to outdo each other in the hot sauce department, like the little kids with their Red Rooster crows. I was as competitive as the next person, maybe even more so, but I wasn't stupid enough to go to the mat over something like hot sauce. My stomach needed its lining.

We all watched as Uncle Rooster took a bite. "Hmmm," he said, shaking his head. "Sorry, Jericho, I'm not feeling it."

"You will," my father replied calmly.

After the second bite, Uncle Rooster leaped up and bolted for the house.

"If you can't stand the heat, stay out of the kitchen!" my dad yelled after him, and everyone shouted with laughter.

"Rooster never could hold his hot sauce," said Grandma G.

"Rusty, you stay away from that stuff!" Aunt True called

down the table to where her boyfriend was seated with my uncles. "You'll get blisters!"

"It'll just warm him up for you, True!" Uncle Teddy called back, making loud kissing noises. "Isn't that right, Professor Hot Lips?"

Aunt True's boyfriend blushed furiously. He still wasn't used to being teased. My dad said it was because Professor Rusty was an only child. I was pretty sure he was enjoying the attention, though. There was a hint of a smile behind the blush.

The back door banged open, and Uncle Rooster reappeared. He'd gotten ahold of Grandma G's lipstick and painted his lips bright red. We gaped at him, and then everyone started to laugh again.

Uncle Rooster gave my father a crisp salute. "I admit defeat. Duly *terminated*, sir!"

One thing you could say for Uncle Rooster, he wasn't a sore loser.

"I don't think I can eat another bite," said Mackenzie after a while. Then she grinned and reached toward the almost empty platter of ribs. "Well, maybe just *one* more bite."

I grinned back, licking the barbecue sauce off my fingers with a sigh of contentment. I'd really missed Uncle Teddy's barbecue.

"Who wants ice cream?" Aunt Louise called from the back steps.

"You've got to be kidding!" protested Uncle Rooster, clutching his stomach.

"Spoken like a man who's just eaten his weight in ribs," teased Aunt Sally.

"Nonsense!" Aunt True retorted, pushing back from the table. "There's always room for ice cream."

"True speaks truth," quipped Aunt Meg as she and Uncle Lenny got up too. Mackenzie looked at me and shrugged, and the two of us followed them.

"Mint chip, please," I told Aunt Louise when it was my turn. "Just one scoop."

"Two for me," said Mackenzie. "Chocolate and strawberry."

"Now there's a true Gifford," said Grandma G approvingly.

I looked at Mackenzie. Five feet nothing and about the size of my little finger, my cousin could really put it away. She smirked at me. "C'mon! After all that swimming we did this afternoon? I earned it."

The two of us took our cones over to the hammock, where we swung back and forth in contented silence.

"I am so full!" Mackenzie groaned a little while later.

"I wonder why, Ms. I'll Have Two Scoops?"

"It was worth it!"

We swung some more. Light streamed through the open window over the sink in the kitchen. I listened to the clatter of pots and pans as Aunt Rose and Uncle Craig did the washing up, and to the soft strumming of Uncle Brent's guitar over by the firepit, where conversation among the grown-ups was punctuated frequently by loud bursts of laughter. The clink of horseshoes and shrieks and giggles from my sisters and younger cousins playing hide-and-seek drifted over from the Mitchells' yard. Closing my eyes, I could almost imagine that we were back on the ranch.

Listening to my family reminded me of listening to birds. The twittering of sparrows would be the younger cousins; the piercing cries of jays the older ones; and the laughter from the adults was like the raucous cawing of crows. What was it that they called a flock of crows? Gramps and Lola had sent me a book on owls for my birthday, and it had a whole list of terms dating back to the Middle Ages for groups of different bird species. *A parliament of owls*—that one I remembered, of course. Owls were my favorite birds. *An exaltation of larks*, which Aunt True said was pure poetry. Ditto for *a charm of finches.* I couldn't remember the term for a flock of sparrows, but I did remember the one for blue jays—*a scold of jays.* That was spot on. The term for a flock of crows had been an odd one, I recalled, casting about in my memory for it. Oh right—*a murder of crows*!

I wrinkled my nose. That was awful. Not the right term for my family at all.

Seagulls, maybe? *A squabble of seagulls.* Better. No, wait—geese! *A gaggle of Giffords.* Perfect!

Swaying lazily in the hammock, I watched my cousins and aunts and uncles, my brothers and sisters and parents. What would those people in the Middle Ages have thought of my family? I wondered.

"What are you snickering at?" asked Mackenzie, giving me a sidelong glance.

"Nothing."

She sighed deeply. "I wish we had more time together! I can't believe we only have one more day left."

"I know."

She sat bolt upright, sending the hammock swaying wildly. "Hey, what if you flew back with me to Austin?"

"What?" I frowned. I loved Mackenzie and would miss her, but Texas was not part of my perfect summer plans.

"I'm sure Coach would be happy to have you back on the Nitros' summer swim team. And we could hang out with all our friends and go to the mall and camping and play with Frankie!" Frankie was Mackenzie's new kitten. She'd taken him home with her when she'd visited in March, courtesy of Belinda Winchester.

I hesitated. My perfect summer dangled in the air between us, glimmering like an ornament on a Christmas tree. "What if you stayed here instead?"

She shook her head. "Can't. My parents have a big family vacation planned to Yellowstone. You could come with us." She looked over at me. "Plus, I've already been to Pumpkin

Falls twice now since you moved here, and you haven't been back to Austin even once. C'mon, Truly—everything will be just like it was before!"

That isn't true, I thought, as she continued to chatter on about all the stuff we could do together. Nothing was going to be like it was before. Not my father, whose arm would still be missing, and not my family, who was still getting used to the unexpected left turn in our lives that had brought us here to Pumpkin Falls.

"So, what do you think?" prodded Mackenzie. "Are you in?"

"I have stuff planned," I told her. "I can't."

She took my hand and gave it a squeeze. "I wish you still lived down the street, Truly. I really miss you. I miss *us*."

I knew exactly what she meant. We'd hit a rough patch over Spring Break, but she was still my best friend in the whole world. Life just wasn't the same without her around. Pumpkin Falls wasn't as awful a place as I'd thought it was when we first moved here, but still, Mackenzie wasn't here.

"I know," I replied, squeezing back. "I miss us too."

CHAPTER 3

"It's going to be a scorcher!" my father announced as I yawned my way into the kitchen the next morning. Mackenzie and I had stayed up way too late talking.

My mother stretched up on her tiptoes and planted a kiss on my cheek. "Happy Fourth of July!" She handed me an apron, and I blinked at it sleepily. "Squad Lovejoy is in charge of breakfast, remember?"

"Where's Hatcher?" I said automatically. My brother was AWOL again, as usual.

My father cupped his hand behind his ear. "What was that? I believe the correct answer is 'yes, ma'am.'"

I sighed. "Yes, sir. I mean, yes, ma'am."

"Looks like your aunt could use some help," my mother said as I draped the apron over my head. I turned around so that she could tie it for me, then shuffled over to the stove, where Aunt True passed me a large spoon.

"Blueberry donut muffins," she said as I joined her in scooping batter into the waiting muffin tins. "My new recipe. You'll have to tell me what you think—I'm considering making a mini version as our signature treat at the bookshop this summer."

My aunt was in charge of marketing for Lovejoy's Books, and she was big on signature treats. She said people came for the treats and stayed to shop, and so far, she'd been right.

A few minutes later, Uncle Teddy and Aunt Louise wandered in, sniffing the air appreciatively. The kitchen smelled of sausage and coffee and muffins.

"Morning, everyone!" said my uncle. "Tables are all set up and ready to go outside, J. T. Anything we can do to help in here?"

"Nope," my dad replied. "Breakfast is still a few minutes out. Grab a cup of coffee and take a load off."

"That's an invitation we won't refuse," said Aunt Louise. She took two of the mugs stacked by the giant carafe that my mother had borrowed from church and poured coffee for my uncle and herself.

Uncle Teddy waggled his eyebrows at me. "Great day for a road race!"

I made a face. Running was so not my thing, and Uncle Teddy knew it. I'd much rather be in the water, especially on a day that was expected to be a "scorcher."

"Do we have to go?" I asked my father. "Can't we just

spend the day at Lake Lovejoy instead?" My voice sounded whiny even to my ears, but I couldn't help it. The prospect of trotting all over Pumpkin Falls in the blazing sun was not appealing.

"Too late! We're Team Lovejoy's Books, remember? I signed us up weeks ago."

Four on the Fourth—a 4K road race on the Fourth of July—was a big tradition in my new hometown. Nobody loved a holiday like Pumpkin Falls did, and nobody had more holiday traditions. Some were normal enough—twinkle lights on Main Street at Christmas, for instance—others, like the annual Halloween Pumpkin Toss, which dated back to before the Revolutionary War, were not. Our Fourth of July race was the oldest of its kind in New England and drew huge crowds of runners. Just about everyone in town got involved one way or another. Most of the local businesses sponsored a team of runners, and whoever's team won got to display the trophy (the big silver pumpkin we'd taken our relatives to see at Mahoney's Antiques) until the following Fourth of July. The winner also got the money raised by the race's entry fees. Well, *they* didn't, but their project of choice did.

Each spring at the town meeting, two finalists were chosen from a list of proposed Pumpkin Falls beautification projects, and those became the projects that the Four on the Fourth teams competed to fund. I knew this because my brothers and sisters and I had been forced to attend the meeting.

"This is democracy in action, kids!" our mother had told us on our way to the town hall that night. She'd gone back to college after our move to Pumpkin Falls, intending to become an English teacher. The American History for Educators class she'd taken with Professor Rusty had her bubbling over with patriotic spirit. "There's nothing more American than a town meeting. Consider it part of your civic education."

I'd heard Gramps and Lola talk about town meetings before, but they hadn't sounded very interesting. And mostly they weren't, if you asked me, which nobody ever did. There were a bunch of boring reports on stuff like budgets and tax revenues, and discussions about things like sewage treatment (eew!), graffiti, and the pros and cons of licensing a food truck. One of the top agenda items at the meeting we attended was a proposal to install parking meters on Main Street, which sparked a surprisingly lively debate. Surprising because seriously, who got worked up about parking meters? Pumpkin Falls, that's who.

Ella Bellow, who used to be the postmistress until she retired last January, had been elected town moderator and ran the meetings. Ella loved being in charge of things even more than my dad did. She had more energy than should have been legal for somebody her age. Giving up her job as postmistress seemed to have given her a new lease on life, too. Instead of retiring to Florida, as everyone in town had thought was her plan, she'd stayed put, opened a knitting shop, and become involved in town politics. She was busier and bossier than ever.

"As always, only two worthy causes will be chosen from this year's proposed list of beautification projects," Ella had announced that night. "Of course, I can't pretend to be impartial about one of the projects," she added coyly, flinging the fringe of her sparkly blue knitted shawl over her shoulder. Ella used to dress mostly in black, but she'd been wearing brighter colors since opening A Stitch in Time. My father had dubbed her new shop "A Snitch in Time," thanks to Ella's favorite sport, which was gossip. "It's a scandal, the shape that the Pumpkin Falls Grange is in!"

I nudged Hatcher. "What's a grange?"

"You know, that old building on the edge of town where they put on plays and stuff."

"My father was a founding member of the Pumpkin Players," Ella continued, "and he'd be as shocked and saddened as I am if he saw what poor stewards we have been of that historic building. Back in its heyday it was one of the crown jewels of this town. I should know; I practically grew up within its hallowed halls!"

"During the Jurassic era?" whispered Hatcher, which made me giggle and earned us a stern glance from my father.

After Ella finished trying to convince everyone to vote for her pet project, Mr. Henry, the children's librarian at the Pumpkin Falls Library, leaped to his feet.

"The Pumpkin Falls Grange is a worthy cause, of course," he said. "The arts are vital to the health of a community, as are its open spaces"—he tipped his red baseball cap at Reverend Quinn, who was slated to speak next on a project with the überthrilling title "Revitalizing our Village Green"—"but what could be more important to the future of Pumpkin Falls than its children? And providing them with an attractive, modern space in our library, which is undeniably one of the gems of our community, is an investment in that future. Let's use this year's earnings to revitalize the children's room!"

Ella Bellow tried and failed spectacularly to keep a neutral face. I could tell she was itching to snatch the microphone back from Mr. Henry.

"May I remind you all," she snapped, finally doing just that, "that the Pumpkin Falls Grange is even older than the library—"

"Jurassic Ella," Hatcher whispered again, more quietly this time, so as not to attract my father's attention.

"—and therefore more historic."

"Your point is interesting," Mr. Henry conceded, deftly plucking the microphone away from her again. "However, age alone does not equate with value." The two of them continued in ping-pong fashion until Scooter Sanchez's father, who was assistant moderator, had to step in and ask them to wind things up so that other people could speak about their proposed projects.

The meeting ran late. Pippa fell asleep on the floor. My sister Lauren read not just one but two books, and my mother finished knitting an entire sock. Unlike my brothers who at least had their cell phones to distract them, I'd left mine at home and was stuck having to listen to Reverend Quinn try to whip up some enthusiasm for repainting the benches and bandstand on the village green, and then some guy I didn't know drone on about replacing the rusted rivets in the covered bridge, which he claimed were an eyesore and possibly an actual hazard. Ethel Farnsworth got excited during that discussion and leaped to her feet, recommending that the town expand on the project and install hanging flower baskets on the bridge as well, but she was quickly shushed by Ella.

When the vote was finally taken, Ella and Mr. Henry emerged triumphant. The children's room at the library and the Pumpkin Falls Grange would vie for this year's Pumpkin Falls Beautification Project. The outcome of the Four on the Fourth race would determine the winner.

Not surprisingly, Team Lovejoy's Books chose to support Mr. Henry and Team Library. Ditto for Team Starlite Dance Studio and Team Kwik Klips, our town's hair salon. Ella pledged Team A Stitch in Time to the Grange restoration, of course, and her friends fell in line behind her: the Farnsworths and Team General Store, the Mahoneys and Team Mahoney's Antiques, and Reverend Quinn and Team Speedy Geezers, which was made up of some of the older gentlemen from the men's choir at First Parish Church.

The screen door leading out to the backyard slammed shut, startling me. I looked up to see Uncle Brent come in. "When's chow?" he asked. "The troops are getting restless."

My father handed him a platter of scrambled eggs. "Perfect timing. We're ready to go. How about you ladies?"

"Enough muffins to get started," said Aunt True, putting the last tray into the oven and setting the timer.

"Look alive, then, Truly-in-the-Middle, and hustle outside with what you've got."

I opened my mouth to complain again about my brothers not pulling their weight when Hatcher sauntered in. He grabbed a tray loaded with yogurt containers and fruit and gave me a sly grin. "Yeah, Drooly, what are you standing there for?"

"Hatcher," warned my mother.

"Sorry," he said to me, as I stalked past him out the back door.

"BREAKFAST!" my brother Danny hollered from the back steps, which apparently was his contribution to our family's assigned task. In a flash, just like every other meal all weekend, hungry Giffords descended from every direction.

Mackenzie was the last one to appear. "Sorry I didn't get up in time to help," she told her father, rubbing her eyes sleepily. "I forgot it was our turn to set up."

Uncle Teddy gave her a hug. "No big deal, petunia. We thought we'd let you sleep in."

I watched them, wishing my father could be more chill like Uncle Teddy. "Sleeping in" wasn't part of Lieutenant Colonel Jericho T. Lovejoy's vocabulary.

Hatcher came up behind me and gave me a companionable hip bump.

"What do you want?" I snapped. I hated it when he insulted me and then tried to act like nothing was wrong.

He took a bite of the muffin he was holding. "These are great."

"Thanks," I muttered.

He gave me a blueberry-stained grin. I scowled at him, but it was hard to stay mad at Hatcher. His smile was infectious, even when it was smeared with breakfast. Honestly, it could be raining toads, and my brother would still walk around smiling. He'd inherited the happy gene, along with the Gifford sunflower smile, as Grandma G called it. It was identical to the smile my mother almost always wore, as did my sister Pippa and my cousin Mackenzie and a bunch of my other uncles and cousins. Me? I was a Lovejoy through and through, and only smiled when I meant it.

"I can't wait for the race!" Hatcher said.

I grunted. My brother loved to run. "I can."

"C'mon, it'll be fun. I think our team has a good chance of winning, too."

I shrugged. "Maybe."

My father may have lost an arm in Afghanistan, but both his legs worked just fine. He was fast, and he'd been training hard. He and Danny had been running together just about every morning since it finally stopped snowing last spring. Hatcher joined them often, although he wasn't as fanatical about it as they were. Lauren was pretty zippy for an almost fifth grader, plus there was Professor Rusty, who apparently had been on the track team in high school and college. Aunt True called him our "secret weapon." *Emphasis on 'secret,'* I thought, looking over at her boyfriend's pale skinny legs and knobby knees. None of us had ever seen him so much as walk fast. As for me—

"I just hope I can finish," I said glumly.

"Don't be such a wet blanket, Drooly!"

"Shut *up*, Hatcher!"

My mother passed us, carrying a pitcher of orange juice. "That's enough, you two!"

"Sorry, ma'am," we replied simultaneously.

I waited until she was out of earshot, then turned to my brother and peered closely at him, feigning concern. "I think your nose looks bigger this morning."

Hatcher's hand flew up to his face. He gave his nose an exploratory squeeze, and I suppressed a smile. He was terrified that he was going to inherit the famous "Lovejoy proboscis," as Gramps called it—the big nose visible on our ancestor Nathaniel Daniel Lovejoy in the portrait in the living room, and on Gramps and our father, too.

"Come on, Mackenzie." I crossed to where my cousin was standing and grabbed her arm. "Let's eat."

CHAPTER 4

Breakfast was over practically before it started, the food vacuumed up by my hungry relatives in nothing flat. Afterward, everyone scattered to put on their race day clothes so we could head downtown. No school bus for us this morning—we were hoofing it, as Grandma G called it.

"Pumpkin Falls will be jammed," my father had warned our relatives last night. "As the oldest road race in New England, Four on the Fourth is a big deal. Runners come from all over to check it off their bucket list."

My sisters and the younger cousins all ran ahead along Maple Street, excited in the way that only little kids who don't know what's waiting for them can be excited. I slouched along next to Grandma G, who was pushing the stroller containing Bella and Blair. The rest of my family streamed down Hill Street, all of us in our matching T-shirts—red, white, and blue today in honor of the holiday. *Hey, kids! Check it out!* I thought, cringing inwardly. *The circus is in town! Step right up and see a gaggle of Giffords!*

"What's up with you?" asked Mackenzie, giving me a sidelong glance.

"Nothing."

"So, are you going to try out for the play?"

I frowned. "What play?"

"Weren't you paying attention? It was all Cha Cha and Jasmine could talk about."

"Really? When?"

"Yesterday. Downtown. After we all got our pictures taken."

I shook my head. I'd probably been too busy keeping an eye on Calhoun, but I wasn't about to admit that.

"Well, anyway, it's called *The Pirates of Penzance*, and tryouts are tomorrow at the Grange."

"The pirates of what?"

"Penzance."

"That's a play?"

Mackenzie nodded.

"Technically, it's a musical," Hatcher interjected, wedging himself between us. "A really famous one, by these guys called Gilbert and Sullivan." He draped his arms—already sweaty, thanks to the rapidly rising temperature—over our shoulders.

"Eew!" I protested, pulling away. "It can't be that famous,

if I've never heard of it before." But the names Gilbert and Sullivan sounded vaguely familiar. Had my mother mentioned them at dinner a few nights ago? Or maybe Aunt True?

"The flyers are all over town," said Hatcher. "You can't miss them."

I shrugged. Somehow I'd managed to.

"Cha Cha says that Calhoun's father is directing," Mackenzie continued.

This was a surprise. "I thought Dr. Calhoun was only interested in Shakespeare."

"Apparently he makes an exception for Gilbert and Sullivan," my cousin told us. "At least that's what Calhoun said."

"Since when were you talking to Calhoun?"

"Since you were feeding Bilbo yesterday. He rode his bike over to say hi."

"And you didn't tell me?"

"Sorry. I forgot. Anyway, Cha Cha and Jasmine are both going to try out."

"I might too," said Hatcher.

I gaped at him. My brother had never in his life expressed the remotest interest in acting. I wondered if this sudden burst of enthusiasm for the theater had anything to do with the fact that Cha Cha was planning to try out. Hatcher seemed unusually interested in Cha Cha Abramowitz lately.

"You should try out too," he added.

"Fat chance." Singing was way up on the long list of things

I wasn't good at. My mother, who rarely said anything critical about anybody, liked to joke that I couldn't carry a tune in a paper bag. Even Miss Marple, my grandparents' elderly golden retriever, who had inexplicably latched onto me as her favorite Lovejoy, whined and scratched to be let out of the bathroom whenever I sang in the shower.

And it wasn't just the singing—I'd never had any desire to be onstage, period. It was the whole stealth mode thing, which had kicked in big time after my überweird sixth-grade growth spurt. I hated drawing attention to myself. Piano recitals were an agony, and I dreaded oral reports at school. I tolerated swim meets only because I was mostly underwater. Being onstage, in the spotlight, in a *musical*? No way.

We reached the bottom of the hill and crossed the village green. My father was right about the streets being jammed. Dozens of runners were already assembled by the church, signing in at the long registration tables and putting on their numbered race bibs.

"Huddle up, Giffords!" my father shouted, using his official Lieutenant Colonel Jericho T. Lovejoy voice in order to be heard about the crowd. My extended family crowded together as closely as thirty-seven people could. Thirty-nine, counting Aunt True and Professor Rusty.

My father proceeded to explain how things would work. Technically, our relatives wouldn't be running for Team Lovejoy's Books, since the officially sponsored teams were limited to six runners each. "But we hope you'll run alongside us for moral support anyway," he told them. "Pace us, pass us, cheer us on, make fun of us"—Uncle Rooster gave an enthusiastic whoop at this—"just get us across that finish line!"

That was the only catch to winning the Four on the Fourth race: The whole team had to cross the finish line in order for the official time to count.

"Once you've got your race bibs, we'll gather on the green for warm-ups and stretching," my father added as he led us over to the registration tables. While we were waiting in line to sign in, two big buses with CAMP LOVEJOY lettered on the sides pulled up to the curb. A little girl in a pixie haircut leaned out of one of the windows and waved at my littlest sister in excitement. "PIPPA!" she shrieked.

"TARA!" Pippa shrieked back. She flew over to the bus. Lauren was hot on her heels.

I watched as a river of girls in navy blue shorts and white polo shirts with the official Camp Lovejoy logo flowed from the bus, engulfing my sisters. Should I have gone to camp this summer too? Gramps and Lola had offered to pay for it, and my sisters were obviously having fun. But I'd turned down their offer in favor of my perfect summer.

After Mackenzie and I signed in, we joined the rest of my family on the village green. I looked around as my father led us through a series of stretches. Pumpkin Falls had gone all out for the Fourth of July. In addition to the requisite flags flying from every shop and building in town, all of the flower containers hanging from the lampposts had been planted in patriotic colors, and there was red-white-and-blue bunting hanging from every conceivable spot, including the bandstand.

"The town that time forgot," Mackenzie intoned in her radio announcer voice, as the Pumpkin Falls Brass Band struck up a Fourth of July medley. I had to smile. She was right. Pumpkin Falls was kind of stuck in a time warp.

Most of the benches scattered around the village green were full of racegoers and their families and friends. I watched as people set up lawn chairs in the shade and lined up by Emily's Eats, the town's sole food truck (the one that had been green-lighted at the town meeting this past spring).

"Looking forward to the race?" asked Aunt True, who had come to cheer us on.

I made a rude noise, and she laughed. Aunt True and my mother weren't part of Team Lovejoy. "For one thing, we're walkers, not runners, and for another, every team needs a cheering section," my mother had said firmly when my father had invited them to join.

"The only thing I'm looking forward to is the fireworks," I said, which was the truth. I loved fireworks, even though the ones they had in Pumpkin Falls couldn't rival the ones in Austin. As the capital of Texas, Austin always pulled out all the stops.

"Cassidy!" Aunt True called out suddenly, waving to a

tall red-haired girl who was stretching nearby with a bunch of campers.

The red-haired girl waved back, then loped over to join us. She was older than me, and obviously a counselor. "Nice to see you again," she told my aunt.

"Truly, this is the girl I was telling you about," said Aunt True. "Cassidy Sloane and some of her fellow counselors are the ones who started the book club for their campers." I vaguely remembered her saying something about that.

"How are you enjoying *Understood Betsy*?" asked Aunt True.

"We love it so far," Cassidy replied. "And we *adored* your pumpkin whoopie pies!"

Pumpkin whoopie pies were one of Aunt True's signature treats. She'd been alternating between those and her Bookshop Blondies in the store for the past few months. I'd be sorry to see either of them retired for the season—but Hatcher was right, the blueberry donut muffins were pretty great too.

Aunt True laughed. "Stop by the bookstore anytime, and I'll make sure you head back to camp with goodies as well as books."

"I'll definitely take you up on that," Cassidy replied. Just then, one of the campers trotted over and grabbed her hand, tugging her back toward their group. "Gotta go! Good luck, Team Lovejoy!"

Hatcher poked me in the back as she left. "Hey, Professor

Rusty's research assistant is here!" He pointed to Aunt True's boyfriend, who was standing in the shade talking to a girl in a Camp Lovejoy uniform. "I'd know those cinnamon buns anywhere."

I grinned. He was talking about her hair, which she wore coiled over her ears in Princess Leia–style poufs. "What's her name again?"

"Felicia something."

"Grunewald," Aunt True told us. "Felicia Grunewald." She gave us a sly smile. "Maybe I should add cinnamon buns to our signature treats at the bookshop."

Hatcher and I stared at her, then burst out laughing.

"What?" said Aunt True, the picture of innocence.

The loudspeaker crackled. "Runners, make your way to the starting line, please!"

"Team Lovejoy's Books!" barked my father. "Follow me!"

As Hatcher, Danny, Lauren, Professor Rusty, and I set off after him, I surreptitiously sized up the other teams.

Team Library was led by Mr. Henry, who had pulled his dreadlocks back into a ponytail for the occasion. Beneath his racing bib he wore a red-and-white-striped tank top over red shorts. No surprise there—Aunt True called red and white Mr. Henry's signature colors. Hatcher said he looked like Waldo in *Where's Waldo?*

"I'm so E-X-C-I-T-E-D!" squealed Annie Freeman, skipping along beside Mr. Henry. Annie was the reigning winner of the Grafton County Junior Spelling Championship and my sister Lauren's best friend. Annie herself wouldn't give us too much of a run for our money today, but there was also Annie's brother Franklin to consider, along with Calhoun and his sister, Juliet, and my friend Jasmine's brother Scooter.

Jasmine herself was running for Team Starlite, which was definitely stiff competition. Jasmine was a star basketball player, and Cha Cha and her parents were in great shape, thanks to all the dancing they did at their studio. Plus, they'd recruited two guys from the high school track team.

The Team Kwik Klips "krew members," as they called themselves, were looking pretty competitive too. They'd all sprayed red, white, and blue streaks into their hair, and were clearly fired up for the race.

Oh well, I thought, whether or not we won, at least we were all running together in support of Mr. Henry's library project. That was the main goal. Our real competitors were the teams running in support of Ella Bellow's Grange project.

Ella wasn't running in the race herself, but she'd twisted the arms of a bunch of her customers to join her team, including my swim coach's wife and Bud Jefferson. Mr. Jefferson was a huge bear of a man who I hoped was as slow as he was big. Technically, he was Ella's landlord, not her customer, although he'd taken up knitting after getting roped into a class on socks that my mother and I had signed up for over Spring Break.

Team Mahoney's Antiques looked stronger. Like my

father and Danny, the Mahoneys were both dedicated runners, and their friends on the team looked equally fit. Team General Store, on the other hand, was a bit of a wild card. None of the Farnsworths were running—they were all older than Grandma G, for one thing, and hardly what you'd call athletic. Four of the people on their team I'd seen around town but had never met. The only two that I knew were Mr. Burnside, our school principal, and Mr. Bigelow, my science teacher. Like Professor Rusty, Mr. Burnside was tall and skinny—thanks to my weird habit of classifying people as birds, I'd always thought of him as a flamingo—and he had the look of a runner, with long legs and a lean build. But any potential edge he might give to the team was probably offset by Mr. Bigelow, who was short and kind of tubby and reminded me of a duck. On the other hand, I knew from experience that Mr. Bigelow had an enormous amount of enthusiasm—he was one of our school's most popular teachers—and sometimes that made up for lack of athletic ability.

The only team I was almost positive that we'd be able to beat were the Speedy Geezers. Reverend Quinn had been bragging about his team for weeks and making pronouncements about "dark horses" and "underdogs," though, so maybe he knew something the rest of us didn't.

I scanned the crowd of onlookers, searching for my mother. I spotted her and waved. She waved back, and so did Aunt True, Pippa, and Grandma G, who coaxed Bella and Blair into waving their chubby little fists from their stroller too.

"Go, Team Lovejoy!" shouted a deep voice. I caught a flash of purple and recognized Augustus Wilde, the romance author who was our town's celebrity. For once, Augustus wasn't wearing a cape. Instead, he sported a purple T-shirt emblazoned with the words GO TEAM LOVEJOY! Belinda Winchester was dressed in an identical T-shirt, and both of them were fanning themselves with matching purple baseball caps. I gave them a thumbs-up.

"Runners, take your marks!" cried the voice over the loudspeaker.

My mouth suddenly went dry. The dread that I'd been feeling earlier came flooding back in a rush. Why had I let myself be talked into running this stupid race?

Hatcher leaned over to me. "Remember, Drooly, all you have to do is finish."

"Don't call me Drooly."

He grinned. "That's the spirit!"

Finish, I thought. I could do that.

Couldn't I?

CHAPTER 5

As it turned out, I could, though just barely.

Even my little sister Lauren beat me to the finish line, which I knew I'd never hear the end of. How was it that I could swim as fast as lightning for what felt like hours on end and barely be short of breath, but an easy 4K loop completely knocked me out?

Mackenzie had doubled back at one point to run alongside me. "How's it going?"

I'd given her a curt nod. My cousin hadn't even broken a sweat, which was almost as irritating as the fact that she felt she needed to check on me.

She'd trotted alongside me as the two of us turned onto Main Street, the official halfway mark in the race.

"There are the girls!" called my mother, who was standing in front of Lovejoy's Books, and my family cheered for us. Aunt True was balancing a baby on one hip. Bella, maybe? I couldn't tell. The twins were dressed alike today, both wearing matching red, white, and blue onesies and floppy stars and stripes sun hats.

My friend Lucas Winthrop and his mother were there too. Lucas was smeared with industrial-strength white sunscreen, his face practically hidden beneath a floppy hat similar to the ones worn by the twins. Poor Lucas! His mother still thought he was six. He'd wanted to run, but she wouldn't let him.

"Heatstroke," she'd warned when he asked. "We can't risk that."

A huge smile spread across Lucas's face when he saw Mackenzie. He waved, trying to attract her attention. Ever since she'd come to visit last Spring Break, Lucas had been smitten with my cousin.

"Go, Bud!" Mrs. Winthrop shouted, and I looked over my shoulder to see Mr. Jefferson lumbering along behind Mackenzie and me. He was red in the face and sweating profusely, and if you asked me, which nobody ever did, he was the one that Mrs. Winthrop should have been worried about when it came to heatstroke, not Lucas.

After a disagreement last March during the big Maple Madness Bake-Off (Maple Madness, a celebration of all things maple, was another of our town's traditions), the blooming romance between Lucas's mother and Bud appeared to be back on track. The town's residents were keeping a close watch on all of the current couples, thanks to Ella Bellow's frequent bulletins from A Stitch in Time. Over at the General Store, I'd heard a number of bets placed as to who'd get engaged first: Mrs. Winthrop and Bud, Belinda Winchester and Augustus Wilde, or my aunt and Erastus Peckinpaugh.

Secretly, my money was on Aunt True. And secretly, I couldn't help thinking it would be fun to have a wedding in the family. I hadn't been to a family wedding since I was eight, when Uncle Brent married Aunt Angie.

"Go on ahead," I panted, flapping my hand at Mackenzie as we spilled out the other end of Main Street.

She nodded and broke away, and I didn't see her again until I managed to huff and puff my way up Hill Street and then circle back to the finish line, where what seemed like the entire gaggle of Giffords was waiting for me.

"Well done, Truly-in-the-Middle!" said my father, giving me a sweaty hug, and Hatcher dumped a bottle of water over my head.

After all of the runners were accounted for, the judges withdrew inside First Parish Church to tally the scores. Meanwhile, the crowd drifted over to the bandstand to wait for the results.

"We still have a chance," Hatcher told me as the brass band struck up another medley of tunes, John Philip Sousa this time.

"You've got to be kidding! I was one of the last ones across the finish line."

"Yeah, but Professor Rusty delivered the goods. Aunt True was right about him being our secret weapon. Our average time is way up there."

A podium had been set up on the bandstand, and behind it stood Augustus Wilde, who had been selected by the race organizers to hand out the prizes. I watched as he taped a poster of his latest novel to the front of it. Augustus didn't have a stealth mode. He was what Aunt True called a guerrilla marketer, someone willing to go to great lengths to promote their own work. Not surprisingly, after the judges emerged and passed him an envelope with the results, during his moment in the spotlight he also managed to wedge in a plug for his new book.

"As I wrote in my latest best seller, *Fortune's Forbidden Fruit*," he told the crowd with a sweeping gesture toward the poster on the front of the podium, "there are no winners in life, only finishers."

This didn't strike me as the most inspiring of quotes, but it brought a ripple of polite applause anyway. Pumpkin Falls supported its own.

Hatcher nudged me with his elbow. "Captain Romance strikes again."

I smiled. "Captain Romance" was our secret nickname for Augustus.

The awards presentation began with the low-hanging fruit—gift certificates for free ice cream cones at the General

Store, which were given to everyone in the crowd wearing a race bib; a prize for the youngest racer to finish (Annie Freeman got that one, which she accepted with a squeal of "G-R-A-T-I-T-U-D-E!"); another for "most improved time from last year" (that went to Principal Burnside); and finally, an award for the last person to cross the finish line—which I was really truly grateful I didn't win.

Reverend Quinn took a bow as he stepped forward to accept the bright orange ribbon with LAST BUT NEVER LEAST emblazoned on it. "Blessed are the meek," he quipped, holding it up.

Overall fastest time was awarded to an elite runner from Connecticut who regularly qualified for the Boston Marathon.

"This race has been on my bucket list for years," he told the crowd. "I'm only sorry we out-of-towners don't qualify for your famous trophy. There's nothing I'd like better than to add that to my shelf. In fact, I may have to move to Pumpkin Falls so I can have a shot at it next year!"

He took his seat again to cheers of encouragement from the crowd.

"And now," said Augustus, striking a dramatic pose, "the award we have all been waiting for—the silver pumpkin!"

Ella Bellow was standing beside me, arms folded tightly across her chest. Much to her displeasure, Team A Stitch in Time had been disqualified. Bud Jefferson had dropped out halfway up Hill Street. On the other hand, one of the Team

Kwik Klips members had stumbled and hurt her ankle, and they had also ended up disqualified. That meant the odds were still even, as far as the Pumpkin Falls Beautification Project competition went. As for the winning team, Hatcher had said our time was solid. Was there a chance we might pull it off? I started envisioning a window display at the bookstore featuring the coveted trophy.

Augustus turned to the brass band behind him. "May I have a drumroll, please?" They obliged. He opened the envelope and peeked inside. "And the trophy goes to"—he paused again to wring every last drop of drama from the moment—"Team Starlite!"

Hatcher and I exchanged a rueful glance.

"Oh well," said Mackenzie. "At least Mr. Henry's project won, right?"

I nodded. The children's room at the library would get its renovation.

"There's always next year," Mr. Henry said to Ella, whose expression looked like she'd soaked it in pickle juice. She gave a curt nod and stalked off. Ella was not a good sport.

The gaggle of Giffords were, though. My relatives and I all whooped and cheered as Cha Cha, her parents, and the other members of Team Starlite climbed the steps of the bandstand to collect their prize. The big silver pumpkin was going to look great in the Starlite Dance Studio window, gleaming under the twinkle lights.

Augustus bent down and reached under the podium for the trophy. A moment later, he snapped upright again. He was frowning.

"Where did you put it?" he asked Belinda in a stage whisper.

"Under the podium," Belinda whispered back. "You saw me."

"Well, it's not here!"

Belinda clambered up the bandstand steps to look for herself. Ella joined her, as did Mr. Henry. The four of them scoured the podium, then the bandstand itself and the bushes that surrounded it.

But Captain Romance was right—the silver trophy was gone!

CHAPTER 6

One good thing came from the Great Pumpkin Trophy Heist, as the *Patriot-Bugle* quickly dubbed it: The Gifford Family Reunion got knocked off the front page.

At first, everybody thought that Belinda Winchester was confused, and that maybe she'd just forgotten to retrieve the trophy from the window of Mahoney's Antiques before the race. But she protested that she most certainly had retrieved it, and she even had a cell phone photo to prove it—one she'd taken on the bandstand earlier in the day that showed Augustus Wilde hoisting the trophy in mock victory.

Residents and tourists alike quickly spread out all over town looking for it, but in the end, everyone came up empty-handed. The silver pumpkin was definitely gone.

"Who would want to steal a dumb trophy?" I asked, as Mackenzie and Cha Cha and Jasmine and I retreated to the shade of one of the trees on the village green. The rest of my family was gathered nearby, and over by the bandstand, the town council was holding an emergency meeting with the police—well, policeman. Pumpkin Falls only had one: Officer Tanglewood.

"It's not dumb," Cha Cha scolded in her deep voice, the one that had earned her the nickname "the kazoo" from Hatcher. "It's tradition." She was obviously disappointed. I'd be disappointed too if my team had won, and the trophy we were entitled to show off all year had vanished.

"You have a point, though, Truly," said Jasmine. "I can't think of anyone around here who would do something like that."

We were quiet for a moment, considering.

"Ella?" I suggested, glancing over at the bandstand, where our former postmistress-turned-knitting-shop-owner was lecturing Officer Tanglewood. "She was pretty unhappy about losing."

Cha Cha didn't look convinced. "Ella wouldn't sink that low, would she?"

"It could be anybody!" said Mackenzie. "A local, a visitor—there were a ton of people at the race today who aren't from around here. Including all of us Giffords."

I looked at her, astonished. "None of us stole it!"

"I *know* that. I'm just saying!"

"I'll bet it was one of those marathoners." Jasmine's dark eyes narrowed as she watched the runner with the winning time laughing with his friends. “That guy, for instance. I’ll bet he made that joke about moving here so he’d be eligible to win the trophy next year just to throw everyone off track.”

“We shouldn’t jump to conclusions,” Cha Cha cautioned. “Don’t forget what happened over Spring Break.”

This past March, during Maple Madness, the sap lines at Freeman Farm and Maynard’s Maple Barn had been cut. Everyone suspected sabotage, and things had gotten pretty heated for a while. It had been like the Hatfields and the McCoys around town, with accusations flying and neighbors taking sides against neighbors before my friends and I had finally caught the real culprit.

“Hey,” said Scooter, sauntering over. Calhoun and Lucas were with him.

“Hey back,” I replied.

“Did you guys have any luck?”

We shook our heads.

“Neither did we,” said Calhoun.

The three boys sat down on the grass beside us.

“If the trophy were smaller, I’d say maybe a magpie took it,” I told my friends.

“What’s a magpie?” asked Scooter.

“A bird that likes shiny things.”

The problem was, you’d need a bird the size of an ostrich to carry away a trophy like the silver pumpkin, and ostriches were in short supply in New England. We did have eagles, though. Gramps had taken me to see them out at Cherry Island on Lake Lovejoy.

"Sounds to me like a case for the Pumpkin Falls Private Eyes," said Scooter, glancing at Mackenzie. Like Lucas, he had a crush on her too.

"This is the last day of our family reunion," I told him. "We don't have time for that."

"Where's your civic spirit?" he protested. "We should at least pool our knowledge and do a little preliminary investigating together."

I didn't want to investigate. I wanted to go the lake, where Grandma G had a big picnic prepared, and where there were paddleboards and kayaks and swimming. It was my reward for running the stupid road race.

"Mackenzie's leaving tomorrow," I told him. "We want to spend the day together."

"You would be," Lucas pointed out, crossing his pale arms over his chest and trying to sound grown-up and important. "Plus, the trail's going to go cold if we don't hop on it."

"Lucas is right," Calhoun agreed. "We should move on this."

"Fine," I snapped, getting to my feet. It was unlikely we could solve this mystery before tomorrow, but it was also unlikely that my friends would shut up about it if we didn't at least try. There was one obstacle, though. "Our parents will say no," I warned. "They're sticklers about us all staying together during our family reunion."

Surprisingly, though, this time they weren't.

"Sure," said both my father and Uncle Teddy, when Mackenzie and I asked if we could hang out with our friends for the afternoon instead of joining everyone at the lake.

"Just be back home in time to freshen up for the clam-bake," my mother added.

My sister Lauren, who had officially become a member of the Pumpkin Falls Private Eyes over Spring Break, was torn between staying with us and going swimming with our younger cousins.

"This is a wild-goose chase," I told her. "Go to the lake. You have to go back to camp tonight after the fireworks, remember? It's the last chance you'll get to hang out with everyone."

"Promise you'll tell me if anything interesting happens?"

I nodded. "I promise."

Hatcher opted for the lake too. "Sorry, Droo—I mean Truly," he corrected himself. "I won't see our cousins for a whole year otherwise."

Uncle Teddy gave Mackenzie money to treat us all to lunch at the food truck, and then my family left. After we ate, we retreated to Lovejoy's Books, which was air-conditioned, for our meeting.

The bookshop was busy. We'd been planning to close for the Fourth of July, but with all the tourists in town, my father and Aunt True had changed their minds.

"Gotta make hay while the sun shines," Aunt True had said.

Good call, I thought, eyeing the throng of customers. Belinda had volunteered to man the fort so that my father and aunt could spend the afternoon at the lake, and she'd corralled Augustus into helping. He was holding court over at Cup and Chaucer, dispensing beverages along with recommendations for books—most notably his own.

"I see you like Earl Grey tea," I overheard him tell an older lady who was hanging on his every word. Augustus had a lot of fangirls. "You may enjoy my own *Earl of Hearts*."

I smothered a grin. I'd have to tell Hatcher about that one later.

"It's too crowded to meet here," said Calhoun, glancing around.

I agreed. "The library is open. How about we go there?"

The library was usually closed on Sundays, but Mr. Henry and the staff had decided to keep it open for race day, so that visitors could use the restrooms. No unsightly porta-potties for Pumpkin Falls, no sirree. We headed back down Main Street toward the village green. Our town's lone police car was parked outside the library. Inside, we found Officer Tanglewood at the front desk, chatting with Mr. Henry.

Officer Tanglewood smirked at us. "Well, if it isn't Nancy Drew and—what is it you call yourselves? The Pumpkin Falls Private Eyes?"

"As I recall, John," said Mr. Henry, giving us a discreet

wink, "these enterprising young people were the ones responsible for finding the sap rustler last March. And Truly here proved herself a real-life Nancy Drew indeed! You'll remember that she was the one who found her sister when she went missing."

That wiped the smirk off Officer Tanglewood's face.

"What can I do for you?" asked Mr. Henry, and I explained that we were looking for a quiet spot to meet.

"There's no one in the children's room at the moment," he told us. "It's all yours. I assume you're turning your attention to the missing trophy. Any strategies you can share?"

My friends all looked over at me. For some reason they'd decided I was in charge of the Pumpkin Falls Private Eyes. Which I wasn't.

"Well," I began, then stopped. We didn't really have a plan yet. Officer Tanglewood saw me hesitate. His lips started to curl again, and I felt my face flush with annoyance. "I thought we'd ask Janet at the *Patriot-Bugle* if we could look over the photographs she took of the race this morning," I said, plunging ahead with more confidence than I felt. "She may have taken one that shows where the trophy went, or who took it, if it's been stolen."

"Brilliant!" said Mr. Henry. "Now we're getting somewhere. Unless you've already taken care of that, John?"

Now it was Officer Tanglewood's turn to redden. "I was just about to."

"Crowdsourcing!" blurted Lucas. We all turned and stared at him, and not just because his voice had cracked.

"Crowd what?" asked Jasmine.

"Sourcing," said Mr. Henry, who was a walking dictionary. Most librarians are. "Also brilliant. It means tapping the collective wisdom of the public—asking for their help, often through social media."

"Plenty of people besides Janet took pictures," Lucas continued. "I saw them. We can put the word out online to send us anything that looks suspicious."

Mr. Henry turned to Officer Tanglewood. "I'm sure you've thought of that, too."

"Of course," the policeman blustered, making it perfectly obvious that he hadn't.

"Well, it certainly can't hurt to have these intrepid young people here duplicate your efforts," Mr. Henry said smoothly. "The more the merrier when it comes to solving a mystery, right? Especially one involving such an important symbol of our town's heritage."

Officer Tanglewood looked like he was wishing we'd all just disappear, Mr. Henry included. My friends and I headed upstairs, only too happy to oblige.

"I love this place!" said Mackenzie happily.

I did too. I'd been coming to the children's room at the Pumpkin Falls Library since I was a little kid, and despite the fact that it was definitely in need of renovation—the paint was faded and peeling, for starters, and the chairs and sofas were nearly threadbare, and I suspected that the weird blotch on the ceiling meant there was a leak in the roof—it was one of the coziest places in town.

We headed automatically for the floor pillows under the big bronze sculpture in the corner that depicted a scene from *Charlotte's Web*. Everyone in the room except Calhoun, who had only moved here a couple of years ago, and Mackenzie, who had visited for the first time over Spring Break, had grown up sitting in the doorway of Zuckerman's barn for story hour, beneath the bronze cobweb that contained Charlotte. At least now, at our age, we didn't fight over who got to sit next to Wilbur and who got stuck next to Templeton.

"What do we have so far?" I asked, pen poised over my notepad to start making a list. We almost always began our meetings by making a list. I jotted down two headings: *What We Know* and *What We Don't Know*.

"We know the trophy is missing," said Lucas.

Scooter shot him a look. "Duh!"

"Scooter!" Mackenzie chided, which earned her a worshipful glance from Lucas.

"Sorry," mumbled Scooter. If anyone could make him behave, it was my cousin.

"Maybe add a column for 'Suspects,' and one for 'Action Items,'" suggested Calhoun. "I like Lucas's idea for crowdsourcing—and yours, Truly, for looking at Janet's photos."

He smiled at me, and I smiled back, then wrote down his suggestions.

"We should find out what time Belinda picked up the trophy from Mahoney's," said Jasmine.

I wrote that down under *What We Don't Know*.

"And when it was last seen," added Cha Cha.

I wrote that down too. "How about suspects? Do we have any?"

In the end, we came up with the marathon runner, an older man whom Lucas claimed to have seen lurking outside Lou's Diner and, after some discussion, Ella Bellow. I stared at the list glumly. There was discouragingly little to go on. We brainstormed for a while, not making much progress. When I finally looked up at the clock, I realized with a start that Mackenzie and I had less than half an hour before Lobster Bob was due to arrive for the clambake.

"To be continued," I told my friends, leaping to my feet. "Our parents will have our heads on a platter if we aren't home in time to change for dinner."

As we were leaving, Mackenzie paused by a rack of brochures advertising all the tourist attractions in the area. Gramps and Lola had taken us to a lot of them over the years. We'd been to Story Land when we were little (kind of like a smaller, lamer version of Disneyland) and hunted for souvenirs at Clark's Trading Post. We'd climbed Mount Monadnock when we were older and gone swimming and boating at

Lake Winnipesaukee and ridden the Mount Washington Cog Railway to the highest spot in the northern Appalachians. Other places I hadn't been to and had no interest in visiting included the World's Second-Largest Chainsaw (the largest was in Michigan, apparently) and New Hampshire's Favorite Dairy Museum. I knew that some people called our state "Cow Hampshire," but who would want to visit a museum about cows? And did "favorite" mean that there was more than one?

"Hey, check this out!" Mackenzie plucked a brochure from the bottom row.

"Check what out?"

"This." She thrust it into my hands.

A woman wearing a bikini top and a fish tail floated on the brochure's aquamarine cover, smiling broadly and waving. I read the words in her thought bubble aloud: "'Do you dream of being a mermaid?'"

Can't say that I do, I thought, and handed it back.

"Sounds like fun, right?" said my cousin.

"For Lauren and Pippa, maybe," I replied.

For me? Not in a million years.

CHAPTER 7

By the time we got home, the school bus filled with my relatives had returned from the lake, and the house was awash in Giffords getting ready for the clambake. Mackenzie and I took quick showers and changed out of our sneakers and smelly race clothes into sandals and sundresses—Grandma G liked us all to dress up for our annual "farewell banquet," as she called it.

"Obadiah, Abigail, Jeremiah, Ruth," Mackenzie sing-songed as the two of us headed back downstairs from my bedroom. I'd made up the rhyme when I was younger, to help me remember the names of all my Lovejoy ancestors in the portraits that lined the staircase.

"Matthew, Truly, Charity, and Booth!" I finished, pausing momentarily to blow a kiss at my namesake. I'd gained a new respect for the original Truly Lovejoy this past Spring Break, when I learned how she'd risked everything to help runaway slaves on the Underground Railroad.

"Here come my two beautiful eldest granddaughters!" announced Grandma G as Mackenzie and I entered the kitchen. She was sitting at the table with Professor Rusty and Aunt True, who was holding one of the twins while Aunt Angie nursed the other. At least I assumed that was what Aunt Angie was doing. There was a blanket draped over her shoulder, and I figured that the slightly squirmy lump she was cradling underneath it must be either Blair or Bella. I watched Professor Rusty making silly faces at whichever baby Aunt True was holding, startled by an unexpected thought: *Do they want a baby of their own?*

I figured the two of them would get married someday, but it had never occurred to me that they might want to start a family. Would Aunt True still want to work at the bookshop if she had a baby? My stomach lurched as I realized what a huge hole it would leave in my life if she didn't.

My father poked his head in the back door. "Truly! Grab some newspapers from the recycling bin, would you? Brent could use a hand out here."

"Yes, sir."

"I'll help too, Uncle Jericho," said Mackenzie.

The two of us rummaged through the recycling bins in the mudroom and took a stack of old newspapers outside. Uncle Brent was the sole member of tonight's setup squad, since Aunt Angie was busy with the twins. We helped him spread the newspapers on the picnic tables, then set out paper plates with a plastic bib on top of each one. Clambakes were notoriously messy.

"Where's that hot sauce of your father's at?" my uncle asked me.

I wrinkled my nose. "Hot sauce? On lobster?"

Uncle Brent grinned. "First rule of Texas cuisine, darlin': Ain't nothing on the menu that hot sauce don't improve."

I laughed and retrieved the box from the kitchen. After Mackenzie and I set the little Terminator bottles out on the tables, there wasn't much else to do, since dinner was being catered. And from what I could tell, it was nearing completion. Over by the portable stoves that had been set up, Lobster Bob, a white-haired gentleman with big bushy white eyebrows and a mustache to match, was tending a pair of huge, steaming pots.

We Lovejoys were on cleanup duty tonight, which would be a snap. All we'd have to do was roll everything up in the newspapers, stuff it into garbage bags, and boom, we'd be done. Mackenzie and I would have plenty of time afterward to enjoy our last evening together.

A few moments later, Lobster Bob started banging a wooden spoon on a pot. "Who's ready for a CLAMBAKE?"

In the stampede that followed, Giffords scrambled for seats as the caterers paraded over to the tables bearing platters of freshly-boiled lobsters and buckets of steamed clams, piles of corn on the cob and homemade rolls, and giant bowls of coleslaw. I'd been skeptical about the whole clambake idea, especially after so many years of great barbecue from the Salt Lick. But my mother's instincts had been right. The clambake was a huge success, after a bit of a rocky start when some of the littlest cousins ran away screaming at their first sight of the fire-engine red lobsters. It didn't help that my cousin Matt egged them on by chasing after them with one in each hand. Lobster Bob was clearly used to this reaction, though. He'd set up a lobster-free zone for the younger kids at the far end of the tables, complete with a hot dog station.

"I see you waited until now to reveal your true colors, J. T.!" teased Uncle Rooster, as my father took a seat across from him. He pointed to my father's baseball cap. Unlike my Texas uncles, who were all sporting matching Longhorn caps—University of Texas is practically a religion in the Gifford family—my father had chosen to wear his favorite faded Red Sox cap.

"Hey! My team is playing the Yankees tonight, and it's my lucky hat." My father had been a Red Sox fan since he was a little kid. Most New Englanders are.

"No hats of any kind at mealtime, boys," Grandma G decreed from the head of the table, and despite the fact that they were grown men, not little boys, my father and uncles obeyed her instantly, removing their caps and setting them down beside their plates. Grandma G's word was law.

Since it was our farewell banquet, my grandmother made

us all hold hands while she said grace. Then it was time to dig in.

"Messy little suckers, aren't they?" said Uncle Rooster, showing Mackenzie how to extract a clam from its shell and remove the membrane from its tubelike neck. "Think of it as rolling down a turtleneck."

She grimaced but did as he instructed, dubiously eyeing the unappealing lump that dangled from her fork.

"I know," I told her. "They look kind of gross. But trust me—they're delicious."

"Dip it in hot water first to clean it and then in the melted butter," said Hatcher, pointing to the paper cups lined up in front of her plate. "Your taste buds will thank you."

Mackenzie hesitantly followed his directions. A big smile spread across her face as she ate her first steamer, as this style of cooked clam is called in New England.

"Told you so," said my brother smugly.

"Even better with hot sauce," said Uncle Brent, shaking a couple of drops of the Terminator into his butter.

Mackenzie shuddered. Like me, she's not a fan of hot sauce.

Lobster Bob inspected one of the Terminator bottles curiously. "May I?" he asked, and Uncle Brent handed him a clam. Lobster Bob dipped it into the spiced butter and took a bite. His bushy eyebrows nearly disappeared under the brim of his chef's hat. "Wow! That'll make your eyes water—but in the best possible way." He ate the rest of the clam enthusiastically.

"Where'd you get that stuff? Bring it with you from Texas?"

Uncle Brent jerked his thumb at my father. "Nope. J. T. made it."

"Seriously?" Lobster Bob looked over at my father. "Are you willing to part with a few bottles? You can name your price. If it catches on, we'll make it an exclusive line."

My parents exchanged a glance. Our family was always looking for ways to make extra money. "Income streams," my parents called them.

My father nodded. "Sure, why not?"

"It can't be exclusive, though," Aunt True said firmly. "We already carry the Terminator at Lovejoy's Books. It's one of our best sellers."

I happened to know that this was a teeny white lie. Maybe even a medium-size one. I'd overheard my parents and Aunt True *talking* about carrying the hot sauce at the bookstore as one of our sidelines—the official name for everything that bookstores sell that aren't books—but nothing had come of it yet, as far as I knew.

Lobster Bob nodded. "I understand. Still, I'm definitely interested."

Teaching Mackenzie how to liberate the lobster meat from its shell was harder than teaching her how to eat a steamed clam. We Lovejoys had all had lobster before, of course. Gramps and Lola had taken us over to the seacoast plenty of times when we visited. But most of the Gifford clan hadn't.

Lobster wasn't exactly a Lone Star State specialty. It took a lot of work to get through that armorlike outer shell, and the nutcrackers and picks that Lobster Bob had brought along to help were practically airborne as my family members passed them back and forth.

"Check it out!" crowed my father. We looked over to see him pick up a lobster claw in his prosthetic hand's titanium fingers. He squeezed, and there was an audible *CRACK!*

"Sweeeet!" hollered my cousin Matt. "Do it again, Uncle Jericho!"

The younger cousins abandoned their hot dog feast at the far end of the table to scamper over and watch this new trick. "No one wins against . . . *the Terminator*!" my father cackled, and they all squealed obligingly as he cracked another claw.

Across the table, my mother gave Aunt True a misty smile. Aunt True smiled back. I knew exactly what they were both thinking. They were thinking what I was thinking, that my father had come a long way this past year since his injury. He'd gone from soldier to civilian, pilot to entrepreneur, and most importantly, from Silent Man—our name for the brooding stranger who had returned to us from Afghanistan—back to his own silly, fun-loving self, the father we'd always known and adored, who could joke around with his brothers-in-law, effortlessly entertain his nieces and nephews, and make light of his own hardship.

"That high-tech device of yours could come in mighty

handy in this line of work," deadpanned Lobster Bob. "If you ever need another job, Mr. Lovejoy, I'll hire you."

My father raised the lobster claw in a mock salute.

"Clambake coma!" declared Hatcher a little while later, slumping forward and pretending to do a face-plant on his paper plate.

"No kidding," I groaned. I hadn't been this full since—well, since dinner last night.

As the catering crew circled the long row of tables passing out warm washcloths so we could wipe off our hands and faces, I helped my brothers bundle up the lobster shells and clamshells and corncobs and other trash in the newspaper table coverings and carry them away to the garbage cans in the barn. Then I helped Uncle Brent pass out clean plastic silverware and napkins. The clambake came with dessert, too—homemade blueberry pie and vanilla ice cream, which Lobster Bob was busy serving up.

"What have we here?" asked Uncle Teddy, taking the piece of paper that Mackenzie handed to him along with his fresh napkin. He read it aloud: "'Sirena's Sea Siren Academy'?"

I looked over, surprised to see him holding the brochure from the library.

"I was wondering if maybe we could go," said Mackenzie. "Me and Truly."

I stared at her, aghast. She shrugged and smiled. "You said

you wished we could spend more time together this summer."

"Yes, but—"

"And since you don't want to come to Texas, how about I stay and we do something fun together instead? We don't just have to hang around Pumpkin Falls."

Not wanting to go Texas didn't mean I wanted to go to some dumb mermaid camp. But before I could say so, my cousin turned back to her father. "Please?" she begged. "Could we? It's just for a week. I'd be home in plenty of time for our trip to Yellowstone."

Uncle Teddy passed the brochure across the table to Mackenzie's mother. "What do you think, Louise?"

"What do I think of what?" Aunt Louise paused her conversation with my mother and Aunt True and glanced at the brochure. She looked up at Mackenzie and smiled. "Aww, honey! Mermaid camp!" Panic rose inside me. "You'd have loved this when you were little."

The panic subsided a bit. Aunt Louise understood exactly—Sirena's Sea Siren Academy was for little kids. Not teenagers like Mackenzie and me.

"You have to be thirteen to attend," Mackenzie continued, pointing to the fine print at the bottom. "Truly and I are just the right age."

Was this conversation really happening? "But I don't want to go!" I protested, my panic level spiking again. No one seemed to be listening to me.

Mackenzie had always been the one fixated on mermaids, not me. When the two of us were little, she used to make me call her Ariel, like in the movie. She wore Ariel pajamas and slept under an Ariel bedspread and dressed up like Ariel for three Halloweens in a row, and probably would have done it for a fourth, except she couldn't stuff herself into her toddler-size costume anymore.

I'd always loved being in the water, but I'd never actually dreamed of *living* there. The closest I'd ever gotten to the whole "under the sea" thing was swim team. That and painting my bedroom back in Texas a gorgeous shade of aqua called Mermaid. Although now that I thought about it, Mackenzie had been the one who had picked the paint out for me.

Aunt Louise inspected the brochure more closely. "Cape Cod, huh?" She passed the brochure to my mother. "That's just a few hours south of here, right, Dinah?"

My mother nodded, slowly turning the pages.

"We'd be happy to pay for Truly to go along and keep Mackenzie company," said Uncle Teddy. That was his polite way of saying, *I know money is tight in your family—let me help out*. Uncle Teddy was really generous.

This was one time that I wished he weren't, though. I shook my head violently at my mother behind his back, drawing a finger across my throat and then pretending to stick it down inside for good measure. Didn't she understand that I had no interest in learning to be a mermaid? None! But my mother pretended not to see me.

"Well, it would certainly be a nice opportunity for her," she said, glancing over at my father. "And for us, too, don't you think, J.T.? Just imagine! All five of them away at once!"

I couldn't believe my ears! She was trying to get rid of me! What about all our plans for pedicures and shopping and day trips to Boston?

"What about me?" I asked indignantly. "Don't I have a say in this?"

"Really, Truly," said my father, frowning. "You could be more gracious. Your aunt and uncle are offering to do something very nice for you."

For you, you mean, I thought, but for once I didn't put my size-ten-and-a-half foot in my mouth and say so. I cast around frantically for another reason not to go. "But you need me at the bookstore!"

My father wasn't budging an inch. "Your aunt and I can handle things just fine without you. Right, True?"

My aunt nodded. There was no support there, either. They were all traitors!

"Who'll take care of Bilbo?" I said, playing my trump card. "You need me for that—Lauren has to go back to Camp Lovejoy tomorrow."

That would definitely get me off the hook. No way would my mother want to deal with changing ferret litter.

"I'm sure Belinda will watch him if I asked," she replied calmly.

I opened my mouth to retort and shut it again. There wasn't much I could say to that. My mother was right. Belinda Winchester was very much like my sister Lauren when it came to animals. At least in the kitten and cat department, which was pretty close to the ferret department.

"What on earth are you two going to do without any children underfoot?" asked Aunt Louise in mock horror.

My mother didn't even hesitate. "Sleep. Go to the Fabulous Fifties film series with Rusty and True. Not have to cook for anybody, or do laundry for anybody, or drive anybody anywhere."

My father reached over with his good hand and gave hers a squeeze, smiling. "Sounds like heaven."

And just like that, my perfect summer flew out the window.

CHAPTER 8

The rest of the Fourth of July passed in a shell-shocked blur. After the clambake, my father loaded us all into the school bus and drove back to Lake Lovejoy for the fireworks. I sat slumped in my seat in a daze as Mackenzie prattled on about Sirena's Sea Siren Academy. My perfect summer hadn't just been whisked out from under me—it had been turned inside out and flipped end to end. It was enough to make anybody's head spin.

Things only got worse when we reached the lake. The beach was packed with people in lawn chairs, happily anticipating the fireworks to come. My friends spotted our bus as it pulled in and came over to join us.

"Any news?" asked Lucas, screeching to a halt in front of Mackenzie. Scooter was right behind him.

My cousin smiled her Gifford sunflower smile. "About what?"

"The missing trophy."

Mackenzie looked over at me.

I shrugged. "Don't look at me—I don't know anything."

His main reason for conversation exhausted, Lucas dangled there, growing pinker by the minute until my cousin took pity on him.

"We do have a bit of news, though, don't we, Truly?" she said.

I shook my head grimly. "Nope. We do not. No news at all."

She turned to my friends. "Truly and I are going to mermaid camp!"

Lucas was rendered even more speechless, if that were possible. Scooter and Calhoun stared at us. So did Cha Cha and Jasmine, before they started squealing so loudly that they attracted a herd of my younger cousins, who came charging over to see what was going on.

"What the heck is mermaid camp?" asked Scooter.

Mackenzie took out her cell phone and showed our friends the video ad she'd found online for Sirena's Sea Siren Academy. It sent the boys into gales of laughter—and sent Cha Cha and Jasmine running off to ask their parents if they could go too. The result was that in nothing flat all four of us were signed up and would be heading together to Cape Cod.

"I can't wait!" exclaimed Jasmine happily. "C'mon, Truly, how could this not be fun?" she added, noticing the sour expression on my face.

Let me count the ways, I thought bitterly. First of all, it turned out that it wasn't just a camp for teenagers; it was for adults, too, which meant we were going to be spending a week with a bunch of seriously deranged people obsessed with mermaids. Second, I was going to have to wear a stupid clamshell bra, or at least something that looked like one. Competitive swimmers didn't do bikinis. Okay, maybe some of them did, but not me. And then there was the tail!

Aunt Louise had called the number on the brochure right after dinner. "You girls are in luck—they still have a few open slots this week," she told us. "Sirena says we'll have to rush-order mermaid tails for you, though. I'll have them shipped directly to Cape Cod."

This was rapturous news to Mackenzie, who had begged my mother to knit her a mermaid tail back in second grade (who knew there were knitting patterns for mermaid tails?) and then happily worn it to shreds. She made a beeline to the computer and found the website.

"What do you think—Calypso, Waverly, Oceana, or Marina?" Aunt Louise asked me. "Those are the styles that Sirena told me were most suitable for teen mermaids."

I scowled. Like there even were such things!

"Blue or green?" asked Aunt Louise, when I finally settled on Marina.

"Blue," I muttered.

"Sequins?"

"No sequins."

Mackenzie went with Calypso in green—with sequins, of course.

My mother sucked in her breath when she saw the price. "Say thank you, Truly," she urged. "This is incredibly generous of your aunt and uncle."

Aunt Louise smiled. "How often do I get to spoil my daughter and my niece in one fell swoop?"

The only bright spot in the rest of the evening, was, quite literally, the fireworks show. Well, that and the fact that I got to spend a few minutes alone with Calhoun. While waiting for the festivities to start, I drifted down to the edge of the lake, leaving Mackenzie and Jasmine and Cha Cha to hyperventilate about mermaid camp. I was skipping rocks morosely when Calhoun wandered over to join me.

"Sorry you won't be around for the film festival," he said, bending down and picking up a rock. "I was looking forward to it."

Looking forward to the movies, or to going with me? I wondered, but couldn't quite work up the nerve to ask. Instead, I just nodded. "Yeah, me too."

He hurled his stone, and we stood watching as it skipped far out across the water.

"Good one."

"Thanks." There was a pause. "I guess your camp thing will be fun, though."

I snorted.

"You don't think so?"

"You saw the video! Would you want to spend a week at something called Sirena's Sea Siren Academy?"

The corners of his mouth quirked up. "I guess not, but mermaids aren't my thing."

"They're not mine, either!"

"Really?" He looked surprised. "I figured since you like to swim so much—"

"Just because I like to swim doesn't mean I want to be a mermaid!"

"You don't have to be so touchy about it!"

I blew out my breath. "Sorry. It's just that I'd planned for my summer to go one way, and now it's turned into something completely different and completely awful."

We picked up more rocks and skipped them.

"I'm thinking of trying out for the play tomorrow," Calhoun told me.

This was a surprise. But Calhoun was full of surprises. He could be cool and aloof on the exterior, but he was a bit of a marshmallow on the inside. That much I knew. I also knew that he was almost as knowledgeable about Shakespeare as his father. "I didn't know you liked to sing!"

He lifted a shoulder. "In the shower mostly. But yeah, I kind of like to sing." He skipped another stone. "So Mackenzie said you're not planning to try out."

I shook my head.

"Not even for the chorus? They just sing and dance in the background."

"Nope."

"You play the piano, right? They always need accompanists for rehearsals."

I shook my head again. "No way. I'm not good enough."

"Seriously, Truly, working on a show is fun! How about stage crew? They have a blast building stuff."

I gave him a sidelong glance. Calhoun was being unusually persistent. And he seemed to know an awful lot about theater. But then, he knew a lot about a lot of things. Romeo Calhoun was smarter than he let people know.

One thing I knew for sure—*The Pirates of Penzance* was not for me.

CHAPTER 9

Exactly twelve hours after the last of the fireworks flickered out over Lake Lovejoy, I was on a bus to Cape Cod.

My cousin and friends and I napped most of the way, worn out from the mad dash to get packed, say good-bye to our families, try out for *The Pirates of Penzance* (Cha Cha and Jasmine, who actually ended up singing for Calhoun's father right there at the lake), and stumble out of bed at zero dark thirty to catch the early bus to Boston. Hatcher and Danny traveled with us as far as South Station, where they saw to it that we made our connection before heading off to their wrestling clinic at Boston University.

"Have fun!" Hatcher called over his shoulder to us as he trotted off after Danny.

"You too!" I called back.

A couple of hours after that, we finally pulled into the bus station in Hyannis.

"Oh great," I mumbled.

Mackenzie yawned, rubbing her eyes. "What?"

I pointed wordlessly out the window. Our ride to Sirena's Sea Siren Academy was waiting for us. It wasn't hard to spot. For one thing, the minivan was aqua, the same color as the manicure on the woman standing next to it. For another, there was a huge mermaid painted on its side.

Mackenzie squealed, waking Cha Cha and Jasmine. "Check it out!"

Our friends did, and then they squealed too.

"Wheee!" I muttered, as we gathered our things and clambered off the bus. "We get to ride in the mermaid-mobile."

"Knock it off, Truly!" Mackenzie sounded exasperated.

I'd been doing my best to suck all the fun out of our upcoming "adventure," as my mother persisted in calling it, ever since my cousin had roped me into it. I figured it was the least I could do to thank her for derailing my perfect summer.

"Welcome to Cape Cod, ladies!" gushed the woman by the minivan. She trotted over to meet us, her shoulder-length red corkscrew curls bobbing like a buoy at anchor. "I'm Sirena."

Sirena didn't look like mermaid material. Not that I knew what mermaid material looked like, but for some reason I'd expected someone with a name like Sirena to be tall and willowy. Sirena was even shorter than my mother and round as an apple.

She helped us load our luggage, then slid in behind the

steering wheel. "We've got about a half-hour drive ahead of us. You girls just sit back, relax, and I'll have you there in time for lunch. Most of the other guests have already arrived."

Mackenzie bounced up and down on the seat beside me. "We're going to mermaid camp!"

"Mermaid *academy*, please, mermaid *academy*," Sirena corrected, wagging an aqua-tipped finger in the rearview mirror. "This is not *camp*! What we are undertaking this week is much too serious an endeavor to be trivialized by that term."

I snorted, and Mackenzie elbowed me in the ribs.

As we left bustling Hyannis, Sirena turned onto a quieter, tree-lined road. It wound along past tidy houses whose white picket fences spilled over with roses and hydrangeas. We passed through several little towns, some of them with village greens nearly identical to the one back home.

"Cape Cod looks like an overgrown version of Pumpkin Falls," said my cousin.

"Isn't it awesome?" Jasmine replied. "The Cape is one of my favorite places in the whole world! We come here on vacation every year—wait until you see the beaches!"

We drove along in silence for a while. My eyelids drooped. A few minutes later Jasmine shrieked, and they flew open again.

"What?" boomed Cha Cha, and the minivan swerved as Sirena glanced at her in alarm. Cha Cha's voice always surprised people the first time they heard it.

"It's the Brewster Store!" Jasmine exclaimed. "It's like our General Store back in Pumpkin Falls, only better. Their penny candy counter is amazing. And they have homemade ice cream, and fudge, and all sorts of cool stuff for sale!"

Sirena smiled. "The Brewster Store is always a big hit with our guests. It's just a short walk from the academy."

A few moments later she turned onto a narrow lane. Up ahead, I spotted Sirena's Sea Siren Academy. Like the minivan, it was hard to miss, thanks to the sign out front with a life-size mermaid painted on it.

I peered out the window as Sirena pulled into the driveway. The academy was a little more run-down than it appeared in the flyer. The white clapboards of the large house at the front of the property were peeling, and the lawn was ragged around the edges and rapidly turning brown in the summer heat. The window boxes were cheery, though, painted a soft blue and filled with bright red geraniums. And there were matching window boxes on the row of tiny cabins that stretched out behind the main building.

"Here we are," said Sirena, parking the minivan next to an identical one. She gestured toward the main house. "This is Mermaid Headquarters—Mermaid HQ for short—where you'll find the dining room, the communal living room, and everybody's favorite, the screened-in porch. We call it Mermaid Crossing."

Of course you do, I thought crossly. I was already sick of all the mermaid references. This was shaping up to be a long week.

"And that will be your second home while you're here!" Sirena pointed toward a large pool beyond the cabins. Its blue water gleamed invitingly. There were bleachers set up on the far side, partially shaded by the fringe of pine trees that I assumed marked the edge of the property.

I caught a quick flutter of yellow on a branch high up in one of the trees, and my spirits lifted a bit. A goldfinch! Maybe I'd end up adding a bird or two to my life list while I was here. That would be some consolation. That and the fact that I'd be in the water most of the day. I wondered if I'd have time to sneak down to the pool for a quick dip before lunch.

"One of the most important rules of Sea Siren Academy," Sirena warned, as if reading my thoughts, "is to never swim alone. Always make sure you have an experienced buddy to watch you when you're in the pool. Now, let's get you girls settled into your quarters. Delphine will be ringing the lunch gong shortly."

Lunch gong? Seriously? My gaze slid over to my cousin. Normally, something like this would strike Mackenzie as funny too, and we'd share a smirk, if not an outright laugh. But she was oblivious, her eyes shining in rapturous anticipation of all things mermaid.

We unloaded our luggage and followed Sirena down the path toward the cabins. Like the driveway, the path was made of what looked like white gravel, but on closer inspection turned out to be some sort of crushed seashells. They made a pleasant crunching sound underfoot. I figured it must be a Cape Cod thing, as I'd seen a lot of similar driveways on the ride over from Hyannis.

"We've put you down at the end, in Whelk," Sirena told us.

What the heck is a whelk? I wondered. Then I noticed the signs over the doors to the cabins. They were painted the same shade of blue as the window boxes, with each cabin's name carved into them and painted a contrasting gold: NAUTILUS, ABALONE, OYSTER, and SAND DOLLAR. There was a pattern here, I quickly realized. A whelk must be a shell.

"Your quarters, ladies," Sirena told us, opening our screen door with a flourish.

It was dark inside. As my eyes adjusted to the dim light, I could see that the space was small and cramped. Two bunkbeds, two dressers, two windows in front, two in back. One tiny bathroom, and one even tinier closet.

Good luck with that, I thought, eyeing our collective suitcases.

"Your tails arrived earlier this morning," Sirena told us, gesturing to a pile of packages at the foot of one of the lower bunks.

This brought fresh squeals from Mackenzie and my friends.

"Please don't try them on yet," Sirena cautioned. "The unveiling and tailing ritual is part of our evening activity tonight."

Unveiling and tailing? My gaze slid over to Mackenzie again, but there wasn't even a flicker. She was taking this all completely seriously.

"Yes, ma'am," I said automatically, knowing an order when I heard one. *No calling it mermaid camp. Never swim alone. No trying on of tails.* Sirena had as many rules as Lieutenant Colonel Jericho T. Lovejoy.

After Sirena left, there was a scramble for the bunks. Jasmine and Cha Cha each claimed a top one; Mackenzie and I ended up on opposite sides of the room on bottom ones. I pressed my nose up against the screen on the window at the foot of my bunk and gazed longingly at the pool. Laughter floated over from Sand Dollar, the cabin next door.

"How many other people are here this week, do you think?" I asked.

"Maybe twenty?" Cha Cha ventured. "If the four other cabins are like ours."

They weren't, as we learned during introductions at lunch. Not quite, anyway. Two of them, Abalone and Oyster, contained just two beds each. Abalone was occupied by the two eldest "aspiring mermaids," as Sirena referred to all of us.

"This is Zadie Malone and her friend Lenore Sullivan," she announced, peering at her clipboard through aqua-framed reading glasses as we took our seats around the dining room table. "They worked together years ago in Los Angeles before marrying and moving to opposite ends of the country—Oregon for you, Lenore, and Vermont for you, Zadie, correct?"

The two ladies nodded.

"But you've remained best friends all these years—"

"—and every year we go on an adventure together, don't we, Lenore?" finished the one named Zadie.

There was that word "adventure" again. Had Zadie been talking to my mother?

Lenore nodded again. With their halos of white hair and wrinkled, smiling faces, the two of them reminded me a bit of Belinda Winchester. I felt a pang of homesickness. If I were back in Pumpkin Falls right now, I'd be hanging out at the bookshop with Aunt True and Belinda instead of a bunch of "aspiring mermaids."

"Last year we went on a raft trip through the Grand Canyon," boasted Zadie. "And the year before that we went bungee jumping in Australia."

"My, aren't you the thrill seekers," said Sirena admiringly.

"Next year we're planning to celebrate the big nine-oh by learning how to skydive."

Wait. *What?* I stared at them. "The big nine-oh"—did that mean what I thought it did? As in Zadie and Lenore were eighty-nine going on *ninety*? I was at mermaid camp with ladies older than Grandma G!

I was still digesting this bit of information when Sirena introduced the mother-daughter duo who were staying in Oyster, the other cabin with just two beds. "Meet Helen and Hayden Drake, who have come all the way from Seattle!"

"We're here for some special mother-daughter time, aren't we, princess?" said the mother part of the duo, reaching over and patting her daughter's hand.

"Princess," who looked to be around my age, rolled her eyes. "Yes, Mom."

The other guests were a mix of adults and teens. Nautilus was occupied by four girls from St. Louis who'd been given the week together as a high school graduation gift. Sand Dollar, the cabin next to ours, housed four women who didn't know each other at all, but who were quickly bonding over the tuna fish salad that Delphine—Sirena's daughter and the academy's only other employee—had served up for lunch.

"Mermaids eat fish," Sirena announced, as if it were a fact. She poked her fork into a chunk of tuna and hoisted it aloft. "I hope you like seafood, because you'll be eating a lot of it this week."

The conversation ebbed and flowed around me as we ate. I glanced around the dining room. The table and chairs had seen better days, as had the faded seashell-themed wallpaper. The air conditioner in the corner wheezed and grumbled as it grudgingly eked out a coolish breeze. Instructing aspiring mermaids didn't seem to be a very lucrative business. If the property was a bit shabby inside and out, though, at least the food was good. I wasn't a huge fan of tuna fish salad, but this wasn't gloppy with mayonnaise, and it had an unexpectedly yummy twist: chopped apple. I was pretty sure the rolls were homemade, and the gingersnap cookies, which finished off our meal, most definitely were. Somebody knew how to cook—Delphine, maybe?

I watched Sirena's daughter as she circled the table, clearing away dishes. She was in her late twenties, I guessed, and as tall as Sirena was short. Nearly as tall as me. The differences between mother and daughter didn't end there. Delphine's fingernails were free of polish, and her hair was blond, short, and spiky, not curly and red. I caught a glimpse of a mermaid tattoo on her left ankle as she passed by.

"We'll take an hour's siesta back in our cabins," Sirena informed us when we finished our meal. "Mermaids need their beauty rest! After that, I have a special treat in store to provide us with a little inspiration before we plunge into the hard work of learning to be mermaids. I've booked us seats at *Beauty and the Buccaneer*, the daily matinee at the Jolly Roger!"

If she'd expected us to be overjoyed at this announcement, we disappointed her. The table fell silent as we all looked at each other, puzzled. *Jolly Roger?*

"You mean the pirate museum?" said Jasmine finally, and Sirena nodded. "Oh, I love that place! We go every summer!"

I perked up at this. Pirates beat the pants—or should it be

tails?—off mermaids any day of the week. But my hopes were quickly dashed when Sirena went on to explain that the daily show featured not only pirates but also professional mermaids.

"There are professional mermaids?" I blurted, astounded at this news.

"Yes, indeed," Sirena replied. "I used to be one myself."

As we got up from the table to return to our cabins for rest hour, Sirena looked me up and down. "My, you are a tall one, aren't you?"

There was really no point in replying to that kind of comment.

"Delphine!" Sirena called, and her daughter poked her head in from the kitchen. "What do you think? We haven't had any guests in a while who were tall enough to pull off the sea serpent costume."

Delphine gazed at me, considering. She nodded slowly. "That would certainly spice things up a bit."

I could feel my face redden. I wanted to be a sea serpent even less than I wanted to be a mermaid. Folding my arms across my chest, I gave the two of them my best impression of a Lieutenant Colonel Jericho T. Lovejoy glare. If my mother could see me now, I knew exactly what she'd say: *Really, Truly, where are your manners?* I didn't care. No way was I going to spend a week at stupid mermaid camp learning how to be a stupid sea serpent.

Sirena and Delphine were too busy discussing the idea to

notice my expression, though. A moment later, Sirena clapped her hands. "Ladies! The vans will be leaving Mermaid HQ at two o'clock sharp! Don't be late."

I stalked out of the dining room after my cousin and friends, who were chattering happily about the Jolly Roger and tonight's unveiling and tailing. There was no talk of any of them being sea serpents, I noted bitterly. Obviously they were perfect mermaid material.

Me, on the other hand? Mermaid camp—pardon me, mermaid *academy*—hadn't even started yet, and I was already flunking out.

CHAPTER 10

"Wow!" Mackenzie whispered. "Those ladies can really swim!"

We were sitting front and center in the Jolly Roger's "showquarium," as the theater was called, watching *Beauty and the Buccaneer*. Any closer and we'd have been onstage ourselves.

Onstage underwater, that is.

All that stood between us and the quartet of mermaids currently performing their routine was a thick pane of glass. It was like sitting in front of a giant fish tank. Most of the showquarium, including the seats we occupied, was underground. All we could see was a carefully constructed "amazing undersea world," as the program trumpeted, complete with a fake castle, fake seaweed, fake seahorses that the mermaids rode in on, and a fake sparkly coral reef. A fake treasure chest in one corner spilled over with the kind of plastic jewelry that my sister Pippa loved to play dress up with. The only thing that was real, as far as I could tell, were the fish that darted here and there. Far above, sunlight filtered down through the water, illuminating the whole scene.

It was incredibly cheesy.

If only Hatcher were here to poke fun at it with me! This kind of thing was right up his alley. It was usually up Mackenzie's alley too, but when I glanced over at her, I could tell by her shining eyes that she was not in the mood for mockery. Ditto Cha Cha and Jasmine. I seemed to be the only one who noticed how silly it all was. Especially the pink seahorses. They looked like giant pool toys.

Mackenzie was right about one thing, though, I had to admit. The professional mermaids really could swim.

I watched the four women glide through the water, propelling themselves with an effortless flip of the flukes at the bottom of their surprisingly realistic tails. They swam in and out of the castle, waving at us from the windows (Mackenzie waved back, like she was five). They looked at themselves in hand mirrors and pretended to brush each other's hair. They performed what looked like underwater ballet moves, arcing forward and back in graceful somersaults. They swam over to the treasure chest, where they pulled out strands of fake beads and pearls and hung them around each other's necks. Occasionally, one of them would dart over to the back corner, grab one of the long black tubes hidden among the fake seaweed—

oxygen tubes, I presumed—and take a quick breath. Otherwise, they just swam around with their eyes open, big smiles on their perfectly made-up faces (hello, waterproof mascara), as if water really were their natural element.

"Ooo, look! Here comes Beauty!"

Behind us, Hayden suddenly came to life. She'd been watching mostly in silence until this moment, when the quartet of mermaids pointed in excitement toward the castle as a fifth mermaid emerged. She wore a gold bikini top and a gold crown, and she was riding in a carriage shaped like a giant gold shell. It floated toward us, pulled by two of the pink seahorses, although I was pretty sure there was a motor involved somewhere.

"Check out her tail!" Mackenzie whispered, mesmerized, as the carriage stopped directly in front of us, and Beauty emerged. She swam out and hovered before the window, waving and smiling at us as she showed off her long golden tail, which was much fancier than the ones belonging to the other mermaids.

"A *shimmertail!*" breathed Hayden.

I was impressed in spite of myself. Glimmering scales in iridescent shades of peacock blue and green were scattered up and down the tail's golden surface, and the oversized flukes at the bottom looked like butterfly wings.

"Wow!" Mackenzie exclaimed, her eyes shining again. I was guessing "shimmertail" had just shot right to the top of her Christmas list.

All of a sudden the mermaids drew back in mock horror.

A sinister figure plunged into the water from above. Dressed in a black-and-white-striped T-shirt and what looked like the bottom half of a wetsuit, he descended toward the bottom of the showquarium on a big black anchor. In one hand he held a fluttering black flag with a white skull and crossbones on it.

"The buccaneer!" exclaimed one of the girls from St. Louis at the same time that Mackenzie said, "The pirate!"

"Boo! Hiss!" called Zadie, who was enjoying the show almost as much as my cousin.

The pirate gave an evil grin, revealing a gold tooth. He hopped off the anchor and swam toward the mermaids, who fluttered their hands in pretend panic.

"C'mon, Team Mermaid!" I shouted. "Whack him with your tails!"

Whether it was my encouragement or just the script, the mermaids finally sprang into action, forming a guard around Beauty. The pirate tried to reach over them and grab her crown, but they successfully fended him off. Finally, he gave up and turned his attention to the treasure chest.

"Not the treasure!" hooted Zadie, who was surprisingly feisty for someone who was nearly ninety, if you asked me, which nobody ever did.

As the pirate rifled through the contents of the chest, the mermaids set off after him in furious pursuit. I knew they were furious because of the way their tails lashed the water. In the end, he was no match for them, though. Everyone cheered when Beauty gave him a final thwack with her shimmer-tail, sending him somersaulting across the bottom of the showquarium. Her mermaid guards snatched away his pirate flag, put him in handcuffs, and sent the buccaneer back to the surface on one of the seahorses in defeat.

"That was amazing!" said Mackenzie as we emerged from the theater. "I can't believe how long they all could hold their breath."

"At least ninety seconds, and some of them for up to two and a half minutes," Sirena told her. "I used to be able to hold mine for two minutes, back when I was performing."

I tried to imagine her as a professional mermaid. Sirena was shaped more like one of the bobbers my brothers used when they were first learning how to fish, but when she was younger, she was probably built more like Cha Cha or Mackenzie, pint-size and cute.

"Were you a mermaid here at the Jolly Roger?" asked Hayden's mother.

Sirena shook her head. "No—Florida. But that was many years ago. Delphine worked here every summer during college, though." She clapped her hands. "Ladies! You have about forty-five minutes to enjoy the museum before we head back to Mermaid HQ."

As the rest of the group made a beeline for the gift shop, Cha Cha and Jasmine and Mackenzie and I entered the "Wreck of the *Windborne*" exhibit.

"Ooo, spooky," said my cousin, shivering in anticipation as we pushed past a curtain of fishing nets into a dark tunnel. We emerged onto a gangplank that led onto a replica of a ship. A costumed guide motioned us over.

"The tour is just getting started," he told us, adjusting his tricorne hat. A fake stuffed parrot was perched on his shoulder. "Welcome aboard the *Windborne*, mateys!"

Mateys? Seriously? I glanced at my oblivious cousin. Where was Hatcher when I needed him!

"The tale of the *Windborne* is a tragic one," our guide began. "While sailing home to England in 1765 with a hold full of South American gold and silver, she was attacked off Jamaica by Benjamin 'Black Tooth Ben' Buttonwood and his band of pirates. They trussed the *Windborne*'s captain up like a Thanksgiving turkey and set him ashore on a small island. His crew was given the choice of being marooned with him or joining the buccaneers. Most chose to go rogue."

"I want to be a pirate too!" announced a little boy about Pippa's age.

"Arrrrgggghhh!" growled our guide approvingly. "Bully for you, lad!"

Frustrated actor, I thought. Couldn't get a real job, ended up here. That's what my father always said about the employees these kinds of museums.

The guide continued with his tale. "The *Windborne* spent the next couple of years sailing under the black flag—that's what they call the skull and crossbones, that or the 'Jolly Roger'—preying on other ships. Then, in the spring of 1767, she set a course for Black Tooth Ben's home port in Maine. Legend has it he planned to meet his sweetheart there and spirit her off to a life of luxury in the West Indies. Alas, fate had other plans. The *Windborne* was nearing Nantucket when she ran afoul of a nor'easter. The monstrous storm blew them back toward Cape Cod, and they foundered on a sandbar just off Marconi Beach."

Jasmine gasped. "I've been swimming on that beach!"

The guide nodded solemnly. "As have I, lass, as have I." His voice dropped low. "As the ship's bell tolled the alarm, the *Windborne* broke apart. Nearly all hands were lost, including that of the cabin boy, who was just about your age." He pointed at the little boy who'd announced that he wanted to be a pirate. He didn't look so certain now. "Only two men made it to shore. Isaiah Osborne, the ship's carpenter, was quickly found, arrested, and hanged for piracy. The other managed to escape and was never seen or heard from again. Dandy Dan, his shipmates called him, but his real name has been lost in the mists of time."

"What happened to the treasure?" asked Cha Cha.

"They say that Dandy Dan spirited some of the booty away with him when he vanished, but no trace of it has ever been found. The *Windborne* lay in her silent grave at the bottom of the sea for three hundred years. Bits and pieces of her washed ashore from time to time, tantalizing beachcombers and treasure seekers alike. But her exact location eluded all who sought to find her."

The tour guide knew how to spin a tale. We were hanging on his every word.

"All, that is, except Skipper John Dee, Cape Cod's own intrepid underwater explorer. Ten years ago, after spending most of his life searching for the *Windborne*, he mounted one final expedition, and this time he found her! Thanks to his recovery efforts, we now have this museum and all of the priceless historical artifacts that it contains." He whipped off his hat and threw it into the air. "Huzzah for Skipper Dee!"

"Huzzah for Skipper Dee!" echoed the tour group.

I laughed out loud, which earned me a puzzled look from the tour guide. Just the other night Mackenzie had read *Eloise*, Pippa's favorite book, to a group of our younger cousins. Skipperdee was Eloise's pet turtle's name. I looked over at my cousin, expecting to see her grinning too, but she was too busy huzzahing to notice.

After the tour, we meandered on through the other exhibits, looking at the cannonballs and swords and other artifacts that had been recovered from the ocean floor.

"Hey! There's the ship's bell!" said Jasmine.

We followed her to the large tank in which it hung submerged. It reminded me of the Paul Revere bell in the steeple of our church back in Pumpkin Falls. This one was similar in style, only smaller. The name WINDBORNE was engraved around the middle. I stared at it, imagining the storm and the howling wind and the cries of all those doomed men, including the poor little cabin boy. And above it all, the ringing of the bell as the ship sank beneath the waves.

I jumped as someone touched my arm. It was Mackenzie.

"What's the matter?"

"Nothing."

"Come on," she said, "this room gives me the creeps. Let's go look at some pirate treasure."

CHAPTER 11

There was plenty of treasure to see. The *Windborne* sank loaded with plunder from nearly two dozen ships, and my cousin and friends and I lingered over the displays of gold and silver coins and jewelry from Africa and South America.

Another costumed guide was standing by one of the exhibit cases, letting people hold a real coin—a silver piece of eight. When it was my turn, I held out my hand as directed.

"Wow!" I exclaimed as she placed the coin in the center of my palm. My fingers closed over it reflexively. "I wasn't expecting it to be so heavy."

She smiled. "Nobody ever is."

I managed to find some decent souvenirs in the gift shop, including fake pieces of eight for Hatcher and Danny, a plush stuffed parrot toy for Pippa, a book called *The Pirate Queen* for Lauren, and for my mother and Aunt True, the museum's special blend of *Windborne* tea. I hesitated by a rack of T-shirts, wondering if my father would get a kick out of one that said CAPTAIN HOOK on it. I finally decided that he would. Lieutenant Colonel Jericho T. Lovejoy had a good sense of humor, and I was guessing he'd wear it proudly with his matching prosthetic arm with the hook on it, the one he'd received before upgrading to the Terminator.

"Ladies!" called Sirena, poking her head in the door of the shop. "Time to set sail for home. Dinner awaits! It's fish and chips night, our traditional welcome meal."

We arrived back at Mermaid HQ just in time to stash our loot in our cabins before the dinner gong sounded. *Sirena wasn't kidding when she said we'd be eating a lot of fish this week,* I thought, surveying my plate. It was a good thing that I liked seafood.

"Oh man, this is so good!" said Mackenzie, and Delphine smiled.

"You know your way around a kitchen, that's for sure," agreed Zadie.

"Indeed she does," said Sirena proudly. "I'd say she's a chip off the old block, except I can't even boil water! I'm hopeless at cooking."

"I had to learn in self-defense," joked Delphine.

After dinner, it was time for the "unveiling and tailing."

"Change into your swimsuits, gather your tails, and meet at Mermaid Crossing—the back porch—in fifteen minutes," Sirena told us, and we all scattered to our cabins.

Mackenzie skipped happily down the path toward Whelk. "I can't wait to try mine on!"

I could. Watching the professionals today at the showquarium had given me a little more respect for the whole mermaid thing, but I still wasn't looking forward to turning myself into one. And my mood did not improve when I got my first glimpse of Mermaid Crossing.

"Over the top much?" I muttered at the same time that Mackenzie exclaimed, "It's perfect!"

Twinkle lights in the shape of seashells were draped across the porch's broad screens, and there were fishing nets and glass floats strung up everywhere. Big cushy chairs and sofas covered in faded blue denim were arranged in a semicircle, and scattered atop them were throw pillows that sported jaunty sayings like LIFE IS BETTER AT THE BEACH! and SEAS THE DAY! and MERMAIDS AHOY!

I eyed the enormous full-length mirror that leaned against the back wall of the house. It was encrusted with a haphazard pattern of seashells glued to its frame and looked like something Pippa might have made in kindergarten. Above it was a colorful mural featuring a trio of mermaids seated on a rock, brushing their long hair while whales frolicked in the distance. MERMAID CROSSING was written above their heads in shiny silver paint.

We all found seats and looked over at Sirena, who had changed into a gauzy white dress that fluttered and swirled around her knees as the ceiling fan spun overhead in slow circles. Sparkly flip-flops, full makeup, and yards of costume jewelry completed the look.

"And now," she said dramatically, "it's time for the unveiling and tailing!"

At Sirena's signal, we all opened the packages containing our tails. At first glance, Marina, the style I'd chosen, didn't look all that bad. I held it up. The tubelike part at the top was made of shiny blue fabric printed with scales, and the flukes fluttered limply at the bottom. I gave it a tentative tug. The whole thing didn't look very long, but it was stretchy.

"You'll need to insert the monofin first," Delphine told me. Unlike her mother, she was dressed simply in denim shorts and a Brewster Store T-shirt.

I gave her a blank look.

Leaning over my shoulder, she rummaged in the box that the tail had arrived in and pulled out a stiff, black crescent-shaped thing. "It's like a single swim flipper," she explained. Picking up the fluttery fabric at the bottom of the tail, she inserted the monofin into a hidden opening along the edge, then pulled the stretchy fabric back in place to cover it.

"Voilà!" she said, smiling. "Flukes!"

When everyone was finished prepping their tails, we all held them up.

"We're quite the rainbow, aren't we?" said Zadie, whose tail was hot pink.

"It always ends up this way," said Sirena. "Mermaids are a colorful bunch."

"Isn't mine gorgeous!" Mackenzie crowed, scattering audible exclamation points like the glittering sequins on her green Calypso tail.

The last time I'd seen Mackenzie this happy was over Spring Break, when her parents had given her permission to bring a kitten home. But even the thrill of picking Frankie out of a litter seemed to pale in comparison to this.

No two tails were alike, except for Hayden's and her mom's. They had ordered matching ones covered in flat, pearly disks.

"I think those are a style called Atlantis," Jasmine whispered to us. "I saw them on the website. They're custom and *really* expensive."

This didn't surprise me. Mrs. Drake was clearly a nothing-but-the-best-for-my-princess kind of mom.

"Delphine, would you like to demonstrate how a mermaid puts on her tail?" Sirena asked her daughter.

Delphine nodded and stepped out of her shorts, revealing her bathing suit underneath. She picked up a shiny turquoise tail that was draped over the back of the sofa and rolled it down like a sock. Then she sat down and deftly placed her feet into the openings in the monofin. With one graceful movement, she stood up again, pulling the fabric upward while she shimmied. The tail unfurled smoothly over her long legs. She gave a final tug to the waistband, removed her T-shirt to reveal a matching turquoise bikini top underneath, then perched on the arm of the sofa, smiling at us as she swished her flukes back and forth.

"Couldn't have done it better myself," said Sirena, as we gave Delphine a round of applause. "Now it's your turn, ladies. Let the tailing begin!"

The porch grew quiet as we concentrated on copying Delphine. Sixteen pairs of legs were inserted into sixteen fabric mermaid flukes. Thirty seconds after I started to pull my tail up, though, I knew something was wrong. Marina was supposed to fit mermaids five foot eight and over, but no matter how hard I tugged and shimmied and yanked on it, the stupid thing wouldn't go past my knees.

"Oh, honey," said Zadie, looking over at me, "they sent you the wrong size!"

Cha Cha laughed her raspy laugh until her legs went weak and she collapsed on the floor. That set Jasmine and Mackenzie off, and pretty soon everyone was laughing. Everyone except me. I stood there wearing half a mermaid tail and feeling like a big idiot.

Sirena finally took pity on me. "Don't worry," she said, wiping her eyes, "if there's one thing we have here at Mermaid HQ, it's plenty of tails." She crossed the porch and flung open an old trunk that was serving as a makeshift coffee table. "See if you can find one that fits you."

As the rest of the group hopped around looking at themselves in the full-length mirror and snapping selfies, I tried on one tail after another. A couple of them almost worked, but nothing was quite right for my size-ten-and-a-half feet and extra-long legs.

"Any luck?" asked Sirena a few minutes later.

I shook my head.

"Delphine, surely there must be one of your old tails floating around here that would work for her."

"I'll go check," said Delphine.

"And while you're upstairs, bring down the sea serpent costume, would you?"

Delphine nodded, shimmied back out of her tail, and disappeared into the house. I steeled myself to put my foot down. I'd rather be sent home than have to be a sea serpent!

In the end, though, I didn't have to. Delphine returned a few minutes later bearing a rueful expression and a sad, droopy brown mess riddled with so many holes it almost looked like lace draped across her shoulders. At one end lolled a sea serpent head, grinning spitefully at me.

"Moths," Delphine reported to her mother. "They got into the old practice tail of mine, too."

"Oh no! What a shame!" Sirena frowned, drumming her aqua-tipped fingers on the arm of her chair.

"There's always my tail from the Jolly Roger," Delphine suggested. "It would fit her."

"That's against the rules," said her mother sharply.

I perked up at that. "Against the rules" sounded a whole lot better than "sea serpent."

"She's probably got the strength for it," Delphine continued, the two of them discussing me as if I weren't standing right there. "It said on her application that she's on a swim team."

Sirena thought it over. "Well, perhaps we could make an exception." She nodded at Delphine, who withdrew inside the house again, and returned a few moments later carrying what looked like a floppy rubber tube made of glimmering aquamarine.

"A *shimmertail*!" cried Hayden. "No fair! Only professional mermaids are supposed to wear shimmertails!"

Sirena silenced Hayden with a stern wag of her finger. "Mermaids are never envious. And this is a special case. Truly is too tall for any of the other tails that we have on hand."

"Truly *enormous*," Hayden muttered resentfully. She said it under her breath, but I heard her just fine. My face flushed.

"Now, Hayden," said her mother, half-heartedly scolding her.

Delphine handed over the shimmertail. I gasped and nearly dropped it.

"Thirty pounds of sculpted silicone," she told me. I was familiar with silicone. My father actually had three prosthetic arms to choose from, and silicone was what Ken, his name for the lifelike but useless option, was made of.

I hefted the tail. It was going to be interesting trying to swim in this thing. I might as well strap a cinder block to my feet. I sat down to put it on.

"Wait," said Delphine, "you'll need these first." She passed me a pair of black socks. "They're neoprene and will keep your feet from slipping out of the heel straps." She also handed me a spray bottle.

I squinted at it. "What's this?"

"Hair conditioner mixed with warm water. Spray your legs with it, and the tail will go on easier."

I wrinkled my nose but did as I was told. Putting first one foot in and then the other, I felt around for the heel straps that would secure my feet in place.

"Take your time," said Delphine. "Pull it up inch by inch."

The silicone tail didn't stretch as much as the fabric tails had. It took a lot of encouragement and instruction from Delphine, and I was red-faced and sweaty by the time I was done, but I finally managed to wiggle into the gleaming tube.

Mackenzie's eyes widened in admiration. "Wow! You look amazing, Truly."

"Truly amazing," quipped Zadie. "Right, Lenore?"

Lenore nodded.

Delphine turned to her mother. "See? I told you. Fits like a glove."

More like a corset, I thought. The waistband was so tight I could hardly breathe.

"Don't try and stand up," Delphine instructed. "That's pretty much impossible in a shimmertail."

"Okay," I said, scooting myself awkwardly over to the mirror. The shimmertail *was* pretty awesome, I had to admit, smoothing it over my hips. Realistic-looking 3-D scales were molded along the length of it, and glitter had been embedded into the silicone itself, giving the surface an iridescent sheen. The graceful arch of the fluke at the bottom was nearly twice as big as the ones on the fabric tails. I looked—well, I looked like a real mermaid.

If there were such things.

Over my shoulder, I caught a glimpse of Hayden's face. She was staring at my tail with unmistakable envy.

"There's a matching bikini top," said Delphine, handing me what looked like two aquamarine potholders sewn together.

I gulped. "I don't—"

"Come on, Truly!" Mackenzie begged.

I sighed. *In for a penny, in for a pound,* I thought. Awkwardly tugging my arms inside my Pumpkin Falls Swim Team T-shirt, I managed to pull the top of my one-piece racing suit down and squirm into Delphine's bikini top.

"It's perfect!" said Mackenzie, after I reluctantly removed the T-shirt to show off the results. "Right, Cha Cha? Right, Jazz?"

My friends nodded enthusiastically.

"I think we've found our queen," Sirena said to Delphine.

Wait. What? I thought in alarm. Who said anything about a queen?

I looked in the mirror again. There was nothing remotely regal about what was looking back at me. My worst nightmare had just come true—I was wearing a clamshell bra!

I grabbed my T-shirt and yanked it back over my head.

Sirena arched an eyebrow. "We've got our work cut out for us," she murmured.

Delphine patted her on the shoulder. "We've dealt with worse."

As everyone wriggled onto the sofas and chairs, Delphine went back inside, reappearing a few moments later with a tray.

"Mermaid snacks!" Sirena announced. "Time to celebrate your new tails!"

The snacks turned out to be a flavored sparkling water and shortbread cookies cut into fish shapes. We helped ourselves while Delphine passed around some handouts.

"You'll be choosing a mermaid name for the week," Sirena told us. "This list will provide you with some suggestions, but feel free to let your imagination take you where it will."

Mine was taking me right out the door and onto the bus for home, I thought as I glanced down at the name at the top of the list. Malibu? Seriously?

"If your mermaid name has an interesting meaning, please share it with us," Sirena continued. "Sirena, for instance, is

Greek for 'enchantress'—a siren was a mythical sea creature whose beauty and song lured sailors to their deaths."

That sounded like something to aspire to, I thought, suppressing a smile. I made a mental note to add this to the growing list of things I couldn't wait to tell Hatcher.

"And Delphine is French for 'dolphin,'" Sirena went on. "We encourage you to come up with a backstory for yourself as well. Spin us a tale! Who is your mermaid? Where did she grow up? What are her hopes and dreams?"

"My mermaid name is Shellina," blurted Hayden, like she couldn't hold it in any longer.

If I'd been drinking anything just then, it would have spurted out my nose for sure. Shellina? Even Mackenzie let out a sound that was close to a giggle.

"I was born in the undersea kingdom of Tritonia," Hayden continued, throwing us side-eye. "My father is the ruler there, and I have six younger sisters, and I will grow up and marry a prince."

Shellina's backstory sounded suspiciously like the plot to Pippa and Lauren's favorite mermaid movie, but nobody else said anything, so I didn't either.

"And someday, I shall be queen." Hayden looked pointedly over at me as she emphasized this last bit.

Queen Shellina? I sat up a little straighter in my shimmertail. Not if I had anything to say about it. I didn't ask to be queen, but I wasn't about to just hand the role over to a spoiled brat, either.

"Wonderful!" said Sirena. "You've obviously come prepared, Hayden. The rest of you have a little homework to do. But don't stay up late! Remember, mermaids need their beauty rest. 'Early to bed, early to rise, keeps mermaids fit and their fins looking nice!'"

I groaned inwardly. Where did she *get* this stuff?

"Off with your tails now, and then off to bed with you. Tomorrow is a big day. Class will convene at the pool before breakfast. We have less than a week before the revue to transform you into mermaids."

Review? I didn't like the sound of that. "You mean, like a test?"

"Not review, R-E-V-U-E," said Sirena, spelling the word out like Annie Freeman. "It's our performance for the general public. We do it at the end of every session here at the academy."

My face must have registered my shock.

"It's a very popular event here in Brewster," Sirena hastened to assure me.

"There wasn't anything in the brochure about a revue!" I protested. It was one thing to be forced to goof around privately in somebody's backyard, and a whole other kettle of fish to have to appear as a mermaid in public!

"Just think of it as a piano recital," said Mackenzie.

I shot her a look. She knew exactly how I felt about those. Plus, I'd never worn a bikini top to a piano recital in my life, let alone a tail. And only parents and relatives showed up for piano recitals, not the "general public."

So much for stealth mode. Unless I totally caved and let Hayden—make that Shellina—get her way, I was destined to be front and center in Sirena's Sea Siren Academy pool for all of Cape Cod to gawk at.

This was quickly shaping up to be the worst week of my life!

CHAPTER 12

I lay in my bunk, listening to the soft murmur of voices that floated in the window from the cabin next door. The ladies of Sand Dollar were busy getting better acquainted from the sound of it. All was quiet in Whelk, apart from Cha Cha's and Jasmine's steady breathing and an occasional snuffle-snore from Mackenzie across the room. I was the only one awake. I turned over again, trying to get comfortable. But sleep was impossible.

What was I doing here? How had I let myself get talked into coming to mermaid camp? I should be home, helping out at the bookstore and trying to find the missing trophy.

Unplugging my cell phone from its charger, I slipped out of bed and crept as quietly as I could across the bare wooden floor to the cabin door. Outside, I tiptoed behind Whelk, then sprinted across the back lawn toward the cover of the pine trees beyond the pool. I stood there for a moment in the shadows, hoping no one had seen me. But the windows in the main house and all the cabins remained dark, and the ladies of Sand Dollar were still busy whooping it up, clearly not interested in anything going on outside. Like a fellow aspiring mermaid making a desperate phone call.

Aunt True answered on the first ring.

"Truly? It's late—is everything all right?"

At the sound of her voice, I burst into tears.

"Oh, honey, what's wrong?"

"Everything!" I wailed. "I hate it here! I want to come home!" I knew I sounded like a homesick little kid, but I didn't care. The words came tumbling out in a rush. "My stupid mermaid tail didn't fit because they sent me the wrong size, and Sirena wanted me to be a sea serpent instead but it had moth holes and now I have to wear something called a shimmertail and be a queen in front of the *entire world!*"

There was silence on the other end of the phone as my aunt tried to digest this burst of information. "Um, I get the picture, I think?"

Just in case she didn't, I expanded on my list of complaints: Sirena and her dumb "mermaids eat fish" and "mermaids need their beauty rest" and other pronouncements; Mackenzie's complete lack of a sense of humor about all the things that struck me as funny; Hayden's designs on my throne, which I didn't really want anyway; the revue looming at the end of the week. "I even have to wear a stupid clamshell bra!" I finished indignantly.

I could hear Aunt True smiling. "You do realize, of course, that you're going to have great stories to tell about this experience for the rest of your life."

I grunted. "That doesn't help."

"I know, sweetheart." She sighed. "I wish I could fix this for you."

"You can! I really want to come home, Aunt True! I called you because I know Mom and Dad were looking forward to some time alone, but couldn't I stay with you?"

There was another long pause. "I tell you what," she said finally. "Before we go with the nuclear option, how about you sit tight for forty-eight hours? Things might get better. And if they don't, and you still want to come home, I'll drive down and get you, okay?"

I could live with that. "Okay."

"Good girl. Meanwhile, call me any time, or zap me a text. Tall timber sticks together. Now, go get some sleep. I hear that mermaids need their beauty rest."

I laughed grudgingly. After we hung up, I decided to text Calhoun and Scooter and Lucas. No point waiting until tomorrow.

ANY PROGRESS? I waited for a response. Nothing. They were probably all asleep. As I was slipping my phone back into my pocket, though, it buzzed.

It was Calhoun!

A LITTLE, he told me. LUCAS'S CROWDSOURCING—#MISSING

TROPHY #PUMPKINFALLS #FOURONTHEFOURTH—IS STARTING TO PAY OFF. WE'RE REVIEWING THE PHOTOS AS THEY COME IN.

VIDEO CHAT TOMORROW?

SURE. HOW'S MERMAID CAMP?

DON'T ASK, I replied, adding an eye roll emoji.

LOL! NIGHT

NIGHT

There was one other person I thought about calling, but I knew from personal experience that athletes at sports camps went to bed early. I typed out another text instead: HELP! HAVE BEEN KIDNAPPED BY ALIENS DISGUISED AS MERMAIDS! I added an alien emoji, along with a mermaid one for good measure, and sent it to Hatcher. And then I went back to bed.

Morning came way too early. I trailed down to the pool behind my cousin and friends, yawning. I wasn't the only one who'd stayed up too late. The four women from Sand Dollar looked even less awake than me. They'd still been talking and laughing when I'd finally managed to fall asleep last night.

Sirena wagged a finger at them. "Next time, ladies, do as I tell you. Mermaids—"

"—need their beauty rest!" the four of them chorused in unison.

"That's exactly right." Sirena was bright-eyed and bushy-tailed, as Grandma G would say. Today she was wearing a bright floral swimsuit, matching floral flip-flops, sunglasses whose frames were studded with rhinestones, and a wide-brimmed hat. From what I'd seen, just about everything Sirena owned was decorated either with sequins, fake jewels, or glitter.

Delphine looked more like a normal person. Her racer-back swimsuit was similar to the one I was wearing, and over it she'd pulled the same denim shorts she'd worn last night.

The high school girls from St. Louis were in high spirits, laughing and joking around with one another. Hayden still looked grumpy. Her mother, who was probably used to her moods, calmly sipped coffee out of a travel mug with MER-MAMA emblazoned on the side. Zadie and Lorena were going through a series of stretches on the pool deck. I watched them, impressed. They were pretty flexible for ladies pushing ninety.

Sirena clapped her hands. "Into the water with you!"

"What about our tails?" asked Hayden.

"We'll get to that later. First, morning mermaid exercises."

This sounded suspiciously like warm-ups at swim team practice, which it pretty much was. Sirena and Delphine led us through stretches along the wall first, and then made us swim laps while they watched.

"We want to get a sense of your overall comfort in the water, and of your general level of ability as swimmers," Sirena told us. Delphine stood beside her, taking notes.

I felt myself relax the minute I slipped into the pool. Ever since I was a little girl, I'd loved the feeling of being in the water, whether it was a pool, a lake, the ocean, or even a bathtub. I loved that moment when the water closed over my head and the outside world fell away. As Sirena put us through our paces, the anxiety that had crowded in on me last night began to fade away. Was it really that big a deal if I had to swim in public? I'd done it a zillion times before, after all, at countless swim meets over the years.

Maybe Aunt True was right, and things would get better. And if not, all I had to do was stick it out for forty-eight hours. Forty-two, now.

I'd been happy to see that Sirena's pool was a regulation-size twenty-five-meter one. As I churned my way to the far end, I thought maybe I'd ask if I could swim some extra laps each day, to help keep me in shape for summer swim team. This mermaid stuff seemed like it was going to be a snap. I was easily the strongest swimmer here. Well, along with Mackenzie. When I reached the far edge of the pool, I paused, treading water as I awaited further instructions.

"Swim back to me underwater!" Sirena called. "Let's see how far you can go."

Like I said, easy.

I took a deep breath and pushed off, diving beneath the surface into the streamline I used for races, then dolphin-kicked my way back down the length of the pool. I inspected the bottom as I swam. The pool had been nice once, with tiny colored tiles that formed an intricate mural of King Neptune holding his trident aloft, surrounded by dolphins. Now, though, the picture had faded, and some of the tiles were missing.

Thirty seconds later, I reached the shallow end.

Sirena checked something off on her clipboard. "Excellent, Truly. Impressive breath control."

"Thanks." At least now they knew that I could swim.

So could Zadie and Lenore, as it turned out.

When Sirena asked if anyone knew any synchronized swimming moves, Zadie and Lenore looked at each other, smiled, and swam out to the middle of the pool. They extended their arms overhead like ballerinas, then slowly and gracefully arced backward through the water in perfect unison, one knee bent, one straight, toes pointed.

"Perfect knee-back dolphins!" gasped Delphine.

We all clapped as the two older ladies resurfaced.

"We appear to have a pair of ringers in our midst!" Sirena exclaimed, putting her hands on her hips. "Out with it, you two. Where on earth did you learn to do that?"

"From Esther Williams," Zadie replied smugly, swimming back over to join us. Lenore was right behind her.

Sirena's mouth fell open. "You're kidding, right?"

"Nope. We weren't much older than these girls here"—Zadie gestured toward Mackenzie and Cha Cha and Jasmine and me—"when a Hollywood talent scout discovered us in a water ballet class in Laguna Beach. That was the start of our film career."

"You mean to tell me that you two swam with Esther Williams in the *movies*?" If Sirena's jaw dropped any farther, it was going to hit the pool deck. I had no idea what she was talking about, but Delphine and Hayden's mom and the four ladies from Sand Dollar clearly did, as they all looked equally astounded.

Zadie and Lenore nodded again, clearly pleased by the attention.

"We thought about telling you ahead of time, but Lenore thought it might be more fun to surprise you," Zadie explained. "Isn't that right, Lenore?"

Lenore gave a modest smile.

"Oh. My. Goodness," said Sirena, for once at a loss for words. She stood there, shaking her head in disbelief. "Which of her movies were you in? I have them all!"

"Let's see, *Million Dollar Mermaid*, of course, *Neptune's Daughter*, and *Easy to Love*—a whole slew of them. They even brought us out of retirement to help choreograph the water ballet scene in *Funny Lady*."

Turning to the rest of us, Sirena announced, "I simply can't believe this. We are in the presence of underwater royalty, ladies. *Royalty!*" It must have been obvious that some of us were still clueless, because she went on to explain. "Esther Williams just about single-handedly popularized water ballet, which is what they used to call synchronized swimming. She was a huge movie star, and an amazing athlete—without her popularity and pioneering influence, synchronized swimming might never have become an Olympic sport! And for many of us who grew up watching her onscreen, she's part of the reason we became mermaids. You could say that, in a way, she was the spark that lit the fire beneath today's interest in all things mermaid."

Thanks a bunch, Esther, I thought.

"As a tribute to Zadie and Lenore, I'm switching up our post-siesta movie today," Sirena continued. "I'd planned to have us watch *Splash*, but we'll watch an Esther Williams movie instead!" She turned back to the two elderly ladies. "And did I hear you correctly? Do you have experience with choreography?"

Zadie nodded.

Sirena clasped her hands together beseechingly. "Would you be willing to help us out this week? Pretty please with mermaid glitter on top?"

"We were hoping you might ask," Zadie replied. "Isn't that right, Lenore?"

Lenore nodded again.

Sirena gave them a rapturous look. "Just think what a marketing hook we'll have! 'All-new mermaid revue, choreographed by Esther Williams's own protégées!' Every senior citizen on the Cape will be begging for a ticket!"

I let the water close over my head and sank to the bottom of the pool. It was quiet down there, and sane.

Later, after breakfast—scrambled eggs, fresh fruit, and bagels with cream cheese and something called "lox," which turned out to be smoked salmon—we returned to the pool.

"Now that I feel confident in your swimming abilities, we're ready to try it with tails," Sirena told us. "It's time for your official mermaid training to begin, ladies!"

Excitement fizzed as everyone rushed to wiggle into their tails. Everyone except me. There was no rushing a shimmer-tail. Once again, I needed Delphine's help putting it on. I was the last one into the pool, slithering awkwardly across the deck to join Mackenzie and my friends, who were perched on the edge, swishing their flukes in the water.

"Group photo, ladies!" said Sirena, taking her cell phone out of a pocket in her swim cover-up. "Lean back on your elbows and lift those tails aloft—jaunty angle now, let's show them off! Smile and say—"

"Cheese?" I suggested.

"—seashells!"

Looking down the long row of multicolored tails sparkling in the morning sun, I had to admit we made a pretty sweet lineup.

"Wonderful!" Sirena gestured toward the water. "When you feel ready, hop on in. We'll stay down here at the shallow end to begin with. Please keep a grip on the edge for now. We're going to take this in baby steps."

I dangled my shimmertail in the pool, swishing its flukes and testing the resistance. I was used to swimming with my legs and feet close together—the dolphin kick was a staple on swim team, and the butterfly was my favorite stroke—but it was a completely different feeling having them encased in a heavy silicone tube.

Around me, my fellow aspiring mermaids began sliding in. Sirena watched the proceedings closely, standing poised with one of the long rescue hooks that Coach Maynard sometimes used to fish swim team members out when they accidentally swallowed a big mouthful of water and panicked. But Sirena was fairly small and some of the other guests—two of the Sand Dollar ladies in particular—were pretty large. If push came to shove, they might yank her right into the pool with them. I hoped I wouldn't have to try to put my junior lifeguarding skills to the test while wearing this heavy tail.

But nobody seemed to be panicking so far. Quite the opposite, in fact. All I could hear were shrieks of delight as the others tested out their tails for the first time. Mackenzie held on to the edge of the deck, flapping her flukes up and down behind her. She smiled up at me. "What are you waiting for?"

I shrugged. "Nothing." Scooting forward, I pushed myself in.

And sank instantly to the bottom of the pool.

CHAPTER 13

I thrashed around in a panic, struggling to heave the tail into a position that allowed me to stand. The water was only four feet deep, but it might as well have been forty. When the pool hook appeared beside me, I grabbed it and let myself be hauled up.

"I'm not so sure this is a good idea, Delphine," said Sirena when I emerged unharmed but flustered. "This may be beyond her abilities."

Beyond my abilities, my eye! I thought. I'd show her beyond my abilities.

Lovejoys are competitive. We can't help it; we just are.

Taking a deep breath, I let go of the hook, pushed off the wall, and launched myself into a streamline. Arms stretched out in front of me, I undulated back across the pool for several lengths, exactly the same way I'd done a few minutes earlier when Sirena tested my breath control. The tail was heavy, there was no doubt about that. I could feel the powerful resistance as I forced the flukes up and down, up and down through the water. But my legs were powerful too, their muscles honed from years of swim team practice.

Suddenly I felt a subtle shift as I found my groove. I was no longer fighting the shimmertail, and in a flash it went from enemy to ally, rocketing me forward with each dolphin kick. I shot to the surface and threw my arms overhead in the classic butterfly arm stroke, the shimmertail propelling me through the air faster and higher than I'd ever managed on my own before. I almost laughed out loud. So this was what flying felt like!

At the far end, I slapped my hands on the pool's edge, just the way I would during a race, rotated, then pushed off and swam back toward Sirena and the others.

Right before I reached them, I suddenly reversed into a backstroke position, whipped my tail up and out of the water, and smacked my flukes down as hard as I could.

My fellow aspiring mermaids squealed as a tsunami engulfed them.

"Really, Truly!" sputtered Sirena. "Was that necessary?"

Hayden glared at me. "Show-off."

Everyone else was laughing, though. Delphine grinned as she marked something down on her clipboard. "You have to admit that was quite an advanced move, Mom."

Sirena, who was mopping her face, grudgingly agreed. "I guess we don't need to worry about her abilities." She turned to the rest of the group. "That's quite enough tricks for one morning. I want to see laps now and plenty of them. Take it slow while you get used to swimming in a tail."

Sirena and Delphine put us through our paces for the next hour, alternating laps with stretches and basic ballet arm gestures. Nothing too strenuous, but I was definitely getting a workout, thanks to the heavy shimmertail.

"You've danced before, haven't you?" Delphine said, watching Cha Cha.

My friend smiled. "A bit."

"Her parents own a dance studio," Jasmine explained. "She doesn't just dance—she helps teach."

Sirena beamed. "We are just overflowing with talent this week! This is going be a standout revue. Definitely one of the academy's best, I can already tell." She looked at her watch. "Okay, ladies, let's take a break! We'll be back in the pool later this afternoon, and meanwhile, I'm going to give you a choice. You can stay in the water for another half hour with Zadie and Lenore, who are keen to share a few of their synchronized swimming moves, or you can enjoy a little free time before lunch."

The high school girls opted for free time. So did the Sand Dollar ladies. As Delphine headed for the kitchen, Sirena retreated to a seat by the cabana, as she referred to the shed where the pool supplies were stashed, and kept one eye on us and one on her cell phone. That left Mackenzie and

Cha Cha and Jasmine and me in the pool, along with Hayden and her mother.

If I'd ever thought synchronized swimming wasn't real swimming, I quickly learned otherwise. Zadie and Lenore started with a few basic moves. I already knew how to tread water, but they demonstrated how to do it invisibly, sculling our arms underwater with our elbows glued to our sides as we waved our flukes back and forth. It took a surprising amount of effort to stay afloat.

"Being a good synchronized swimmer takes the lung power of a long-distance runner, the leg strength of a water polo player, the grace and rhythm of a ballet dancer, and the muscle control of a gymnast," Zadie explained. "That's what Esther Williams always used to say."

Next, they had us try the ballet leg double position. Lying back in the water, we drew our knees in to our chests, then extended our legs straight up and waved our flukes in the air.

"See how I'm sculling underwater again to keep myself in place?" said Zadie.

We also tried the oyster, lying flat on our backs in the water and then closing up like clamshells—or oyster shells in this case—by bringing our legs and hands up and touching them together, then sinking down bottom first into the water.

"Good job!" said Zadie. "Now form a circle and try some of the moves in unison."

Swimming in a tail was a lot harder than the professional

mermaids had made it look at the pirate museum. By the time Delphine rang the lunch gong, my legs were aching, and my arm and back muscles were sore from the constant sculling needed to counter the downward drag of the heavy shimmertail.

"This isn't mermaid academy; it's mermaid boot camp," I grumbled as we trooped back to our cabins to change.

At lunch, I nearly fell asleep in my clam chowder. My head was bobbing as Sirena outlined the rest of the day's packed schedule.

"And don't forget, we're all going to reveal our mermaid names tonight after dinner!" she told us. "Get busy on those backstories, ladies!"

Mackenzie and Cha Cha and Jasmine had to practically carry me back to Whelk for our siesta. I flopped onto my bunk as the three of them huddled together to work on their back-stories. I was too tired to lift my head off the pillow, let alone lift a pen. They'd been swimming all morning in tails made of spandex and neoprene, not thirty pounds of silicone. I was out like a light in ten seconds flat.

I awoke with a start as Mackenzie shook my shoulder.

"Siesta is over, Truly!"

"Already?" I groaned. "We were supposed to have a Pumpkin Falls Private Eyes videoconference." I checked my phone. Sure enough, there was a whole string of text messages from the boys.

"We can do that later," my cousin said. "Hurry up! You'll miss the movie!"

I texted Calhoun to let him know the change of plans, then headed back to Mermaid HQ, where Sirena and Delphine had giant bowls of popcorn waiting for us in front of the big-screen TV.

"Which movie did you decide on?" Zadie asked Sirena.

"*Million Dollar Mermaid*, of course!"

Zadie laughed. "I figured you might choose that one." She patted the sofa next to her. "Come on, Lenore. This is going to be fun."

The movie was as cheesy as the rest of mermaid camp. Zadie was right, though—it was fun. It wasn't about a mermaid, but rather a real woman named Annette Kellerman who was a famous Australian swimmer a century ago. She had to wear leg braces as a kid, but overcame them by learning to swim. She went on to win all sorts of prizes before moving to America and becoming a star, performing in this giant aquarium theater in New York called the Hippodrome. I liked how feisty Annette was, sticking up for herself when she got in trouble with the law for wearing a one-piece bathing suit. That was considered scandalous back in 1907, when women were supposed to wear "bathing costumes" that looked like long dresses, or bloomers with stockings.

The best parts, though, were when Annette—Esther Williams—dove and swam. I could tell the minute I saw the muscles in her legs that she was a real athlete. Sirena had been right about that. Esther did her own stunts, and even without knowing much about synchronized swimming, I could appreciate the level of difficulty most of the dives and tricks took.

I had to admit that I liked the choreographed water ballet stuff, too, even if it was over the top Hollywood, with Esther almost always wearing full makeup and something sparkly.

"There we are!" yelled Zadie at one point, and Sirena immediately hit pause on the remote. Zadie sprang out of her seat and rushed to the TV screen, pointing to a circle of girls in gold swimsuits and matching caps who were emerging from the water on a platform. "That's us, right behind Esther!"

Sirena hit play again, and we watched as the swimmers all rose into the air, thanks to what Zadie explained was a hydraulic lift. Esther Williams was wearing a glittering gold bodysuit and matching crown for this scene, and Zadie and Lenore framed her like a pair of shiny gold bookends.

I glanced from the youthful onscreen images to the two wrinkled faces beaming at us from across the room. Would I look like that when I was their age, I wondered? On the other hand, if I could swim as well as they could when I was nearly ninety, who cared?

My favorite scenes were the ones filmed from above. As the swimmers' arms and legs moved in changing formations, they created a sort of human kaleidoscope, which was really cool to watch.

"Such precision! Such artistry!" cried Sirena, pausing the movie again a few minutes later when the camera zoomed in on Zadie and Lenore. The two of them were smiling big red-lipstick smiles and laughing as they were towed across the Hippodrome pool by an invisible underwater mechanism.

"That was our big close-up!" Zadie said. "And those smiles weren't fake—we were genuinely having fun. We thought we had the best job in the world!"

We all clapped after the grand finale, when the two of them were once again lifted out of the water on a platform with Esther Williams and a bunch of other swimmers, this time against a backdrop of fireworks that fizzed and flamed.

Zadie sighed with satisfaction. "Esther really knew how to make an entrance—and an exit."

"How come they don't make those kinds of movies anymore?" asked Cha Cha.

"Aqua-musicals, you mean?" said Zadie.

"There's an actual name for them?" Cha Cha's deep voice went up an octave.

"Oh yes. Aqua-ballet, aqua-musicals—they even named us in one of the films. We were billed as 'the Neptunettes' in *Neptune's Daughter.*"

For some reason this struck Mackenzie as funny. She

started to laugh. "That could be your mermaid name, Truly—Neptunette!"

I gave her the stink eye. But she'd reminded me that I still needed to pick a name and a backstory. So far, I had nothing.

"Were you ever in the Olympics?" asked one of the girls from St. Louis.

Zadie shook her head. "No. By the time synchronized swimming became an Olympic sport in 1984, we were way too old. But they asked Esther to be an official commentator. She was wonderful! We watched together from my house that year, cheering her on."

Sirena stood up. "Ladies, you have about an hour of free time until our afternoon pool session. If anyone wants to make a trip to the Brewster Store, the van is available."

"Or you can walk," suggested Delphine. "It's less than half a mile from here."

My cousin and friends and I chose that option, and a few minutes later we were crunching down the shell-covered driveway toward the road.

"I'm going to live here when I grow up," Jasmine announced. "Cape Cod is so cool! I love being near the ocean."

Cha Cha shook her head. "Not me. New York City is where I want to be. It's the only place for a dancer. Well, that or San Francisco or London, maybe."

"I'm a Texan through and through," said Mackenzie firmly. "It's the Lone Star State for me. You too, right, Truly?"

I lifted a shoulder. I had no idea where I wanted to live when I grew up. I was still trying to get used to Pumpkin Falls.

Just as Jasmine had promised, there was a long counter at the Brewster Store where they served ice cream and fudge and penny candy. I looked around as we waited for our cones. The creaky wood floors and high ceilings and big windows reminded me a bit of our bookstore back home. The rest of it was similar to the Pumpkin Falls General Store, as Jasmine had said, except that instead of selling mostly practical everyday stuff like seed packets and tools, the Brewster Store was geared completely to tourists. The displays were crammed with postcards and souvenirs, sweatshirts and T-shirts and baseball caps with I LOVE CAPE COD on them, plus beach toys and knickknacks and that sort of thing.

"Hey, check it out!" Cha Cha pointed to a sign in the window:

BOOK SIGNING THURSDAY NIGHT!

AMANDA APPLETON, PHD, PRESENTS HER NEW BOOK—

SAGA OF A SHIP: THE LOST TREASURE OF THE WINDBORNE

"Isn't the *Windborne* that wreck we learned about at the pirate museum?" she asked.

"Yeah," said Jasmine. "Let's tell Sirena. Maybe she can schedule a field trip."

Fine by me, I thought. Pirates were more interesting than mermaids any day of the week.

CHAPTER 14

By four o'clock, we were back in the pool.

"Lenore and I spent our siesta with Sirena, working up a routine for the revue," Zadie told us.

"We focused on simple moves that should be easy to learn and easy to perform," Sirena added, "but the girls"—it took me a moment to realize she was talking about Zadie and Lenore —"put them together in combinations that will add a little razzle-dazzle."

Razzle-dazzle? Did anyone actually use that term? Anyone except Sirena, that was? My eyes slid over to Mackenzie, but predictably, there was no answering smirk.

"And," Sirena continued, "we've got a killer finish that will really show off our mermaid queen."

I wasn't sure I liked the sound of that.

Hayden definitely didn't. I could tell by the look on her face.

"You'll probably recognize a few of the moves," said Zadie. "It's a bit of a nod to *Million Dollar Mermaid*—but without the fancy special effects."

"Unless you call sparklers special effects," said Delphine.

Sirena beamed at Zadie and Lenore. "I can't thank you two enough!" she gushed. "This is going to be our best revue ever! I'm going to call it *A Tribute to Esther Williams*. Delphine, you can help me make up flyers tonight, and we'll distribute them around town tomorrow."

Zadie had us all take seats on the edge of the pool opposite the bleachers while Sirena and Delphine headed for the cabana. They emerged a moment later with a boom box and a whiteboard on an easel. Zadie wrote *DECK WORK* on the whiteboard.

"We're going to break it down into individual positions and strokes," she told us. "Then we'll work on transitions—the movements that connect everything into a routine. But first we're going to start with some deck work."

"Think of deck work as a preshow routine," Sirena added. "You'll perform this part right where you're sitting now, before you get in the water."

Zadie nodded at Delphine, who fiddled with the boom box. A moment later, music wafted from its tinny speakers.

"As the lights go up and the music starts," said Zadie, "you'll all be sitting along the edge of the pool just like you are now, but with your backs to the bleachers and your knees drawn up to your chins. Would you try this, please, ladies?"

We pulled our tails out of the water and swiveled around obediently.

"Sirena? Delphine? Can you see the tails?"

Sirena and her daughter, who had taken seats in the bleachers, both shook their heads.

"Now, I'll be positioned here at the end of the row"—Zadie scampered down to where Jasmine was sitting—"and at my signal, Delphine is going to switch on the spotlight. She'll point it at each of you, one by one. When the light hits you, I want you to turn around, lean back on your elbows, kick your tail up into the air, and hold it for the count of five. Lenore? Would you please demonstrate?"

Lenore did.

"Make the most of it, ladies," said Sirena, as Lenore leaned back and kicked her tail up into the air. "This is your close-up, as they call it in Hollywood!"

"Absolutely!" Zadie agreed. "Flaunt those flukes, smile and wave at the audience, show off a little. After you count to five, you'll sit up and drop your tail in the water. Give it a good splash when you do." She pointed at Lenore, who obediently dropped and splashed. "After the tail drop, the spotlight will move on to the next mermaid. Everyone will get their moment to shine. All except you, Truly. Our mermaid queen will be safely hidden in the cabana until closer to the grand finale."

Hayden looked pleased for the first time all day.

It was our turn next. Even though I'd be waiting in the wings—well, the cabana—during the opening number, Zadie had me practice with them anyway. She went down the row, tapping each of us on the shoulder to represent the spotlight. We spun around one by one to face the bleachers, leaned back and hoisted our tails into the air and waved them around for the count of five, then sat up and dropped our tails into the pool.

The next move involved diving into the water like a row of dominoes. Once again, Lenore demonstrated as Zadie walked us through it.

"After the final tail drops, the lights will come up, and on my cue, it's arms up, palms together"—Lenore put her arms over her head and pressed her palms together—"and you'll peel off one by one and dive into the water from where you're sitting, just like we did in *Million Dollar Mermaid*. And don't forget that big smile!"

Lenore dove neatly into the pool, smiling for all she was worth. Zadie had us run through the domino dive a few times, and then it was time to connect the moves together.

"What do you think, Sirena?" asked Zadie when we were done.

"I think we have ourselves a genuine school of mermaids!" Sirena replied, doing a little victory shimmy. Her red curls shimmied happily too.

"Excellent work, ladies!" said Zadie. "That's our deck work, done and dusted."

Sirena told us we'd learn the next part of the routine tomorrow, and suggested we swim laps while Delphine got dinner ready.

A few lengths of the pool later, Mackenzie surfaced beside me. "This is great, isn't it?"

I grunted.

"Mermaid camp—I mean mermaid *academy*—is even better than I thought it would be. I love it here, don't you?"

If anyone had told me a few days ago that I'd find myself in a pool on Cape Cod, wearing a mermaid tail and learning synchronized swimming moves from a pair of elderly ladies, I'd have told them they were crazy.

What was crazier was the fact that Mackenzie was right—it was better than I thought it would be. I was actually starting to enjoy myself. At this rate, I might not need Aunt True to come rescue me.

"It's okay, I guess."

Mackenzie laughed. "C'mon, Truly! Admit it—you're having fun."

I grinned at her. "Yeah," I admitted. "I'm having fun."

And then I flipped over onto my back and splashed her with my shimmertail.

CHAPTER 15

"Ladies!" Sirena clinked her knife against her glass to get our attention. Dinner had been another Delphine special—crab cakes, salad, and corn on the cob—and rumor had it that it would be followed by something called Mermaid Chip Cookies, which sounded intriguing. "Let's take a quick break and then gather at Mermaid Crossing for dessert, and the big reveal of your mermaid names!"

I stiffened. I'd completely forgotten to pick one!

"I'm eager to hear your backstories, too," Sirena continued. "See you in ten minutes!"

I hadn't made a backstory up either! I raced back to Whelk, glancing up at the sign over the door as I entered our cabin.

Hmm, I thought. Whelkina?

No. That was worse than Shellina. I'd have to come up with something better.

Mackenzie and Cha Cha and Jasmine were right on my

heels. The three of them huddled on Mackenzie's bunk, discussing something in low murmurs as I crossed to mine. I started hunting for the handout that Sirena had given us on our first day. I finally found it wadded up under my bed. Uncrumpling it, I scanned the list. No, no, and no. Each of the suggested names sounded worse than the one preceding it.

"It's time to go, Truly!" said my cousin a few minutes later, heading for the door as the gong sounded back at Mermaid HQ.

"I'll be there in a sec. Save me a seat." I scanned the handout again, starting to panic. None of the names were something I wanted to be stuck with all week. Harbor? Please. Echo? Jewel? Stormy? They sounded like something Belinda Winchester would name her kittens. There had to be *something* decent I could call myself! I looked frantically around the room for inspiration.

My gaze fell on the stack of presents I'd bought for my family at the pirate museum. The title on the spine of the book I'd picked out for Lauren caught my eye: *The Pirate Queen*. I grabbed it and flipped through the pages. The story looked interesting. It was about an Irish woman named Grania O'Malley, whose exploits on the high seas back in the 1500s rocked the Elizabethan world.

"Grania." I repeated the name aloud slowly. I could live with Grania.

Slamming the book shut, I ran out the door, spinning

my backstory as I sprinted toward Mermaid Crossing. I flung myself onto one of the sofas beside Mackenzie just as Hayden—make that *Shellina*—began to speak.

Hayden droned on for at least five minutes about her stupid fishy alter ego. We learned that Shellina's favorite color was the deep green of emeralds, and that her favorite hobby was collecting shells (of course), and that she had a pet hermit crab named Crabby. My smile grew broader with each passing minute. I couldn't wait to tell Hatcher about this!

Hayden probably would have gone on for a lot longer, but Sirena finally cut her short. "Thank you, Shellina, for the delightful word-picture you've painted for us," she said smoothly. "Now, how about you, Mrs. Drake?"

Hayden's mother kept it short and sweet. "My name is Coralina. I, too, live in Tritonia, where I serve the princess Shellina." This sounded pretty true to life. Princess Hayden clearly had her mother wrapped around her little finger.

It was Zadie's turn next.

"I'm Isla, which is Spanish for 'island,'" Zadie announced. She gestured to Lenore. "And this is Merissa, which means 'of the sea.'"

"Beautiful names," said Sirena, nodding in approval. "Two of my favorites."

Zadie had come up with a pretty good backstory about a pair of mermaids who were captured and forced to perform in an underwater circus—an "aqua-circus," as she called it.

One by one, everyone shared their chosen names and backstories. The four high school girls from St. Louis had picked Chantal, Morwenna, Genevieve, and Bijoux. Morwenna, who was a really good artist, had drawn a detailed map of the undersea realm where they lived, and we all oohed and aahed over that. The four ladies in Sand Dollar introduced themselves as Rilla, Avalon, Oceana, and Bahari, which we learned was Swahili for "ocean." Some of their stories were pretty good, too—especially Bahari's. She'd invented this whole African legend about an underwater world populated by slaves rescued from ships heading to the New World. They'd been freed by King Triton, who turned them into mermaids and mermen.

Then it was our cabin's turn.

"I'm Nixie," said Cha Cha. "That's German for 'little water sprite.'"

Sirena beamed. "Very appropriate for you, Cha Cha. Good choice."

"This is my twin sister Pixie," Cha Cha continued, pointing at Jasmine. "We live in a cave whose walls are lined with sparkling gems."

I wondered if that idea was inspired by the Starlite Dance Studio, whose walls may not have held sparkling gems, but certainly held twinkle lights.

"Nixie and I were orphaned in a storm when we were just mer-babies," Jasmine said, picking up the thread of the story.

"Fortunately, we were adopted by a dolphin, who taught us how to dive and play and who caught fish for us to eat. And then one day, we happened to meet—"

"Me, Neptunette!" said Mackenzie, with a flash of jazz hands. "I'm their best friend."

So that's what the three of them had been working on back in our cabin! I tried not to feel left out as they giggled their way through their joint backstory.

Sirena arched an eyebrow at my cousin when they finished. "Really? You're going with Neptunette?"

Mackenzie nodded. "As a tribute to Zadie and Lenore, who are awesome."

Zadie jumped up off the sofa, ran over to where we were sitting, and kissed my cousin on both cheeks. "And we think you are awesome too, Miss Neptunette." She made a sweeping gesture that encompassed the entire room. "In fact, we think you are *all* awesome, don't we, Lenore—I mean Merissa?"

As usual, Lenore just nodded and smiled.

Finally, it was my turn. *Last but no way am I gonna be least*, I thought, my Lovejoy competitive spirit kicking in. "I'm Grania," I began in a low and mysterious voice.

"Interesting," said Sirena. "We've never had a Grania before, have we, Delphine?"

Delphine shook her head.

I plunged ahead, channeling Aunt True at our bookshop's story time, and Augustus Wilde at one of his dramatic readings, and Gramps, who'd told the best bedtime stories in the world when we Lovejoy kids were little.

"They called me the pirate queen, back when I had land legs," I continued. "I ruled the Emerald Isle, roving the high seas and plundering all ships that crossed my path. But I ran afoul of the law. They chased me from Dublin to Dover, until I did the only thing I could. I sailed to—" I paused. Sailed to where? My gaze fell on the MERMAID CROSSING sign, and I continued, "Mermaid Bay, a place of dark magic, where I called on all the gods of the watery deep to aid me in my time of peril." This was all completely made up, of course. The real Grania O'Malley had done no such thing. But my audience obviously didn't know that. They were hanging on my every word. Even Hayden. "A great wave sprang up, as if from nowhere, and swept me off my ship before I could be caught and punished for my dark deeds. I tumbled down, down, down, deep beneath the surface of the sea, where King Triton awaited me." I thought about the mosaic at the bottom of the pool. "He touched me with his trident, and suddenly I could breathe underwater! Dolphins came and transported me to a castle, and a bed made of soft seaweed, and when I awoke, I had this fish tail you see before you." I finished with a sweeping gesture like Zadie's, pointing at my legs.

The room burst into enthusiastic applause.

"Now *that's* a backstory!" said Delphine, which earned me a dose of stink eye from Hayden.

The Mermaid Chip Cookies were just as good as they sounded, studded with pastel M&M's and sprinkled with sea salt. When it was time to head back to our cabins for bed, I grabbed a couple of extras when nobody was looking and stuffed them into my pocket.

"Should we try to get ahold of the guys?" I asked when we got back to Whelk.

Mackenzie frowned. "It's kind of late."

"Yeah, but we promised." I punched in Calhoun's number on the videoconferencing app. Scooter's face was the one that appeared on my cell phone screen, though.

"Where have you guys been?" he demanded, scowling. "We've been waiting for hours! Didn't you get our texts?"

"We've been kind of busy."

"Doing what?"

I pulled a cookie from my pocket. "Eating delicious Mermaid Chip Cookies, for one thing!" I took a long, slow, exaggerated bite, just to torture him.

"Being mermaids is hard work," Jasmine explained. "It's not like we're just sitting around on our, uh, tails. We have a lot of stuff we have to do. We're going to be starring in a show later this week."

Scooter's scowl softened into a sly smile. "Wish we could see that!"

Calhoun's face appeared beside Scooter's. "Hey!"

I smiled at him. "Hey back!"

"We may have some leads," he told us.

I paused midbite. "Seriously? That's great!"

"Lucas knew what he was doing with those hashtags. It seems like just about everybody who was at the race that day took pictures and posted them on social media. There's this one guy in particular—show them, Lucas."

Lucas's pale hand shot into view, holding his phone up for us.

"Um, who exactly are we looking for?" asked Cha Cha.

"See the old guy in the Grateful Dead T-shirt and aviator sunglasses?"

"By the bandstand?" Mackenzie squinted at the screen.

"Yeah. He's the guy I saw hanging out near the diner, too," said Lucas. "He shows up in a bunch of the pictures before the race, and then he disappears."

I chewed on that bit of information. "Does that automatically make him a suspect, though? Maybe he was just passing through."

"Just passing through near the *bandstand*? He's right there when Belinda and Augustus are fooling around with the trophy, and he's right there when they put it back in the paper bag under the podium. Then he vanishes. Definitely suspicious."

Lucas had a point.

"So what now?" Jasmine wanted to know.

"Now we see if anyone knows him," Calhoun told her. "We're going to start asking around."

"Excellent work, guys," I said. "I wish we were there to help you."

"No you don't," said Scooter, scowling again. "You'd rather be right where you are, eating Mermaid Chip Cookies without us."

I smiled and took another bite. And then I hung up.

CHAPTER 16

At breakfast the next morning, a FedEx truck pulled into the driveway just as we were starting in on big steaming bowls of Delphine's deluxe oatmeal. Everyone watched with interest as the driver strode up the front path carrying a package. Sirena went to the door to meet him.

"It's for you, Truly," she told me a moment later, setting the package down on the sideboard beside a platter of homemade raspberry rhubarb muffins. I started to get up, but she held up her hand. "Breakfast first! Most important meal of the day for mermaids."

I sighed and sat back down. "Yes, ma'am."

"You need lots of fuel, ladies. We have a busy day ahead. Zadie and Lenore and I have scheduled extra pool time. We have a lot to learn before the revue this weekend."

When Sirena finally excused us from the table, I bolted for

the sideboard and grabbed my package. I looked at the return address label. It was from Aunt True!

"See you all poolside in five minutes!" said Sirena. "Move your tails, mermaids!"

I dashed down the path to Whelk, where I flung myself on my bunk and tore the wrapping off the package. Inside, a big envelope with my name written on it in my aunt's bold handwriting was waiting. I pulled out a card featuring an oval picture of a tranquil forest scene—a stand of majestic redwood trees reflected in a pool of water. *Tall timber,* I thought instantly, and smiled. Aunt True knew how to make a point. A line of her crisp handwriting wound around the oval's edge: *To the Unsinkable Truly Lovejoy, my favorite eldest niece, who really truly knows how to make the best of everything.* Inside, she'd written, *Don't ever be afraid to stand out in a crowd. (Even if it's a crowd of mermaids!)*

Aunt True was the best!

I propped the card up on my bedside table and turned my attention to the rest of box's contents. My aunt had sent maple sugar candy, too! Before I could rummage any further, though, my cousin and friends burst in.

"Where's your bathing suit?" said Mackenzie. "Hurry up—we're due at the pool."

My care package would have to wait.

The rest of the day was a lot like the day before, except that we skipped siesta after lunch in order to squeeze in as much pool time as possible. We paused midafternoon for a snack (homemade energy bars, courtesy of Delphine) and another Esther Williams movie—*Easy to Love* this time, which had more over-the-top stunts, including Esther doing water-ski jumps and diving from a helicopter. Actually, her stunt double did that one.

"The helicopter scene is the only one she ever used a stuntwoman for," Zadie told us. "And wisely so. We found out later that she was pregnant at the time."

For dinner, Delphine whipped up an amazing soup she called "cioppino," which was full of big chunks of fish, along with scallops and shrimp and clams and mussels. She served it with crusty homemade bread.

"Mermaids have excellent manners," Sirena told us, "but dipping your bread in the cioppino is allowed."

As we were finishing, Sirena tapped her glass. "You worked very hard today, and Delphine and I are proud of all of you. As a reward for your efforts, we're rearranging our evening schedule slightly. Instead of Mer-mopoly and the other games we had planned, we're moving up one of the academy's most anticipated activities—Bling Night!"

A chorus of cheers filled the dining room. I looked over at Mackenzie and my friends. They were clearly as clueless as I was.

"Mermaids love bling," Sirena continued, trotting out

another of her fake mermaid facts. She reached into a drawer in the sideboard behind her and pulled out several long sparkly necklaces. She draped them over her head and added a trio of bracelets and half a dozen rings. The result was blinding. "How many of you brought yours with you?"

Every hand around the dining table flew up except ours.

"We didn't know we were supposed to," said Jasmine.

"It was right there in the brochure," scoffed Hayden.

Sirena gave her a warning glance. "Not to worry. You girls were last-minute additions, after all. You'll be making your own tonight! Let's meet at Mermaid Crossing in five minutes."

While our fellow aspiring mermaids scattered to retrieve their bling, Mackenzie and Cha Cha and Jasmine and I helped Delphine carry dessert out to the porch.

Mackenzie looked askance at the bowl full of what looked like green shaving cream that Delphine handed to her. "What *is* this?"

Delphine laughed. "Just whipped cream with a little food coloring in it."

Dessert was something she called "Fruit of the Sea," which was actually fresh strawberries topped with a cloud of the pale green whipped cream. It looked a little weird, but it tasted great. Mackenzie and I both had two helpings.

"Delphine always makes this for Bling Night," said Sirena happily, scooping a little more out of the bowl too. "Now, ladies, tonight is the night you've all been waiting for! You're going to make bling to your heart's content."

My heart was pretty content being bling free, I thought, watching as Delphine placed a large tray on the coffee table in front of us. It was piled high with seashells, fake gems, metallic tassels, glitter, and the like—all the kinds of stuff that I avoided like the plague in real life. Crafts were another item on the long list of things I wasn't good at. But then, mermaid camp wasn't real life, was it? I sighed and reached for a glue gun. The swimming part had turned out to be not so bad. Maybe this would be fun too.

I was just finishing up stringing my second strand of glitter-encrusted seashells when my cell phone vibrated. I pulled it from the pocket of my shorts. It was Hatcher!

"I'll be right back," I told the group, and headed for the powder room off the kitchen. Closing the door behind me, I put my phone to my ear. "Hey!"

"Hey yourself!" my brother replied. "I got your text—sorry I didn't have a chance to answer sooner. You know how wrestling camp goes."

"Yep." Exactly the same as swimming camp, and every other athletic camp on the planet. Eat. Sleep. Practice. Repeat.

We chatted for a few minutes. Aunt True was right about mermaid camp providing great stories. I got Hatcher laughing so hard he almost choked when I told him about Shellina and

Skipper Dee and Sirena and her endless list of mermaid rules and sayings.

"Oops, gotta go," he said finally. "Coach is making us watch videos from practice today. See you back in Pumpkin Falls!"

"See you!"

We hung up, and I went back out to the porch to finish my bling.

Later, before she dismissed us for the evening, Sirena made an announcement.

"We have a special field trip planned for you tomorrow morning before breakfast!" she told us. "Instead of meeting by the pool, please meet in the parking lot at six thirty a.m. sharp. Wear your bathing suits and bring your towels and tails."

This didn't sound good. Especially the tails part. Was she planning to drag us out in public somewhere?

"And, ladies, don't stay up too late this time! I can promise you that this is a trip you won't want to miss. Remember, mermaids need their—"

"—beauty rest!" we all chorused.

Back in the cabin, Mackenzie and Cha Cha and Jasmine and I made another video call to the rest of the Pumpkin Falls Private Eyes. I sorted through the remainder of my care package while we chatted, pulling out a T-shirt with WELL-BEHAVED WOMEN SELDOM MAKE HISTORY on it, a new sudoku book, a stash of my favorite candy bars, a double strand of peacock blue and green glass beads that I recognized from our latest sideline shipment—more bling!—and the latest issue of *Bird Watcher's Digest* magazine.

"Pay attention," Scooter said irritably, watching as I flipped through it. "This is important."

"I'm listening," I replied, and pulled a pair of purple wool socks from the box. I frowned. What was Aunt True thinking? It was July! Then I saw the little note pinned to them. Belinda had knitted them for me.

At least she hadn't sent me a kitten, I thought. But she had included a picture of one, a really cute little gray kitten with a white tip on his tail, like he'd dipped it in paint. On the back she'd scribbled *I've named this little fellow Fog. He's the perfect mer-kitten, and he's up for adoption! Tell your mermaid friends!* Like Aunt True, Belinda had a flair for marketing. Unlike Aunt True, Belinda focused solely on her foster kittens.

"We've had some luck following up on the Grateful Dead guy," Scooter said, still glaring at me. "Lucas's mother remembers seeing him at Lou's that morning when he stopped in for coffee and a donut."

"And Mr. Henry is almost certain he spotted him heading for his car right before the award ceremony," Lucas added. "He remembers because he says the guy's car was awesome, a 1957 Chevy or something."

At the bottom of my care package was a trio of books. I lifted them out and examined the covers, frowning. Aunt True had gone full mermaid on me. There was a copy of *The Little Mermaid* (a sticky note on the cover assured me that this was the original fairy tale by Hans Christian Andersen, and that I'd like it much better than the movie) and something called *The Mermaid Handbook*. Lots of illustrations, gilt edges—I figured Mackenzie would love that one. The third book, at least, looked like something I might want to read.

"Check it out!" I said to my cabin-mates, holding up *Saga of a Ship: The Lost Treasure of the Windborne*. "This is that book we saw at the Brewster Store! The one whose author is doing a book signing tomorrow night."

"Truly!" My head snapped up. It was Calhoun. "Could you please put that down and pay attention?"

"Sorry," I replied meekly.

"We also have some new suspects, thanks to the crowd-sourcing."

"Really?" said Mackenzie. "That's great! Way to go, Lucas!"

Lucas gave her a shy smile.

"Take a look at this one," said Scooter, holding up the first picture for us to see. It was out of focus, but if I squinted I could just make out what was written on the suspect's baseball cap: DON'T MESS WITH TEXAS.

"Um," I began as Mackenzie blurted, "That's our Uncle Rooster!"

Lucas looked crestfallen.

"It's okay," she assured him. "It's still really good detective work."

Scooter showed us the other two pictures, both taken on the morning of the race. One was of a middle-aged woman wearing a Red Sox baseball cap. She was setting up a lawn chair on the village green and appeared to be all by herself. The other was of a pair of teenage boys about Danny's age who were lounging on the steps of the gazebo.

"Definitely suspicious," said Cha Cha.

"That's what we thought," said Calhoun. "We've asked around a little bit, but so far, nothing."

"Keep at it," I told them. "We're with you in spirit."

"Talk to you guys again tomorrow night?" asked Scooter, with a hopeful glance at my cousin.

I held up *Saga of a Ship*. "We might be at a book signing. How about you text us if you get any more new leads or learn anything about our suspects?"

After we hung up, Mackenzie reached over for the book I was still holding. "Can I take a look?"

I passed it to her. Cha Cha scooted closer. Jasmine climbed up onto her bunk and leaned over the edge, her long dark hair trailing down like seaweed.

"Looks kind of interesting," my cousin said, riffling through the pages.

"It's long, though," added Jasmine, yawning. "And

there aren't many pictures." She reached out and fingered the strand of beads I'd looped around my neck. "Ooo, pretty!"

"Mermaids love bling," I deadpanned, and they all laughed.

"So are you really going to read a giant book about pirates?" asked Mackenzie.

I shrugged. "They're more interesting than mermaids. They were real, for one thing."

I shared my maple sugar candy with them, and the three of us talked for a while, and then it was time for bed.

"Night, Pixie. Night, Nixie!" Mackenzie called softly from across the room. "Night, Grania!"

"Night, Neptunette!" I called back, stifling a giggle.

There was an echoing giggle from Cha Cha's bunk, which got Jasmine going, and pretty soon we were all giggling.

"It's not that funny, you guys!" Mackenzie protested, but she was laughing too.

"Yes it is," I told her, which set us all off again.

Our giggle fit finally subsided, and the room grew quiet. Propping myself up with my pillow, I switched on the flashlight app on my cell phone and opened *Saga of a Ship*. I leafed through a few pages, then turned to the index and ran my finger idly down the entries. Something caught my eye under the listings for *C*: *Cherry Island, p. 87.*

I frowned. There was a Cherry Island on Lake Lovejoy.

The book couldn't be referring to that, though, could it? For one thing, Cherry Island was only our island's nickname. Its real name, the one that appeared on maps, was MacPherson's Island. Only locals called it Cherry Island. Curious, I turned to page eighty-seven and hunted until I found the reference: *Rumors persisted well into the 1800s about one of the survivors of the* Windborne. *It was said that he fled with his share of the treasure and buried it in a place called Cherry Island, where it has remained undiscovered to this day.*"

I put the book down thoughtfully, then reached for my cell phone. CHERRY ISLAND'S REAL NAME IS MACPHERSON'S ISLAND, RIGHT?

A few seconds later my phone vibrated. PRETTY SURE, Hatcher texted back. WHY ARE YOU STILL UP? MERMAIDS NEED THEIR BEAUTY REST.

I smiled. I'M NOT A MERMAID, I'M GRANIA THE PIRATE.

WHAT?? DID YOU GET A PART??

HUH?

THE PLAY, DUH.

He thought I was talking about *The Pirates of Penzance*.

NO, I texted back. I DIDN'T TRY OUT, REMEMBER?

"Truly, turn that thing off, you're keeping us all awake," Mackenzie mumbled.

GOTTA GO, I texted. SURROUNDED BY CRABBY MERMAIDS. NIGHT!

NIGHT!

I switched off my phone and lay there in my bunk in the dark, staring up at the bottom of Jasmine's mattress. *Saga of a Ship* had to be referring to a different Cherry Island. It couldn't possibly be our Cherry Island.

Pirates in Pumpkin Falls? Preposterous!

CHAPTER 17

I awoke at the crack of dawn the next morning and lay there with my eyes half-shut, listening to the low, soothing coo of a mourning dove. Above it floated the flutelike whistle of a Baltimore oriole, its song punctuated in turn by the insistent call of a cardinal. I smiled. The dawn chorus was in full swing. I heard a robin's refrain—*cheerily, cheer up, cheer up, cheerily, cheer up!*—and remembered how, when I was little and Gramps was trying to get me to wake up, he'd fooled me into thinking the bird was actually calling to me: *Truly, get up, get up, Truly, get up!*

Which I might as well do, I thought, throwing back the covers. There was time to squeeze in a little bird-watching before we left on Sirena's "mystery trip." I pulled on my bathing suit, then dressed in shorts and a T-shirt, grabbed my binoculars, and slipped out the cabin door. My flip-flops were where I'd left them on the front steps last night. As I slid my feet into them, I glanced toward the pool. An early-morning mist hovered over the water.

It looked irresistible.

Never swim alone, Sirena had said. It was one of her top ten Mermaid Commandments. I hesitated, torn. It wasn't like I needed a buddy—I was on swim team, for Pete's sake. Plus, I could be in and out before anyone else was even up. Nobody would ever know.

A moment later I was skimming over the grass. I couldn't help myself—the gleaming water drew me like a magnet.

When I reached the edge of the pool, though, I stopped short. Somebody had beaten me to it. Two somebodies, in fact.

"Truly!" said Zadie, beckoning to me. "I mean Grania—come on in and join us."

I gaped. "But—"

She gave me an impish grin. "Skinny-dipping is good for the soul. Isn't that right, Lenore?"

Lenore nodded. I quickly covered my eyes as she did a surface dive. "Um, no thanks."

"Suit yourself. Or not, as the case may be!" Zadie laughed and paddled away.

A bird walk it was, then, I thought, veering back toward the driveway. As I passed the hammock, though, I suddenly changed my mind. Switching directions, I detoured to Whelk and slipped inside, where I retrieved the book about the *Windborne* that Aunt True had sent. Then I headed to the hammock to read.

Twenty minutes later, I sat up so fast the hammock flipped over and I went sprawling onto the grass. Scrambling to my feet, I ran back to Whelk and burst through the door.

"Hey, guys, wake up!"

Jasmine groaned. Mackenzie buried her head under her pillow.

"Go away," growled Cha Cha.

"Seriously, you have to hear this!"

Mackenzie lifted a corner of the pillow and peered out at me. "Hear what?"

"It's from the book Aunt True sent!"

"Which one?"

"*Saga of a Ship*!"

"It's too early!" Jasmine protested, as Cha Cha let out another low growl.

"I mean it—this is big stuff! I think one of my ancestors was a pirate!"

"Oh for heaven's sake, you have pirates on the brain," said Mackenzie in disgust. She rolled over, pulling the pillow back over her head.

I pried it away, thrusting the book under her nose and stabbing my finger at the page. "Look, it's right here in black and white!"

She glared at me resentfully. "I'm *sleeping*, Truly."

"Right here, see? It's talking about one of the pirates who survived the shipwreck of the *Windborne*—the one who didn't get caught."

"Dandy Dan?" Jasmine mumbled.

"That's the one! It says that he was described by his shipmates as 'a man most generous of beak.'"

My cousin stared at me blankly.

"*Beak*. You know, nose?"

"What the heck are you talking about?"

"He had a *big nose!*"

"So?"

"So think about it—the Lovejoy *proboscis*?" Mackenzie looked at me like I'd completely lost my mind. "Nathaniel *Daniel*—"

"—looks like a spaniel," she concluded automatically.

"Exactly! My ancestor! You've seen his portrait—his nose is enormous! He's a man 'most generous of beak'!"

The lump in the bunk that was Cha Cha gave a raspy laugh. "Are you kidding me?"

Mackenzie sat up and threw her pillow at me. "You woke us up for *that*? Do you know how many people in this world have big noses, Truly?"

"A lot, that's how many!" said Jasmine. "It's just a coincidence."

"Yeah, but c'mon, guys, think about it—don't you think it's a little too many coincidences? It's not just the big nose, it's the name—Dandy *Dan*. Nathaniel *Daniel*. And there's more." As I explained about Cherry Island, my cousin and friends fell silent.

"It's still probably just a coincidence," Jasmine said finally.

"And even if it were true," said Cha Cha, "how would you ever find out for sure? It's been a secret all these years."

"So was the Underground Railroad hiding spot, and the original Truly's diary, and Professor Rusty's letters to Aunt True," I pointed out.

"Yeah, but we found all those by accident," Cha Cha continued. "The *Windborne* sank three hundred years ago, and people have been trying to solve the mystery of the pirate treasure ever since. And not just any people—really *smart* people. Historians and real-live treasure hunters, like the guy who founded the pirate museum."

Mackenzie nodded, pointing to the book. "The author has a PhD, remember?"

"We're smart too!" I protested. I couldn't believe they couldn't see what was right in front of their eyes.

Jasmine sat up. "Okay, so let's say it isn't a coincidence. Where do we even start?"

I waved the book at them. "We could start by talking to Amanda Appleton at her book signing tonight."

Mackenzie looked doubtful. "What if she doesn't want to talk to a bunch of kids?"

"Authors always want to talk to potential readers," I told them. "Trust me. We've got to talk to this lady. She may know a bunch more than what she put in her book."

While my cousin and friends got dressed, I sat on my bunk and stared at the cover of *Saga of a Ship*. I thought about the portrait of Nathaniel Daniel Lovejoy on our living room wall back home in Pumpkin Falls. Could my distinguished ancestor really have sailed under the black flag?

If Nathaniel Daniel had actually been Dandy Dan, what made him decide to give up his life of crime and become a model citizen? One who founded a college and paid for the Paul Revere bell on our church? Facing the prospect of a public trial and hanging, I supposed it would have been a smart move, heading to a small town in the foothills of the White Mountains, far away from the sea. What better place to hide than in tiny landlocked Pumpkin Falls? No one would think of looking for a pirate there.

I thought of Nathaniel Daniel's wife, Prudence. She looked so prim and proper in her portrait, the very image of a perfect New England housewife—certainly not like someone who would marry a pirate or approve of him spending his ill-gotten gains. Had she known about her husband's wicked past? If he'd even had a wicked past, that was.

I had so many questions!

I wondered if any of my other relatives knew about Dandy

Dan, the pirate "most generous of beak." Was there a reason that Aunt True had sent me this particular book? Was she in on the secret? Was this some big skeleton in the Lovejoy closet that everyone had taken pains over the centuries to hide?

I needed to talk to Aunt True again.

CHAPTER 18

Talking to my aunt was going to have to wait, though.

"No shell phones today," Sirena announced as we gathered as directed at the minivans a short while later. She held out a basket. "It's time to unplug."

Mackenzie clutched her phone, horrified. "Is she kidding?" she whispered to me.

"I don't think so," I whispered back.

She wasn't. Sirena circulated among us, collecting "shell phones." Mackenzie wasn't the only one who was reluctant to part with her hers. Hayden looked equally appalled, as did the girls from St. Louis.

"You will thank me for this later, ladies, I promise," Sirena reassured us. "This is an exercise that all of our classes here at the academy find instructive and restorative. Just imagine—an entire day disconnected from the world, recharging body and soul!" She struck a dramatic pose, her mane of red corkscrew curls looking as if they'd just been plugged into an outlet and were recharging too. "And we're going to start our restorative morning by plunging into the silent world beneath the sea."

"You're taking us to the beach?" squealed Hayden.

"Indeed I am! Now that you are all comfortable swimming in your tails, it's time for me to release my mermaids into the wild. I shall take you to the ocean and set you all free!" She struck another pose, lifting her hands toward the sky. Delphine tapped her watch discreetly, and Sirena dropped her hands and motioned us toward the minivans. "Ladies, your chariots await! Time and tide wait for no man—and no mermaids."

As everyone loaded up their tails and towels, my cousin and friends and I told Sirena about the book signing.

"Hmmm. We have a pretty full slate for this evening. It's Sea Siren Night."

I gave her a blank look.

"It's an opportunity for the musically inclined to show off their vocal talent as we learn some sea shanties," Sirena explained.

Singing? I thought in dismay. *She's talking about singing?*

Noting my expression, she continued, "However, we do like to support community events, and a trip to the Brewster Store would give me a chance to talk to the owner about publicizing our revue. I'm sure she'd be thrilled to meet Zadie and Lenore—I happen to know she's a big Esther Williams fan."

Sirena took a quick vote. Half were in favor of Sea Siren

Night, and the other half, including Mackenzie and Cha Cha and Jasmine and me, voted for the book signing.

"Very well then," said Sirena. "We'll do both. Delphine, you can manage Sea Siren Night without me, right?"

"Sure, Mom. No problem."

"We'll try and be back in time for dessert. I know you're planning something special."

I perked up at that, although I couldn't imagine how Delphine could top Mermaid Chip Cookies.

Sirena made a right turn out of the driveway, away from the Brewster Store. "This is Breakwater Road," she told us. "It leads to the breakwater, or jetty—sort of a wall of rocks that juts out into the water, creating a sheltered cove. You'll see when we get there."

Jasmine gazed out the window as we drove and gave a contented sigh. "The houses are all so pretty!"

Cape Cod was definitely Jasmine's happy place.

"Which house would you guys pick if you had to choose?" asked Mackenzie. This was one of our favorite games. The two of us had ben selecting our future fantasy homes since we were little.

Jasmine and Cha Cha joined in with gusto. Jasmine chose a huge colonial-style house that looked like Gramps and Lola's. Mackenzie did the same. Cha Cha and I went for cozier Cape Cod–style ones with rose-covered picket fences.

Sirena, who'd obviously been eavesdropping, pulled over

to the side of the road for a moment. "The house you like is called a 'half cape,' Truly," she said. "Only two windows on one side of the front door. A 'full cape,' on the other hand"—she pointed to Cha Cha's choice, directly across the street—"has four windows, two on either side of the front door."

Cha Cha's forehead puckered. "Why would somebody only build half a house?"

"Yeah, someone Truly's size wouldn't even fit in it," muttered Hayden. I pretended not to hear her.

"It was the starter house of its day," Sirena explained. "The story goes that sea captains would build a half cape so that their spinster daughters could live independently, and then, if they ever got married, their husbands would build the other half."

"What a dumb idea!" scoffed Mackenzie. "I'd much rather have a big house."

She wouldn't if she had to help clean it, I thought. Mackenzie's parents had a housekeeper who came once a week. Our family had—well, us. "Chores build character," my parents loved to remind us every Saturday morning, when they rousted us out of bed and organized a full-on blitz starring the Magnificent Seven, as my father called our family. I'd had enough dusting and vacuuming to last me the rest of my life. Half a house would suit me just fine. I'd take a quarter, even.

There weren't many people on the beach this early in the morning. I noticed a couple walking their dog, a scattering of joggers, some kayakers out on the water, and a lone fisherman standing far out on a line of boulders that must be the jetty, or breakwater, that Sirena had described. Down by the water's edge, a woman was talking on her cell phone while her daughter busied herself in the sand with a plastic bucket and shovel.

"Look, Mommy! Mermaids!" The little girl tugged on her mother's shorts, pointing to where we had spread out our towels and were busy wiggling into our tails. The woman turned, peered over her sunglasses at us, then began talking animatedly into her phone. She must have alerted the entire neighborhood, because inside of five minutes a line of cars started pulling into the parking lot.

Delphine was still helping me into my shimmertail when the news truck showed up and two people got out.

I looked at one of them and froze. *No way.* It couldn't be! But it was. I'd recognize that big phony anywhere. The last time I'd run into Carson Dawson, host of Channel Five's *Hello, Boston!*, had been right after we'd moved to Pumpkin Falls. He'd managed to embarrass me on television then. But I sure wasn't about to let him do it again now.

"Hurry up and get me into this thing!" I whispered frantically to Delphine, as we struggled to pull my tail into place.

She frowned. "What's the matter?"

"I can't let him see me!"

"Who?" She glanced back over her shoulder. "Oh wow! Mom's going to faint."

Sure enough, the minute she spotted Carson Dawson and his colleague, Sirena let out a yelp and made a beeline across the parking lot. Meanwhile, I scooted across the sand toward the water as fast as I could manage. My fellow mermaids were already sitting in the shallows, shrieking as each cold wave lapped over them. The Atlantic Ocean wasn't exactly the Caribbean. I inchwormed past them and flung myself into the water without a moment's hesitation. Freezing to death was a far better fate than facing Carson Dawson.

A few minutes later, Mackenzie finally got up the nerve to join me. "It's not like Texas!" she gasped, when she came up for air.

"Nope," I burbled. Stealth mode wasn't easy under these circumstances, but I was giving it my best shot. I hunched down in the water, only the top half of my face visible. With any luck, I'd be unrecognizable.

Zadie was next to take the plunge.

"Whoooo-eee!" she hollered, surfacing with a whoop. "Now that's what I call refreshing!"

One by one, the others joined us. Once past the initial hurdle, it didn't take all that long to get used to the chilly water, and pretty soon everyone was splashing each other and goofing around as we showed off our tails for the audience on the beach. I kept a low profile, staying at the back of the pack. *"Pack" isn't the right word,* I thought. Neither was "gaggle." What was it they called a bunch of fish? I giggled when I remembered the correct term—"school"—then started coughing as I accidentally swallowed some seawater. *School* of mermaids—mermaid *academy*—Hatcher and Aunt True would think this was funny too, and I added it to my list of things to tell them.

Swimming in the ocean in a shimmertail was way easier and way more fun than swimming in one in a pool. The salt water was more buoyant, for one thing, which helped offset the weight of the silicone. For another, I could really stretch out and take it for a proper test drive. Staying parallel to the jetty, I butterflied my way out toward the open water, pausing when I reached the end. Then I turned around and swam back.

Breakwater Beach was on the bay side of the Cape, so there wasn't any surf to speak of, but there were plenty of gentle waves. We all floated in the water for a while, bobbing like buoys and enjoying the soothing rhythm of the incoming tide.

"Yoo-hoo! Ladies!" Sirena called to us from across the parking lot. "Look who I found!"

Uh-oh, I thought, hunching lower in the water as she headed toward the beach with a determined look on her face. Carson Dawson and his cameraman were right behind her.

As the three of them approached the water's edge, the cameraman trotted ahead and turned to start filming Sirena and the television host.

"Helloooooooo, Boston!" hooted Carson Dawson,

launching into the famous opener for his TV show. "Real mermaids, folks! Right here on Cape Cod! And Channel Five is here to check it out!" He smiled his fake smile for the camera, then motioned to the cameraman, who slowly panned over to where we were all bobbing in the waves. "I'm here with Sirena of Sirena's Sea Siren Academy—say that three times fast"—he paused and chuckled at his own joke—"who assures me that we are in for a treat."

"Indeed you are, Carson," Sirena chimed in smoothly, leaning in close to the microphone he had in his hand. "A magical nautical treat."

"If the mermaid academy thing doesn't work out, she could always pursue a career on TV," I burbled to Mackenzie, who shushed me.

"Ladies? Are you ready to strut your stuff?" Sirena's question caught us off guard, and for a long moment nobody moved. Then Zadie leaped into action.

"Back layout, mermaids!" she ordered. "Tails in, heads out, arms interlocked."

A soldier's daughter knows an order when she hears one. I snapped into position. So did everyone else, and within seconds we had formed a circle on our backs in the water, flukes touching in the middle, arms extended to each side so that we were connected shoulder to shoulder. From above, we'd look like the spokes on a bicycle wheel.

"Ballet tails!" called Zadie, and we lifted our tails straight up into the air and flapped our flukes. Carson Dawson and the crowd of onlookers gasped in delight.

Zadie led us through a few other simple formations that she and Lenore and Sirena had taught us for the revue. We ended with surface dives, showing off our flukes again. I made sure to smack the water hard with mine and make the biggest splash that I could, in hopes of drenching Carson Dawson. Unfortunately, he was out of range.

"Mommy! I want to be a mermaid too!" piped the little girl who'd first spotted us.

"And you can do just that on Saturday night," Sirena told her, whisking the mic from the Channel Five host and smoothly serving up a pitch for our upcoming show. "Sirena's Sea Siren Academy is located right here on Breakwater Road. We'll be presenting our all-star mermaid revue this Saturday at seven p.m.—we're calling it *A Tribute to Esther Williams.*"

"Esther Williams!" said Carson, reaching for the mic again. I could tell from the creases on his tanned forehead that he was worried his news segment was at risk of being hijacked. "Now there's a name I haven't heard in years."

Sirena's aqua-tipped fingers were closed firmly around the microphone. She tugged it toward her. "Yes, the *Million Dollar Mermaid* herself!" She bent down toward the little girl, who was looking up at her with shining eyes. I recognized that expression. It had been on my cousin's face all week. *Mermaid fever.* "Two of Esther's former protégées will be performing with us and offering pointers after the show for aspiring mermaids just like you! Come early to get a seat, and don't forget your swimsuit!"

Sirena straightened up again and beckoned to Zadie and Lenore, who swam closer to shore. I hung back, watching as they charmed the crowd with a few more of their synchronized swimming moves.

"Wow," said Carson Dawson, finally regaining control of the mic. "They're really something!" He looked over at the rest of us. "And these are all your students?"

"Yes, indeed. Sea sirens, all! Swim on over and say hello to Mr. Dawson, ladies!"

As the rest of the mermaids obeyed, I hung back, still keeping as much of me underwater as was humanly possible.

The TV host squinted in my direction. "What's wrong with that one?"

Sirena frowned. "Some mermaids can be shy."

"Is that a fact?"

"Oh yes," Sirena continued, nodding sagely. Her red corkscrew curls nodded too. "On the whole they prefer not to be seen by humans."

Suddenly the whole thing struck me funny—two adults, one with a fake tan and faker smile, the other with an aqua mani-pedi and a T-shirt that proclaimed MERMAIDS ARE MER-MAZING!—acting as if it were entirely natural to be discussing the emotions of mythical creatures. I started to laugh and immediately got salt water up my nose again. Turning my back to the shore, I struggled to suppress my coughing fit. The last thing I wanted to do was attract more attention to myself.

Fortunately, Carson Dawson was finished with us. "That's a wrap!" he announced. As he and Sirena retreated back toward the Channel Five news truck, deep in conversation, I rolled over onto my back and floated in the waves again. My cousin and friends swam over to join me.

"Mermaids can be shy," I said, smacking my tail on the water for emphasis.

Mackenzie grinned at me and smacked hers, too. "Mermaids need their beauty rest."

"Mermaids make waves," added Jasmine with an impressive whack.

"Mermaids eat lots of fish," Cha Cha chimed in, twirling around and splashing water in every direction.

"Mermaids talk on shell phones," I said, wondering when Sirena would return ours. Aunt True wasn't going to believe it when I told her about Carson Dawson.

The four of us kept a steady stream of stupid mermaid rules and puns flying back and forth for a while: "Mermaids are never shellfish." "Mermaids send messages by sea-mail." "Mermaids can be crabby." "Mermaids are fintastic." "Mermaid foes are anemones."

Later, as we tossed our tails and towels into the back of the minivans, Sirena reappeared.

"I can't believe our luck!" she said. "Mr. Dawson is here for the week, filming segments for a special about everyday life on Cape Cod. He's going to be spotlighting some local events, and he's going to stop by and film us! Ladies, the all-star revue is going to be featured on TV!"

Everyone cheered.

Everyone but me.

I felt like I'd been kicked right in the shimmertail.

I was going to be on *television*? It was bad enough to have to perform in front of a live audience. Being on television meant performing in front of practically the entire world!

My clamshell bra and I were on a crash course for complete and utter humiliation.

CHAPTER 19

HELP! I texted Aunt True later that day, when dinner was over and Sirena finally relented and gave us our "shell phones" back. GOT TIME TO TALK?

I'd barely pressed SEND before my phone rang in response.

"What's up?" my aunt asked.

"Carson Dawson, that's what!" I paced the back lawn, fuming as I filled her in on our morning at the beach. What I'd thought would simply be a funny story to share had exploded into a looming disaster.

"Don't worry," she said when I was done. "I've got your six."

That was military speak for "I've got your back." If anyone could fix this, it was Aunt True. I had no idea how, or if it were even possible, but I felt better just hearing this.

"So what else did you do today?"

I gave her the rundown. Aunt True was particularly interested in Zadie and Lenore.

"Wow, they're helping Sirena and her daughter choreograph your routine?"

"Uh-huh," I replied. "The stuff they have us doing is actually pretty sweet. Not that I want to perform in public," I hastened to add. "Especially not on TV. Oh, and we've been watching some of their old Esther Williams movies, too, like *Million Dollar Mermaid*."

"Is that the one where she wears a gold swimsuit and crown and dives off a really high platform?" Aunt True is a "cinephile," as she puts it—which is a fancy word for someone who is a big fan of movies.

"Yeah."

"I love that one!"

"I liked it too. And *Easy to Love*. They're kind of corny, but all the water ballet scenes were amazing, and Zadie gave us the behind-the-scenes scoop. Did you know that Esther Williams was pregnant when she did most of those water-skiing stunts?"

I could practically hear Aunt True's eyebrows shoot up. "That's amazing! Wait until I tell Rusty!"

"He likes Esther Williams?"

"Rusty is a man of surprising depths. So what's on the schedule for tonight?"

"A book signing."

"Really? At Sirena's?"

I explained about the Brewster Store, and *Saga of a Ship*.

"That new book I sent you?"

"Yeah." I was just about to tell her my theory about Nathaniel Daniel and Cherry Island, when she interrupted.

"Oops, gotta go. Hair ball."

Memphis, my aunt's cat, was a feline conveyor belt for hair balls. Everyone in my family was used to Aunt True dropping everything when one appeared, which they did with alarming regularity.

"Okay. Bye!" I replied, but she'd already hung up.

I made a detour to Whelk to grab my copy of *Saga of a Ship*, then headed back to Mermaid HQ to meet up with the group that was heading to the Brewster Store. Zadie and Lenore had decided to join Mackenzie and Cha Cha and Jasmine and me, as had the ladies from Sand Dollar. Meanwhile, the four high school girls plus Hayden and her mother had opted for Sea Siren Night. Somehow Hayden had gotten it into her head that she might be able to sing on TV during the revue and get discovered by some big Hollywood talent agent. If you asked me, though, which nobody ever did, the only thing that was going to be discovered was the fact that she was a pain.

The staff at the Brewster Store looked happy to see us.

"Sirena!" cried the woman behind the fudge counter.

"Monica!" cried Sirena.

The two of them leaned in and made air-kissy noises.

"I see you've brought a crowd," said Monica. "We're

gathering upstairs, ladies. Treats are on their way."

"Fudge, I hope," murmured Cha Cha, eyeing the display behind the glass counter. "Mermaids love chocolate."

We took up the entire first two rows. A scattering of people were seated in the back, some with copies of the book in hand, others who were probably just there for the free treats. After working at Lovejoy's Books, I could scan an audience like a pro.

"How nice of you all to come!" The author made the rounds, shaking hands. I'd seen her type before. She was wearing what Hatcher called an I-am-an-artist outfit—the kind a person wears when they want to make a statement, like Augustus Wilde and his purple cape. In Amanda Appleton's case, her statement seemed to be, *I may have been a pirate in a previous life*. Oversize white shirt? Check. Wide black belt with a gold buckle? Check. Large gold hoop earrings? Check. All she needed was a red bandana and an eye patch to complete the outfit. "Are all of you together?" She peered at us from behind a pair of big, black-rimmed glasses, her blue eyes alert.

"We are indeed," Sirena answered.

"A family reunion?"

"You might say that." Zadie gave her an impish smile. "We're sort of a seafaring family."

"You've come to the right place, then!" enthused Dr. Appleton. "I have a salty tale to tell, so let's get started." She turned to face the audience. "The main question every author is asked is, 'Where do you get your ideas?' With *Saga of a Ship*, I didn't get the idea, *it* got *me*." She nodded at my cousin and friends and me. "When I was about your age, girls, I was walking on a nearby beach one day, and I spotted something in the sand. At first, I thought it was a piece of trash. For some reason it caught my attention. When I leaned down to take a closer look"—she paused dramatically, reaching inside the neckline of her shirt to draw out what looked like a slightly squashed fifty-cent piece on a silver chain—"I realized that I'd found something special."

"A piece of eight!" said Jasmine. "Just like at the pirate museum."

"That's exactly right," Dr. Appleton told her. "It's a Spanish coin called a 'cob,' worth eight reales—hence 'piece of eight.' Its shape is somewhat irregular, since they didn't have the equipment to make perfect coins back in the sixteenth and seventeenth centuries. They just sliced off pieces of a silver rod instead and stamped them by hand. This one was minted in Bolivia in the early 1700s."

She handed it to Monica, who passed it around so that we could all take a look.

"This one coin was all it took to shape the course of my life," Dr. Appleton continued. "I was hooked, and from then on pirates and pirate treasure have been my great passion. And since I live here on Cape Cod, it was only natural that I developed an interest in the wreck of the *Windborne*. Fortunately for me, I have friends and colleagues who share my interest, including one who built a whole museum devoted to it! Isn't that right, John?" She smiled at a man with a gray beard and a Jolly Roger T-shirt seated in the back row. *Skipper John Dee!* I thought as he smiled and waved back.

Dr. Appleton went on to explain her research process, and how, in order to try to track down the history of the ship, its crew members, and their tragic fate, she'd sifted through all sorts of stuff called "primary source material." I was pretty sure I'd heard that term before. Professor Rusty, maybe? No, wait—it was that research assistant of his with the weird hair: Felicia Grunewald, the one we'd seen at the road race. She'd used the term over Spring Break, when we were trying to figure out my ancestor's connection to the Underground Railroad. It meant original letters, diaries, newspaper reports, and stuff.

"Most of my research starts at the library," the author continued. "One of the most exciting primary sources I came across recently was a letter that had been accidentally filed with another document, and thus overlooked by previous scholars. It was written to Isaiah Osborne, the ship's carpenter who survived the wreck only to be caught and hanged as a pirate. We already knew from Isaiah's testimony at his trial that after he washed ashore, he'd entrusted his share of the treasure to a shipmate he called Dandy Dan. The two had split up and run in opposite directions, planning to meet up again later. This letter mentions Cherry Island"—I nudged Mackenzie when I heard this—"and names a date for the two to meet, but of course Isaiah never made it to the rendezvous."

Someone in the row behind us raised a hand. "Finding the pirate treasure would be a big deal, right?"

"Oh yes," Dr. Appleton replied. "A very big deal indeed."

"A real career maker," added Skipper John Dee. "Just like finding the *Windborne* was for me."

"Would you get to keep the treasure if you found it?" someone else wanted to know.

The author pursed her lips. "It would depend on where it was found. Many states have so-called 'finders keepers' laws, but they are interpreted differently. In this case, the statute of limitations would have long since run out for heirs to claim it, so I suspect that yes, I would get to keep it."

I blinked. So even if Dandy Dan were actually my relative, Amanda Appleton would get to keep his treasure? That hardly seemed fair.

"Whether or not you got to keep it, finding it would still be very good for book sales," Monica pointed out, and Dr. Appleton nodded.

No kidding, I thought. Forget guerrilla marketing—Skipper John Dee was right. Finding the lost pirate treasure would definitely be a career maker. Dr. Appleton wouldn't need Augustus Wilde–style tactics. All the publicity would send *Saga of a Ship* rocketing to the top of the best-seller lists.

She'd be on the cover of every magazine and newspaper, and interviewed on every news show on TV, including Carson Dawson's *Hello, Boston!*

Monica glanced toward the stairs. "It looks like the refreshments have arrived. Why don't we take a five-minute break, and then I'm sure our speaker will be glad to answer any other questions you might have."

Cha Cha's hand shot up. "My only question is, are you serving fudge?"

Monica laughed. "Of course!" she replied, setting off a stampede for the refreshments table.

"Oh man," I said a few minutes later, reaching for a second piece. "This is really good. You know, fudge would make a great signature treat at our bookshop. I'm going to talk to Aunt True about it."

"Mmmph mmm," replied Cha Cha, which I was pretty sure meant "great idea."

Mackenzie looked over at me. "Are you going to ask about Nathaniel-Daniel-looks-like-a-spaniel?"

"Um," I replied. "Maybe. I haven't decided yet." The discussion about the "finders keepers" laws had made me uneasy. I wasn't so sure now that I wanted to share my hunch.

Mackenzie and my friends went back to their seats. I headed for the drinks at the end of the table and poured myself a lemonade. It was obvious that Dr. Appleton was as obsessed with pirate treasure as I was with birds. Telling her that I might have a clue about Dandy Dan's identity and the treasure's whereabouts would be like somebody telling me they knew where I could go to see a great grey owl—the world's largest owl, and so notoriously hard to spot it was nicknamed "Phantom of the North." If I ever heard of the whereabouts of one, wild horses couldn't keep me away. I had a feeling it might be the same for Dr. Appleton if I told her about Dandy Dan. So the question was, did I really want a professional treasure hunter sniffing around our little town? What if I wanted to find out more about Dandy Dan first—and maybe hunt for his treasure myself? With the help of the Pumpkin Falls Private Eyes, of course.

In the end, I didn't have a choice.

"Excuse me, Dr. Appleton?"

I looked over to see Mackenzie's hand waving in the air. She was going to let the cat out of the bag! I scrambled back toward my seat, but it was too late.

"If you thought you might know who Dandy Dan was," she asked, "how would you go about figuring out for sure?"

Dr. Appleton went completely still. Behind her glasses, her blue eyes focused intently on Mackenzie.

"It's just that we think he might be my cousin's ancestor," Mackenzie continued. "The one who founded Pumpkin Falls."

I slid into my seat and clamped my hand down hard onto her knee.

"Ouch!" She looked over at me and frowned, yanking her leg away. "What's the matter with you?"

"Pumpkin Falls?" Amanda Appleton cocked her head, alert as a chickadee. No, not a chickadee, I thought, watching her. A hawk, maybe. Or a falcon. Definitely a predatory bird.

"No!" I whispered urgently, giving Mackenzie a look that Hatcher would have recognized instantly. It was the one that said, *Warning! Danger! Red Alert! DEFCON Three!*

Unfortunately, my cousin and I didn't share the Lovejoy sibling shorthand.

Mackenzie nodded. "It's a little town in New Hampshire."

I did my best impression of a ventriloquist and forced two words out of the side of my mouth: *"Shut. Up."*

"You might go the library and try to do some research yourself, I suppose," said Dr. Appleton, trying but failing to sound casual. She couldn't hide the rising excitement in her voice. "Or you might consult an expert like myself." She ventured a reassuring smile. "I'd be happy to offer some advice."

I'll bet you would, I thought grimly. Forget predatory bird—how about pirate, plain and simple?

CHAPTER 20

Mackenzie and I weren't speaking.

I was furious with her for spilling the beans about Nathaniel Daniel, and she was furious with me for being a "drama queen," as she put it.

"You're making a big deal out of nothing!" she'd protested as I grabbed her by the arm and hauled her outside after the book signing was over. I didn't even wait to get my copy of *Saga of a Ship* autographed. It was too risky—Mackenzie might give something else away.

"I am not!" I retorted. "A 'career maker,' that pirate museum guy called it! If we give Dr. Appleton any more information, she'll just use it to track down Dandy Dan and the treasure."

"Wasn't that the point?"

I glared at her. "Weren't you listening? *Finders keepers?*"

Mackenzie hadn't spilled the beans entirely, at least. Amanda

Appleton didn't know Dandy Dan's real name yet. And my cousin hadn't mentioned Cherry Island. But how long would it take for a trained researcher to find those things out?

Mackenzie stomped off to Whelk the minute we got back to Sirena's. Cha Cha and Jasmine stood in the driveway looking uncomfortable. I could tell they didn't know whether to stay with the group or console Mackenzie.

"You guys do what you want," I told them, flapping my hand. "No way am I missing out on one of Delphine's desserts."

I made the right choice.

"It's called Siren Song Cake," Delphine told us as she cut into a multi-tiered mocha refrigerator cake layered with whipped cream and something called mascarpone cheese. "Because it sings to you from the fridge, luring you in."

She passed me a slice, and I took a bite. "Oh man," I said for the second time that evening. "This is amazing."

"It's my mom's favorite," said Delphine. Sirena, whose mouth was full, waved her fork happily in agreement.

I ended up surrendering to the cake's siren song and asking for a second piece. The shimmertail had really added to my workouts this week, and I was hungry all the time. I was going to be in great shape by the time I returned to summer swim team.

Thinking about home and swim team got me thinking about our friends back in Pumpkin Falls. I drifted over to the corner of the porch where Cha Cha and Jasmine were standing—they'd both surrendered to the siren song of Delphine's dessert too. "Have either of you heard from the guys today?"

They both shook their heads.

I pulled out my cell phone and tapped out a text to Scooter and Lucas and Calhoun.

A few seconds later the three of them popped up onscreen.

"Are you eating *again*?" Scooter looked incredulous. "And it's always sweets!"

"Mermaids love dessert," I replied calmly, zooming in on the layer cake. I could almost hear him drooling.

"We had fudge earlier too," Cha Cha added helpfully.

Scooter groaned.

"Maybe my dad will make brownies for us if I ask," Calhoun told him. Calhoun's father was an enthusiastic baker.

Lucas peered over my shoulder. "Where's Mackenzie?"

"Back in our cabin," I said, without going into details. I didn't want to get into what had happened at the Brewster Store just yet. "So, anything new on your end?"

"Nothing," said Lucas.

"Nada," said Scooter.

"Zip," said Calhoun. "Well, not entirely zip. Officer Tanglewood's been giving us a hard time because we haven't found the trophy yet."

I wrinkled my nose. "Well, we'll be home soon. See if you can fend him off until then."

"What happens if nobody finds the trophy?" asked Jasmine.

I shrugged. "They'll just make another one, I guess. It's not that big a deal."

"But it won't be the *same*."

"Of course it will," I told her. "It's just a dumb silver pumpkin."

"It's not dumb!" she said hotly. "It's tradition!"

"Guys," said Calhoun, "it's not worth arguing about. And not to change the subject or anything, but my dad says the cast list will be posted tomorrow."

Cha Cha and Jasmine both squealed at this news.

"Ladies! Shell phones off!" said Sirena, who was seated on a nearby sofa deep in conversation with Zadie and Lenore. Well, with Zadie anyway. Lenore seemed to be mostly listening, as usual. "It's almost time for lights-out."

Jasmine grabbed Cha Cha's hand. "Let's go tell Mackenzie!"

I followed them outside, but I wasn't ready to return to Whelk just yet. I tried texting Hatcher to see if he was still awake, but he didn't respond. So I sat in the hammock for a while, brooding about Mackenzie spilling the beans to Dr. Appleton, the likelihood that I was going to make a complete fool of myself in the revue, and how complicated and tangled life seemed sometimes. And then I went to bed.

• • •

Friday was a blur of rehearsals and preparations for Saturday night's show, punctuated by a flurry of excitement after lunch when Calhoun texted us a photo of the cast list.

"I can't believe I'm Mabel!" boomed Cha Cha, clutching her phone and hopping up and down in excitement.

Mabel was the female lead. Jasmine was excited too, even though she didn't have a major part. She'd been cast in the chorus as one of the "maidens"—the daughters of the Major-General.

"That means Hatcher is my father," she said, giggling.

My brother had gotten the part of the Major-General. I could only imagine the jokes that would be flying around our dinner table back at home, since a major general outranked a lieutenant colonel. My father was going to have something to say about that.

It was so typical of my brother to land the lead role! He'd never acted before, never sung in public before—well, besides church, which didn't count—he'd just tried out on a whim and knocked it out of the park. Sunflower smile, sunflower life. It was like he was sprinkled with stardust or something.

"Ooo, Cha Cha!" said Jasmine, looking at the rest of the list. "Calhoun got the part of Frederic, Mabel's true love."

Cha Cha turned pink and laughed it off. I laughed too, but I wasn't laughing on the inside. Neither of my friends knew about my crush. Mackenzie was the only one I'd confided in. I slanted her a glance, but she was still ignoring me.

Calhoun had talked Scooter into auditioning, and like his sister, he was in the chorus, and would be doubling up as a pirate and a policeman. Calhoun's sister, Juliet, had been cast as Ruth, Frederic's nanny, which we all thought was kind of funny. She'd hardly have to act at all—she bossed Calhoun around all the time anyway.

Lucas was the only one of my friends who, like me, hadn't tried out. I was pretty sure it was because his voice was changing and tended to go shooting off into the stratosphere unannounced.

"I wish I could stay and be in the play," said Mackenzie. "You guys are going to have so much fun!"

"Why don't you?" said Cha Cha. "I'm sure there'd be room for you in the chorus."

My cousin shook her head. "I can't—my parents have planned a vacation for us to Yellowstone National Park. We leave next week."

"How about you, Truly?" asked Jasmine. "Are you sure you don't want to get involved?"

I shook my head. "Not my thing."

The rest of the afternoon found us logging serious pool time. Zadie and Lenore put us through our paces, making us practice our routines over and over until we had them down cold. By dinnertime, we were all so tired that the only thing we had the energy for afterward was lolling on the sofas in the living room watching *Splash*.

"Ladies, I think we should declare an early curfew tonight," Sirena said when the movie was over. "Tomorrow is a big day. You owe it to yourselves to be mer-mazing!"

Mer-mazing? Ha! Unless something "mer-aculous" happened, like I got sprinkled with some of Hatcher's leftover stardust, I was pretty sure I was still on a collision course for disaster.

CHAPTER 21

"This week has gone by so fast!"

I cracked open an eyelid. Mackenzie was sitting on the edge of her bunk across the room, swinging her legs back and forth. Was she finally talking to me?

No such luck.

"I know," Jasmine replied, padding out from the bathroom. She perched beside my cousin and put an arm around her. "I wish we could all stay here forever."

I pulled the pillow over my head. Not me. I was ready to go home. On the whole, mermaid camp—excuse me, mermaid academy—hadn't been as bad as I'd expected, but I was eager to salvage what was left of my perfect summer. Bird-watching? Couldn't wait. Swim team? Ditto. Working at the bookstore? Top of my list. And even if I'd missed the film festival, maybe I'd still get a chance to go to a movie or two with Calhoun. Plus, there was the missing trophy to find, and

I was itching to try to solve the puzzle of my ancestor-who-might-be-a-pirate.

At breakfast, Zadie and Lenore and Sirena surprised us by announcing that our morning pool session was canceled.

"There's such a thing as over practicing, ladies," said Zadie. "Trust us, you're ready."

There was another surprise too.

"It's part of graduation day here at the academy," Sirena told us. "Along with the diploma that you will receive, of course, suitable for framing."

A mermaid diploma? Seriously? Who'd want to frame that?

One look at Hayden's face told me that she would. Mackenzie too.

Sirena's surprise turned out to be a professional photographer.

Oh great, I thought when she introduced him. More embarrassing photographs! I'd had my fill of them already this summer, thanks to the Gifford Family Reunion. But everybody else seemed thrilled at the prospect.

The cabana, which was providing the backdrop for our photos, was almost unrecognizable. Sirena and Delphine had stayed up late decorating it, and the little shed was glammed to the hilt, complete with fishnets, seashells, and buoys covered in glitter.

The photographer, a local friend of Sirena's who was used to ladies in full mermaid garb, put us each through a series of poses.

"Nobody better post these pictures on the Internet," I muttered when it was my turn.

Delphine passed me a tiara. "I'll make sure Mom doesn't use yours on our website," she promised. "Now suck it up and look royal."

After the individual photos came the big group photo, and then it was time for the smaller group photos. The girls from St. Louis went first, then Hayden and her mother, and then the Sand Dollar ladies, who had bonded over the past week and were already making plans for a mermaid reunion in Atlanta, where one of them had a pool.

After Zadie and Lenore posed together, it was our turn. As Mackenzie and Cha Cha and Jasmine and I wiggled into position beneath the fishnets, I couldn't help noticing that Mackenzie made sure to put Cha Cha and Jasmine between us.

"Let's get one with just the cousins, too," said Sirena, after our group shot.

Mackenzie gave me a look. And not one that said, *Boy, I can't wait to be in a photo with you.* Delphine must have seen it, because she came over and quietly offered some advice.

"Look, girls, I don't know what's going on, but I know best friends when I see them," she murmured, making a show of arranging our flukes. "Don't let anything spoil that."

There was a long pause, and then Mackenzie looked over and gave me a sheepish smile.

"Sorry," she said. "I guess I shouldn't have spilled the beans at the Brewster Store."

"I'm sorry too. I shouldn't have snapped at you." I put my arm around her, and we both smiled for the camera.

Afterward, we changed back into our regular clothes, leaving our undersea finery in the cabana as Sirena had instructed.

"Graduation day will continue shortly with our farewell banquet," she told us. "We always have it at lunch instead of dinner. You'll be too nervous to eat anything tonight before the revue, and afterward there won't be time before you all head home."

As much as I was eager to sleep in my own bed again, and see Hatcher, who was also due home from wrestling camp tonight, I wasn't looking forward to the long bus ride back to New Hampshire. At least I'd be able to nap. I had a feeling I'd be tired after the revue.

We spent some time back in our cabins packing before the gong announced that lunch was ready. Place cards had been arranged around the dining room table with our mermaid names on them. I was seated next to Mackenzie/Neptunette, and Cha Cha and Jasmine—Nixie and Pixie—were across from us. Zadie (Isla) and Lenore (Merissa) were next to Cha Cha. We all took our seats and reached for our diplomas, which had been printed on parchment paper, rolled into a scroll, and placed on our plates. Each scroll was tied with a blue ribbon, from which dangled a silver shell charm.

"It's so cute!" gushed Mackenzie.

"One last bit of bling," said Sirena, smiling at her.

I unrolled my diploma and read the fancy script:

Sirena's Sea Siren Academy

By the powers of neptune invested in this institution,

I hereby proclaim that Truly Lovejoy

Has proved herself worthy of the name "Grania"

And is officially inducted into the sisterhood of mermaids.

Around the border was a colorful motif of mermaids and dolphins and shells, and Sirena had signed it at the bottom with a flourish.

"Isn't this just the bees' knees!" said Zadie. "Don't you think so, Lenore?"

Lenore nodded, adding her seashell charm to the bracelet that encircled her wrist and jangling it with satisfaction.

Delphine had pulled out all the stops for our farewell meal.

"Can you believe it?" crowed Mackenzie when she spotted the platters that emerged from the kitchen. "Our second clambake in a week!"

As much as I loved lobster and steamed clams and corn on the cob, even they couldn't chase off the herd of leaden butterflies that were stirring in my stomach. I was pretty sure they'd work themselves into a full-blown stampede by the time the revue rolled around.

Dessert managed to distract me, at least temporarily.

"Let's hear it for Delphine!" cried Zadie, and we gave her a standing ovation as she circled the table with a tea cart, showing off the enormous mermaid cake she'd made for us. The mermaid's tail sported sparkly scales, and I figured her curly hair—made of red licorice laces—had to be inspired by Sirena. Fondant seashells coated in edible glitter lined the edge of the platter.

"I can't believe you made all those decorations from *frosting*!" said Cha Cha, and Delphine nodded modestly.

There was a longer-than-usual siesta after lunch, to give us time for naps and to make one last trip to the Brewster Store for souvenirs and to finish packing.

"I'm going to miss being a mermaid," Jasmine lamented as she folded a T-shirt and put it in her suitcase.

My cousin sighed. "Me too."

"At least we have our tails to bring home with us," said Cha Cha. "Maybe we can all get together for a swim next time you're in Pumpkin Falls, Mackenzie."

I wouldn't be going home with a tail—at least not one I could swim in. The shimmertail was only a loaner. I was tempted to throw away the stupid too-short reject I'd started out with, but then I remembered how much Aunt Louise had spent on it, and I stuffed it into my suitcase instead. Pippa would be thrilled to have the hand-me-down.

When the gong sounded again—"The last one!" Mackenzie said mournfully—we gathered back at Mermaid Crossing. There was a light meal of tuna fish sandwiches, chips, and fruit waiting for us, but Sirena was right, we were all too nervous to eat.

"Don't worry, this happens every session," she consoled us. "Delphine will pack everything up for you to take along on the ride home. You'll be starving after the revue."

I glanced up at the clock on the wall. Sixty minutes from now, I would be making a complete fool of myself in front of a bunch of strangers. The butterflies, which had been largely quiet since lunchtime, began to stir.

All too soon it was time to head down to the pool, where people were already starting to show up. Word had gotten out, thanks to Carson Dawson and *Hello, Boston!*

"Into the cabana, mermaids!" said Sirena. "Your tails and costumes are waiting. Delphine will be along shortly to help with makeup."

We crowded inside. Our tails were hanging on a row of hooks that lined the small shed, each one marked with a tag that had our mermaid name on it. Our swimsuit tops and bling were neatly piled on the benches below. I sat down under the hook labeled GRANIA and took a deep breath. There was no going back now.

"Oooo!" squealed Hayden a few minutes later, peeking out the window beside me. "Channel Five is here!"

The other mermaids wiggled over and crowded around us, and we all craned to see. Sure enough, Carson Dawson and his cameraman were just getting out of the news truck. The butterflies in my stomach were rocking and rolling now.

The Channel Five team weren't the only familiar faces to show up, though.

"Hey!" exclaimed Cha Cha, as the Abramowitz's SUV pulled in beside the news truck. "My family's here!"

We watched as her parents and little brother emerged.

"They brought my parents—and my brother!" said Jasmine.

My heart sank. I was going to have to perform in front of Scooter Sanchez?

That wasn't the worst of it, though. There was one more passenger in the SUV.

"I am not going out there in this thing in front of *Calhoun!*" I sputtered, clutching my clamshell bra to my chest and crouching down below the windowsill. The butterflies were legit stampeding now.

"You're the queen," said Hayden. "You have to, or you'll ruin the show, and the rest of us will look stupid."

You already look stupid, I was tempted to reply, but didn't. Not with Delphine standing right beside us. I just glared at her instead.

When it was my turn for what Delphine called the "glam chair," I sat quietly as she swiped bright red lipstick—a nod to Esther Williams—onto my lips. I didn't flinch as she brushed glitter onto my cheeks and eyelids, and onto the strands of fake seaweed she wove into my hair. But when she reached for the can of glitter spray to give me one final spritz, I pulled away. "I'll blind everybody when the lights go up!"

Delphine laughed. "Nonsense. Mermaids love glitter, and so do our audiences."

"Bling too, right?" I said with a reluctant smile, rattling the sparkly necklaces I was wearing. I was loaded with enough of them to send me straight to the bottom of the pool. We all were, I thought, looking around.

Some of the others had even decorated their bikini tops. Hayden and her mother had added plastic pearls to theirs to match their pearly tails, and the high school girls must have spent hours hot-gluing sequins and tiny shells onto theirs.

"Tiara time!" Delphine told me.

I sighed. "Are you sure I need to wear that thing?"

"Quit complaining, Queen Grania! You're going to look very regal."

I didn't feel regal at all. I felt like an idiot.

Hayden watched as Delphine pinned the glittering ornament to my hair. I'd caught her practicing my routine a couple of times this week when nobody was looking, and I was pretty sure she was hoping for a last-minute chance to switch places. *Not if I have anything to say about it,* I thought. Not even if it meant abandoning stealth mode. I didn't intend to give her the satisfaction.

"Truly!" Mackenzie grabbed my arm and pointed out the window.

"What?" I leaned over to take a look, then gave a little yelp of surprise.

My parents had come for the performance too! And not only my parents but also the rest of the Magnificent Seven—Hatcher and Danny and both of my sisters, who must have been sprung from camp for the occasion. As they took their seats, another car pulled into the parking area beside our family's minivan.

"It's Aunt True and Professor Rusty!" The butterflies retreated a bit. Aunt True had promised to help shield me from Carson Dawson. I couldn't imagine how, but she'd said she had my back, and my aunt always kept her promises.

Sirena stuck her head in the cabana. "Curtains up, ladies!"

Delphine flipped a switch by the door, and all the floodlights went out. Excited murmurs rippled through the audience.

"Positions, everyone!" Sirena said in a stage whisper.

All the mermaids except me scooted across the deck to

the edge of the pool. They sat there in the dark, backs to the bleachers and tails out of sight, just as we'd practiced. Delphine waited until everyone was in place, then nodded to her mother.

The loudspeaker crackled. "Ladies and gentlemen, families and friends!" Sirena's voice floated out into the warm summer night. "May I present to you Sirena's Sea Siren Academy All-Star Mermaid Revue!"

A single spotlight flared, illuminating Zadie at the far end of the lineup. As the music started, she swiveled around and leaned back, hoisting her tail into the air expertly. She smiled and waved, and the audience clapped enthusiastically. I watched, counting to myself: "One Mississippi, two Mississippi, three Mississippi . . ." On the stroke of five, down went Zadie's flukes into the pool with a splash, and her head snapped left as she looked over toward the next mermaid in line. The spotlight followed her gaze to one of the girls from St. Louis, who repeated the exact same moves. Each time the spotlight landed on a new mermaid, the audience clapped again.

"There's Cha Cha!" I heard Baxter, Cha Cha's little brother shriek. Cha Cha grinned and waggled her fingers at him.

After the entire row of mermaids was facing the audience, tails in the water, Sirena's voice came over the loudspeaker again: "And now, we bring you tonight's feature, straight from Hollywood—*A Tribute to Esther Williams*!"

The bleachers erupted as the music swelled and the floodlights came up and one by one the mermaids peeled off the edge of the pool, diving into the water like dominoes. Carson Dawson's cameraman was filming everything. I glanced anxiously at Aunt True, who was busy whispering to Erastus Peckinpaugh. She hadn't forgotten me, had she?

Out in the middle of the pool, arms and legs began rising and lowering in unison, and flukes swished this way and that. The choreographed routine was proceeding like clockwork. The tails looked fantastic in the water, I had to admit, and so did the bikini tops, bling, and even the stupid glitter. It wasn't exactly *Million Dollar Mermaid*, but it wasn't half-bad, either.

Our revue didn't have an elaborate plot like the performance at the Jolly Roger showquarium, just a bunch of synchronized swimming moves leading up to my appearance in the shimmertail. The whole thing would actually have been kind of fun, if it weren't for the fact that there was a news camera out there just waiting to humiliate me on TV. And if the boy I liked hadn't been sitting smack-dab in the middle of the bleachers, where he was about to have an excellent view of me wearing mermaid underwear.

I glanced over at Aunt True again, hoping for a sign—something, anything!—that would let me know she had a plan to foil Carson Dawson. But she didn't even glance my way. This time she wasn't just whispering to Professor Rusty—she was kissing him. In public!

I was on my own.

Cut and run! urged the butterflies.

Mermaid up! ordered my conscience sternly. This was no time for stealth mode. It was time to step up and be tall timber, like Aunt True was always telling me. My fellow mermaids were depending on me. Besides, I wouldn't get very far in a thirty-pound tail anyway. Whether I liked it or not, Romeo Calhoun was about to get an eyeful.

Reaching under the bench for the skateboard that was stashed there waiting for me, I lowered myself onto it, hoisted my legs and shimmertail into place, and propelled myself into position by the door. As the music swelled, Mackenzie and Cha Cha and Jasmine and the rest of the mermaids formed a circle in the center of the pool and slowly sank beneath the surface of the water. Delphine cut the floodlights.

That was my cue! I rolled to the edge and slid into the water as quietly and unobtrusively as I could. Taking a deep breath, I did a silent surface dive and dolphin-kicked my way underwater to where the others were waiting.

When the lights came up again a few seconds later, I was hidden within a tight circle of bodies. And then it was goodbye, Truly Lovejoy, and hello, Grania the Mermaid Queen.

"Hey!" I heard Carson Dawson exclaim as the bodies fanned out like petals on a flower and I emerged, tiara sparkling in the spotlight. "I've seen that girl somewhere before!" The news host peered at me, his overly tan forehead wrinkling in concentration. He turned to his colleague. "Zoom in!"

Here it comes, I thought, bracing myself.

But nothing did.

Aunt True hopped down from her seat and disappeared behind the bleachers. She reappeared almost immediately, smiling a big Cheshire cat smile. I'd seen that smile before. It was the one that said, *I've been up to something*.

A few seconds later, Carson Dawson tapped his microphone and frowned. He said a few words to his tech, who inspected the camera, then shook his head and shrugged.

Aunt True must have unplugged their power cable!

As the two men trotted off to investigate, my fellow mermaids circled around me in formation while I used the powerful shimmertail to propel myself slowly straight up out of the water. Beneath the surface, my legs were pumping furiously back and forth. Above, I was cool as a cucumber, regally smiling and waving to the audience.

"Go, Truly!" Calhoun shouted, and he and my brothers and Scooter whistled and stamped their feet in the bleachers. A school—make that an *academy*—of mermaids rotated slowly around me, arms outstretched shoulder to shoulder.

Time for the razzle-dazzle, I thought. As the others fanned out even farther, allowing me more space, I slid down into the water again and leaned back in the ballet leg double position. Lifting my tail in the air, I sculled my arms the way Zadie and Lenore had taught me and waved my flukes back and forth for all I was worth. The audience gave an audible gasp as the shimmertail caught the light.

Out of the corner of my eye, I spotted Scooter filming me with his cell phone. I gritted my teeth and kept smiling. If he put that video online, I was personally going to stuff him into this shimmertail and send him to Davy Jones's locker!

The music shifted, and the circle of mermaids parted. I headed for the opening.

"Swim pretty, now!" Zadie whispered as I passed her, echoing Esther Williams's famous phrase. I could tell from the twinkle in her bright blue eyes that she was having fun. I was surprised to realize that I was too.

"I'll do my best," I whispered back, and began a slow circuit of the pool. The others peeled off and swam after me single file, like a mermaid parade.

We all smiled and waved as we glided by the cluster of little kids in swimsuits who were seated in the front row. They watched us, eyes shining in anticipation. They were obviously eager for the traditional swim-with-a-mermaid part of the show, which was scheduled to begin as soon as our revue was finished.

The music swelled, signaling the approach of the big finale. While I jackknifed into a surface dive, the other mermaids swam over to where Delphine was waiting by the edge of the pool. I brought my tail down on the surface of the water with a loud *SMACK!*, propelling myself into a streamline. Surfacing, I burst into the air and flung my arms forward into the butterfly stroke—my favorite. The rest of the mermaids were all back in the center of the pool by now, and I swam faster and faster around them until I was fairly flying through the air. The audience whooped and cheered.

For a moment, I forgot about being on display in a clamshell bra, and I forgot about the butterflies, and I forgot about everything but the feel of the water and the way the shimmertail rocketed me through it.

For a moment, I almost felt like a real mermaid.

And then disaster struck.

With one final *thwack* of my tail, I dove deep underwater and headed for the center of the tight circle that the others had formed again.

When I emerged this time, they crowded around, lifting me onto the shoulders of the two tallest girls from St. Louis. As they did, I felt a tug on my back and let out a horrified yelp as I started to rise into the air.

Someone had undone the clasp on my bikini top!

My clamshell bra was about to go AWOL, right in front of my family and friends! And possibly a TV audience too, if Carson Dawson managed to get his camera rolling again.

Instantly, I clamped my arms across my chest, trapping my top in place. This wasn't what I was supposed to be doing at this point in the finale. I was supposed to be collecting a fistful of sparklers from my fellow mermaids, who had retrieved them from Delphine just a few moments ago. It wasn't quite Esther Williams and her hydraulic-lift-and-fireworks finale, but it was the best imitation we'd been able to improvise.

"What's wrong with you?" Mackenzie whispered as I hunched over, terrified that I wouldn't be able to keep what was left of my dignity in place.

"Wardrobe malfunction!" I whispered back, and her eyes widened as she saw my bikini top closure flapping freely.

Zadie saw them too. "Just keep smiling," she told me, moving in to hide me from the Channel Five team, who had finally managed to plug the camera in again.

Over her shoulder, I caught a glimpse of Hayden. She was smiling the same Cheshire cat smile that Aunt True had worn a few minutes ago, the one that said, *I've been up to something*.

I gaped at her.

Shellina was the one who'd done this?

Anger surged through me, from the tip of my flukes to the top of my tiara. No way was she getting away with this, grand finale or no grand finale.

Without giving it another thought, I tipped backward into the water and smacked down as hard as I could with my shimmertail.

CHAPTER 22

I went home in disgrace.

My parents didn't even let me say hello—or good-bye—to Calhoun. I barely had time to grab my suitcase before they marched me off to our minivan.

I'd missed Hayden by inches with my tail. From the way she'd carried on, though, you'd have thought it was a direct hit. When my flukes smacked down on the water's surface, I'd unleashed a tidal wave that soaked not only her but also everyone else within a ten-foot radius. Plus it extinguished the sparklers, ruining the grand finale.

Hayden had hollered bloody murder, and I'd hollered right back. We'd gotten into a fight right there in the pool—or as much of a fight as two people in mermaid tails could get into, with one of them clutching her clamshell bra for dear life and the other coughing and spluttering and pretending she was almost drowned.

With some assistance from my father and the lifeguard's hook, Sirena had finally managed to haul the two of us out.

"Try and salvage what's left of the evening," I heard her hiss to Delphine and Zadie as she hustled us off to the cabana. After the ruckus, though, most of the little kids didn't want to get in the water with a mermaid anymore—they were probably afraid that they'd get smacked with a tail too. I felt bad about that. But I didn't feel bad about defending myself. Hayden had been needling me all week, and sabotaging my swimsuit top was the last straw.

Our parents—along with Aunt True and Professor Rusty—came barreling into the cabana behind us. Hayden denied everything, of course. Her mother started threatening to sue me, sue Sirena, sue all of Cape Cod. My mother told her to back off. Sirena was trying to get everyone to calm down. And then my dad started in on me, before I even had a chance to explain.

"You will apologize to this young lady, Truly, and you will apologize now," he ordered.

"J. T., for heaven's sake at least let her get dressed first," said Aunt True, draping me with a towel. My aunt was one of the only people I knew who could stand up to my father. To her, he was just her little brother, not Lieutenant Colonel Jericho T. Lovejoy.

"Stay out of this," my father warned.

"Why am I the one who has to apologize?" I protested,

determined to act like tall timber for once in my life and stand up to him too. "She's the one who tried to humiliate me in public!"

Hayden pretended to look shocked. "I did not! You're lying!"

The muscles in my father's jaw twitched. He was clenching his teeth. This was a warning sign I usually didn't ignore, but I was angry enough that I threw caution to the winds. "She undid my bikini top, Dad! I almost went the full mermaid out there!"

"Don't you dare speak back to me!"

My courage fled under his stern gaze. "No, sir," I mumbled in defeat. There was no point trying to be tall timber. My father always knew how to cut me down to size.

He inclined his head toward Hayden and tapped his foot, waiting for my apology. Hayden shot me a triumphant look.

You win, Shellina, I thought bitterly. Before I could open my mouth to get the words out, though, Professor Rusty held up his cell phone.

"Technically, Truly is right," he announced. "I was filming the revue, and it's all right here, clear as day. This girl *did* undo Truly's swimsuit top."

My father turned on him, his face beet red. "If I want your opinion, I'll ask for it, Erastus," he snapped. "This is a family matter."

"Rusty is family!" Aunt True retorted.

"He most certainly is not."

Aunt True drew herself up to her full height, towering over my father. "Well, he will be soon enough," she told him. "Rusty just asked me to marry him, and I said yes. We were going to tell you all tonight when we got home."

This unexpected announcement stunned everyone into silence.

So *that's* what the kiss in the bleachers had been about! My mother let out a screech of joy, then burst into tears. My father just stood there awkwardly for a moment before giving my aunt a hug and shaking Professor Rusty's hand.

With my side of the family happily distracted for the moment, Sirena swung around and wagged an aqua-tipped finger at Hayden and her mother.

"Given the evidence caught on video, your daughter has a great deal to learn about being a mermaid, Mrs. Drake," she said grimly. Hayden's mother started to protest, but Sirena bulldozed right over her. "Mermaids are polite. Mermaids are kind. Mermaids are honest. And mermaids never, ever bully other mermaids. In fact," she finished, "I am rescinding Hayden's diploma. She is not mermaid material."

It was Hayden's turn to let out a screech.

"Come along, princess," her mother said coldly. "We don't have to stand for this."

Sirena followed them out the door, her red corkscrew curls bobbing furiously. "And if you post one peep about this on social media, or give Sirena's Sea Siren Academy one negative review, I will sue you for slander! And don't think I won't—I have the video as evidence!"

The cabana door slammed shut behind them.

My father turned to me again. "This isn't over, Truly," he told me. "The fact remains that you acted abominably. You're a Lovejoy, and Lovejoys don't behave the way you did tonight."

"But—"

He held up his good hand, silencing me. "Not. One. More. Word. Your mother and I will be discussing your punishment."

Delphine poked her head in just then. "Um, okay if I come in? Truly needs my help getting out of the shimmertail."

My family withdrew to wait outside. Delphine closed the door again and turned to me, smiling broadly. "You were awesome tonight, and don't let anyone tell you otherwise! Hayden has been pushing everyone's buttons all week, including mine. If you hadn't given her a taste of her own medicine, I might have done so myself. What she did to you was unforgivable."

Her words of support were so unexpected, I felt myself tearing up. "But I ruined the whole evening for everyone!"

Delphine flapped her hand dismissively. "Nobody minds a little extra drama when they come to see a show," she continued, tugging at the waistline of the shimmertail and starting to roll it down. "Besides, it served that little blister right. We get a bad apple every once in a while, but I've never seen one who pulled a trick as rotten as that one. Hayden really got my mother's flukes in a flap."

I had to smile at that.

Delphine looked at me thoughtfully. "You're a really good mermaid, Truly. Best I've seen for an amateur. It's not easy to swim in one of these things."

"Um, thanks."

"I've kept this tail because I thought for a while that maybe I'd go pro, like my mother did. You know, move to Florida, join the famous mermaid revue there. But the thing is, I love it here on Cape Cod."

I nodded. "It's a pretty awesome place."

"And here's the other thing—I've discovered that I love cooking even more than I love being in the water. I've been thinking that maybe I'll start my own bakery or café."

"Wow! I'd definitely eat there if you did."

She smiled. "Thanks. It feels really right. I guess what I'm trying to say is, I'd like to give you this shimmertail as a gift."

I stared at her, open-mouthed. She had managed to extract me from it by now, and she rolled it up and stuffed it back into its enormous duffel bag. "Matching top, too," she said with a wink, tossing it in.

I stammered my thanks, although to be honest at that moment I would have been happy never to see a shimmertail—or a clamshell bra—again.

Delphine wasn't the only one who was solidly in my court, as it turned out. Zadie and Lenore intercepted my parents and me on the way to the car. Zadie gave me a big hug good-bye and made me promise to keep in touch. Then it was Lenore's turn. To my astonishment, she spoke the first words I'd heard from her all week.

"Little brat got what she had coming to her," she murmured in my ear, wrapping me up in a bear hug. "There's nothing worse than a bully."

The only other bright spot was that Professor Rusty—I guess I'd be calling him Uncle Rusty pretty soon, which was a weird thought—wasn't the only one who had caught the finale on video. Carson Dawson had also managed to film "the tail end of things," as my aunt jokingly referred to it. With any luck, his video clip would become an Internet meme, and Hayden could relive that epic smack online for years to come.

I, on the other hand, was probably going to be grounded for life.

CHAPTER 23

The next twenty-four hours were painful.

Mackenzie rode home from Cape Cod with Aunt True and Professor Rusty—part of my punishment, I assumed, since it was our last night together before she went back to Texas.

"Really, Truly! I am so disappointed in you" was the only thing my mother said to me on the long drive north. That's what she always said when one of us messed up. Her disappointment was worse than any amount of my father's bluster, or his icy silence, which was what he dished out all the way back to Pumpkin Falls.

As for the rest of my family, Pippa and Lauren, who were returning to Camp Lovejoy first thing in the morning, quickly fell asleep. Danny had his earbuds in and mostly ignored me except for a few sympathetic glances. Hatcher was the only one who addressed the elephant in the room—well, minivan.

"Too bad you're in the doghouse," he whispered. "That tail smack was epic!"

"Hatcher," said my father sternly, "I heard that."

"Sorry, sir."

When we finally pulled into our driveway several hours later, my father reached over the back of the driver's seat and held out his hand. "Cell phone," he said crisply, and I reluctantly handed it over. "Remainder of your punishment still to be determined."

Mackenzie flew home the next morning. I had been quarantined in my room overnight, while she was banished to the guest room, so we didn't get a chance to talk before she left. I wasn't allowed to go with her to Logan Airport, and I almost didn't even get to say good-bye. My father relented at the last minute, though, and let me come downstairs to see her off.

"Make it snappy," he said, grabbing her suitcase and carrying it out the front door.

We stood there for a moment under the watchful gaze of my ancestors' portraits. *They're probably judging me too,* I thought glumly. "Sorry I messed everything up."

Mackenzie hugged me. "You didn't! Hayden totally deserved it. Uncle Jericho is overreacting." She broke away and grinned at me. "Videoconference later tonight, when I get home?"

"If my dad doesn't take my laptop away."

Hatcher and Danny had volunteered to drive her to the

airport. I waved from the front steps as the three of them pulled out of the driveway.

"At least *you're* happy to see me," I said to Miss Marple, who'd been sticking to me like Velcro ever since I got home. She looked at me and wagged her tail. "Let's go back upstairs."

Even there I couldn't hide from trouble, though.

"Truly!" my mother called a few minutes later. "There's someone here to see you!"

I was flopped on my bed with my dog-eared copy of *Owls of the World*. Reading about birds, especially owls, was always soothing. "Tell them I'm not here!" I called back.

"Truly Lovejoy, come down here this minute!" I could tell by the tone of my father's voice that he meant business.

I closed my book reluctantly and stalked downstairs, halting in surprise when I saw Calhoun's father standing in the front hall. He smiled when he spotted me.

"Sorry to stop by so early in the morning," he said. "R. J. told me you were home."

"R. J." was what Calhoun's father called him, short for Romeo James.

"I hear there was a bit of excitement last night at mermaid camp!"

"Mermaid academy," I corrected automatically, the words flying out before I could stop them. My father smelled sass and frowned at me.

"'Academy,' of course." Calhoun's father nodded. "R. J.

showed me a photo of you in—the shimmertail, I believe it's called?"

I nodded, squirming inside. Calhoun had a picture of me in my mermaid outfit?

"It's quite an amazing feat of costumery, young lady. You look like a real mermaid."

I lifted a shoulder, not sure what to say to that. My father's eyebrows flew together as he frowned at me again.

"Thank you," I said, obeying the unspoken order. Like mermaids, Lovejoys were always supposed to be polite.

"I came by to talk to you about *The Pirates of Penzance*. You've probably heard that I'm directing it?"

"Yes, sir."

"Rehearsals start tomorrow afternoon, and R. J. told me that you might be interested in working on stage crew." Noting my surprise, he added, "I realize it's not glamorous, but it's much needed, and it can be a lot of fun."

"Um," I began, wondering why on earth Calhoun had told his father that I was interested in stage crew. Hadn't I made it clear that I wasn't?

"Your friend Lucas has agreed to join us," Dr. Calhoun continued, as if that was an incentive. "Plus," he added, "I'm hoping you might be willing to reprise your role as a mermaid for the opening scene, and perhaps the finale." He held up a hand as I started to protest. "R. J. told me that you're not interested in singing or dancing, and that's just fine. I had in mind a nonspeaking role—something along the lines of set decoration, if you will. You'd be the crowning glory to our briny 'improbable fiction,' as the Bard might term it."

"The Bard" was Shakespeare. Calhoun's father loved quoting him.

Set decoration? I didn't know whether to be flattered or insulted. Mostly I was just flabbergasted. I had no interest in being a "crowning glory," whatever that was, especially not onstage, and especially not while wearing the shimmertail—which was currently banished to the back of my closet, where it couldn't remind me of last night's disaster.

"Of course she'll do it," said my father, pinning me with his steely-eyed gaze. The message couldn't have been clearer: This was to be my punishment.

"Wonderful!" said Dr. Calhoun, rubbing his hands together happily. "Rehearsal starts tomorrow afternoon at four o'clock sharp at the Grange. I'll see you there!"

My father closed the door behind him as he left, then turned to me, looking pleased with himself. "A little community service never hurt anybody. After all, if I'm not mistaken, it was Gilbert and Sullivan who came up with the phrase 'let the punishment fit the crime.'"

"Yes, but that was *The Mikado*, J. T., not *The Pirates of Penzance*," Aunt True told him, emerging from the kitchen just then. She and my mother had been deep in conversation about wedding plans since breakfast. "And for the record, I think Truly has been punished enough." She crossed the hall and put her arm around my shoulders. "If she doesn't want to perform, she shouldn't have to."

I shot her a grateful look, but I could tell by the way my father's jaw was set that his mind was made up. Like it or not, I was going to be in *The Pirates of Penzance*.

CHAPTER 24

"Welcome, players! Come in, come in!" Dr. Calhoun flung open the door to the Grange.

My friends and I filed inside, along with all the other kids who'd gotten parts in the play or who were there, like me, to work behind the scenes. It was hotter indoors than out, thanks to another July scorcher of a day and the Grange's lack of air-conditioning. Overhead, an anemic ceiling fan was straining to stir up a breeze.

I looked around curiously. I hadn't been here since I was younger and Gramps and Lola had brought my brothers and sisters and me to see a production of *The Sound of Music.* "Shabby" was probably the kindest word I could think of to describe the Pumpkin Falls Grange. It was a wonder the place hadn't been condemned. In addition to the garden-variety old building issues—creaky floorboards, peeling paint, cobwebs on the light fixtures, moth-eaten curtains on the stage—there were more serious problems. Some of the glass panes in the dusty windows were cracked, there was a bird's nest in the rafters overhead, and I could actually see daylight through a hole in the roof.

"Ella Bellow is right—this place is a dump," said Cha Cha in a raspy stage whisper.

Calhoun's father pursed his lips. "It is somewhat lacking in charm," he admitted, "but as the Bard says, 'The play's the thing.' And once our stage crew weaves their magic, I guarantee you that by opening night these humble surroundings will be transformed and the audience will be transported." He made a sweeping gesture with his arm, as if seeing it in his mind's eye already. "And in this case, we're going to transport everyone to the 1950s!"

This stirred a ripple of interest.

"I was inspired by last week's film festival," Dr. Calhoun explained. "I had been thinking to myself, *What can we do to present Gilbert and Sullivan in a fresh new way?*—and there was my answer! Instead of nineteenth-century Cornwall, we'll give them midcentury modern, complete with malt shops, poodle skirts, and bobby socks."

I had no idea what he was talking about. And from the looks of it, neither did any of my friends.

Dr. Calhoun had us divide up into our respective groups—actors, costumes and makeup team, and stage crew. Mr. Henry, Lucas's mother, the Farnsworth sisters, and a few other people I didn't recognize were helping with costumes and makeup.

The stage crew consisted of me, Lucas, and three "old hands," as they called themselves: Bud Jefferson, Elmer Farnsworth (who may have been hard of hearing but who apparently was a whiz with a hammer), and Belinda Winchester.

"I've been working stage crew since 1963," Belinda told Lucas and me. "Same year that 'Surfin' USA' was on top of the charts." She popped an ear bud in and hummed along to the Beach Boys as Dr. Calhoun started taking roll call.

My eyes slid over to the wooden bench along the wall, where Augustus Wilde was seated with his laptop perched on his knees. Wherever Belinda went these days, Augustus went too, so it looked like we were getting him as a kind of bonus. Or mascot, more likely. I doubted he'd be much help when it came to actual work—at the moment he was ignoring us completely. He frowned at his laptop, typing furiously. Augustus was on a deadline for his new novel.

"Where's my Frederic?" Dr. Calhoun called, and Calhoun held up his hand. "Ah, there you are, R. J. How about Mabel?"

Cha Cha raised her hand too, and Dr. Calhoun checked her off on his clipboard.

"Major-General Stanley?"

Hatcher, who was seated next to Cha Cha, jumped up and saluted, which got a laugh.

"And Ruth, Frederic's nanny"?

Calhoun's sister Juliet waved from the back of the room. "Hi, Dad!"

Her father smiled and waved back, then checked her name off too.

I noticed that Chanda Patel, my new piano teacher, was the accompanist. She was about Aunt True's age, with dark hair and eyes, and a shy smile. She taught in the music department at Lovejoy College, and we were supposed to start my lessons later this week. I looked at her with interest, wondering whether I'd like her as much as I had liked my teacher back in Austin. I hoped so. I'd really missed taking piano lessons. But there just hadn't been time up until now.

After roll call, Dr. Calhoun enlisted Juliet's help in handing out scripts.

"Friends, we have less than a month to put this show together," he told us as she moved through the hall with the stack of booklets. "It's going to be tricky, but I know we can pull it off."

Belinda Winchester offered to help distribute the rehearsal schedule and the sign-up sheet for costume fittings. When she got to me, she reached into the pocket of her overalls and handed me a kitten along with a clipboard.

I looked down at the ball of fluff in my hand and blinked. "What am I supposed to do with this?"

Belinda shook her head sadly. "Truly," she said, "it's a *kitten,* not a major appliance. It's not that complicated."

Augustus waited until she trundled off down the row of chairs, then took pity on me. "Here," he whispered, leaning over and holding his backpack open. "It's kitten proof—and kitten friendly."

I peeked inside. Sure enough, in the bottom of his backpack was a fleece vest covered in cat hair. Augustus had obviously been down this road before. I deposited the kitten gingerly inside and watched as it curled up on the fleece and started purring. The kitten had been down this road before too.

After all the handouts had been distributed, the three groups scattered to different corners of the Grange.

"Okay, huddle up, stage crew!" said Bud Jefferson. "In a nutshell, our work is pretty much everything the actors don't do. We're in charge of set design, getting props on- and offstage, lighting, that sort of thing. It's hard work, but we always have fun. Right, guys?"

Belinda gave a thumbs-up.

"RIGHT SIZE?" said Elmer, puzzled.

"I SAID 'RIGHT, GUYS'!" Bud repeated loudly, and Elmer gave a thumbs-up too.

Bud had mapped out a schedule of his own for us. I looked it over and winced. At this rate, we'd all practically be living at the Grange.

"When am I supposed to have time to do anything else this summer?" Lucas stared at the schedule gloomily. "The only reason I signed up for this is because my mother begged me to. She's hoping it will be a 'bonding experience' for me and Bud."

I gave him a sympathetic glance. Lucas didn't like change any more than I did. And change was definitely in his future. Bud was probably going to marry his mother and become his stepdad. At least that's what practically everyone in town said. Pumpkin Falls was holding its collective breath waiting for Bud to propose.

"Okay, everyone! Good kick-off meeting," said Dr. Calhoun a few minutes later. "Actors, I want you all off book by the beginning of next week. The faster you memorize your lines, the faster things will start to come together. And speaking of coming together, tomorrow evening we will gather here to clean the Grange before we do a read-through. Bud Jefferson and the stage crew will be in charge. Please come dressed appropriately, and bring brooms, mops, cleaning rags, and any supplies you can spare from home. See you at seven o'clock!"

As we left, I turned to my friends and moaned, "How did I get myself roped into this?"

Calhoun gave me a sideways glance, a smile playing on his lips. "Technically, I got you into this. I didn't want you to miss out."

"Gee, thanks."

"Let's get ice cream," Jasmine suggested. "That will cheer you up."

"Um," I replied. My father had been quite clear about the fact that I was still grounded. Helping out with stage crew was part of my punishment, but I was to go directly home after every rehearsal. I explained my predicament to my friends.

"If we run into your father, we'll just tell him that we kidnapped you," said Scooter.

I snorted. Like that would fly with Lieutenant Colonel Jericho T. Lovejoy.

"I scream, you scream, we all scream for ice cream!" Jasmine teased in a singsong voice. "Mmmm—chocolate chip, your favorite!"

"Fine," I said, giving in. "But keep a sharp lookout for my father."

In the end, there was no sign of him, but I couldn't dodge Ella Bellow.

"Yoo-hoo!" she called, swooping down on me as we mounted the steps to the General Store. Her dark eyes gleamed. "A little bird told me that your aunt is engaged!"

The rocking chairs that lined the porch stopped in their tracks, and a row of gray heads all swiveled in my direction.

I sighed. "Yes, ma'am, that's right."

"Have they set a date for the wedding?"

"Not that I know of."

Ella tried to pry more information from me as the onlookers strained to hear. I didn't have any to give her, however, and wouldn't have shared it with her if I did. I finally managed to extricate myself and follow my friends inside.

Where I immediately froze.

"What is *she* doing here?!" I whispered, grabbing Cha Cha and ducking behind the postcard rack.

Cha Cha looked around, mystified. "Who?"

"Shhhh! Keep it down! She'll hear you!"

We peered out from behind the postcards featuring all the wonders that were Pumpkin Falls—the church steeple with the Paul Revere bell, Lovejoy College, and of course the covered bridge.

Cha Cha's green eyes grew round as she saw who I was pointing to. "Amanda Appleton? What's she doing here?"

"My question exactly."

Jasmine, who had trotted off after the boys to the ice cream counter, came back looking for us. She frowned when she spotted us behind the postcards. "What's going on?"

"*She's* what's going on," I told her, pointing to Dr. Appleton, who was browsing the General Store's selection of local guidebooks.

"No way! What's she doing here?"

"That's what we want to know."

"Should I just go over and ask?"

I clutched Jasmine's arm. "No! I don't want her to see us."

The boys came around the corner with their ice cream cones just then. Hatcher was with them. He stared at me. "Who are you hiding from?"

Lucas looked around in alarm. "Is it your father?"

"He's here?" My whisper went up an octave. That was all I needed.

"Calm down, he's nowhere in sight," Hatcher told me. "But seriously, what's going on?"

"Emergency meeting of the Pumpkin Falls Private Eyes, that's what's going on!" As Dr. Appleton wandered away toward the housewares aisle, I leaped up and bounded past my brother and our friends, racing for the front door. "Follow me!"

I paused at the bottom of the porch steps, suddenly unsure where to go. Our usual meeting spot in Lola's studio wouldn't work. Not with me being grounded. The library was closed by now, and so was our family's bookshop. Aunt True often stayed late, though, and, fortunately, I had a key.

Unfortunately, my father did too, and there was a chance he might be there.

Was it worth the risk?

"Bookstore," I told the others, deciding that it was. "Give me a few minutes head start, then come to the back door and I'll let you in."

I arrived just as Aunt True was ringing up the last customer. She already had the CLOSED sign on the door, but I used my key to let myself in.

She looked up and smiled when she saw me. "Truly! Come and meet Artie Olsen. He and his wife run Camp Lovejoy."

I thought Bud Jefferson was a big guy, but Artie Olsen was

huge. I had to tip my head back to look him in the eye. He stuck out his hand, and mine all but disappeared as he gripped it.

"Howdy, Truly! I've heard a lot about you from your sisters."

I glanced at the counter, noting his purchases: *Men and Fire*—one of our most popular barbecue cookbooks—plus a bottle of my dad's Terminator hot sauce. Aunt True had been serious when she'd told Lobster Bob about adding it to the store's sidelines.

"I'm in charge of the weekly cookouts at camp," he explained. "You and your family have a standing invitation to join us, you hear?"

He left, and Aunt True locked the door behind him.

"Such a nice man," she said. "His wife's a sweetheart too." She sat down on the antique church pew that we used as a bench by the door and patted the seat beside her. "How was your first rehearsal?"

"Belinda tried to give me a kitten."

She smiled. "So not a total loss, then."

"How about you? Busy day?"

"Surprisingly so. Half of Pumpkin Falls came in, supposedly to shop for books but really to gawk at my engagement ring. Ella Bellow's grapevine is working overtime."

"She cornered me at the General Store just now, too, fishing for details." The minute the words were out, I clamped my hands over my mouth.

Aunt True grinned. "Busted! The lure of ice cream is hard to resist. Don't worry—your secret is safe with me."

"How the heck did Ella find out, anyway?"

"How does Ella find anything out? It's one of the mysteries of the universe."

"I still can't believe you're getting married!"

"I know, me neither." My aunt waggled her finger happily. The diamond in her new ring winked and sparkled as it caught the light.

"Want me to close up for you?"

"Would you mind? Rusty's taking me out to dinner, and I need to shower and change. I'd better check with your father first, though. I wouldn't want to get you in deeper trouble."

Apparently helping out at the bookstore didn't violate the terms of my grounding, because a minute later she gave me a thumbs-up as she emerged from the office. "But you're to go directly home afterward."

I nodded, crossing my fingers behind my back. The meeting would have to be quick.

Aunt True gave me a hug and left to go upstairs to her apartment. I counted to ten, then sprinted to the bookshop's back entrance, where Hatcher and my friends were waiting.

CHAPTER 25

The first order of business for our emergency meeting was bringing Hatcher and the other boys up to speed on Amanda Appleton.

"Wait. What? There were *pirates* in Pumpkin Falls?" Scooter's forehead puckered as he tried to grasp what I was telling them.

"Not pirates—pirate. Just one: my ancestor, Nathaniel Lovejoy. Maybe."

"Nathaniel-Daniel-looks-like-a-spaniel?" Lucas looked incredulous.

So did my brother. "You're kidding, right?"

I sighed. They weren't making this easy. "Look, guys, I know it's hard to believe, but trust me: It totally makes sense." I grabbed a copy of *Saga of a Ship* from the new releases table and showed them the passages that had caught my attention.

"It's a bit of a stretch," my brother said when I was done

explaining my theory about Dandy Dan's "generous beak" and Cherry Island.

"It's not that far-fetched if you think about it," Cha Cha insisted, and I shot her a grateful look.

Lucas was still skeptical. "How will we ever be able to find out for sure?"

"There's got to be some evidence somewhere," I told him. "A diary. Letters. Maybe a map. That's obviously what Dr. Appleton is in town to find. We just have to stay two steps ahead of her."

"Why?" asked Scooter, his forehead puckering again.

"Because if she finds the information first, it might lead her to the treasure, if there is one. Apparently there's this thing called a 'finders keepers' law, which means she'd have the legal right to it if she finds it."

"Even though Nathaniel Daniel is our ancestor?" Hatcher was indignant. "That's not fair!"

I nodded. "I know, right? Especially since I'm the one who figured out the connection. But that won't stop Dr. Appleton. She isn't the kind of person who gives up easily. There's too much at stake for her—including fabulous publicity for her book if she finds the treasure. We're going to have to be quicker and smarter than she is if we want to get to it first."

I could tell by the expressions on their faces that the boys were warming to the idea of a treasure hunt.

"We should go explore Cherry Island," said Scooter. "There might be clues there."

I wrote that down.

"We should talk to Mr. Henry," added his sister. "He knows a lot about the town's history."

I wrote that down too.

"You and I should look around and see if there are any Lovejoy family papers at home, Truly," Hatcher suggested. "Like you said—letters, or a map or something. Maybe up in the attic or stashed someplace like the original Truly's diary was."

Last Spring Break, I'd found a diary belonging to my namesake, which had revealed some long-hidden family secrets. Could lightning like that strike twice?

Lucas raised his hand. "While we're here, can we talk about the missing trophy?"

In all the excitement over Amanda Appleton, I'd almost forgotten about the other mystery we were trying to solve.

"Sure," I told him, and he and Scooter and Calhoun showed us a couple more pictures they'd gathered and flagged as suspicious. After inspecting them carefully, we were able to identify one of the people in them.

"I'm pretty sure that's Reverend Quinn's cousin," said Jasmine, examining a picture of a skinny man in baggy shorts. "I remember him from the crowd along Main Street. He almost hollered himself hoarse cheering on the Speedy Geezers."

"We should still talk to Reverend Quinn about him, though," I said, and wrote down a reminder. "Just because we recognize somebody doesn't eliminate them as a suspect. Well, except for my uncle Rooster."

The other picture was a slightly out-of-focus shot of a woman at the finish line. She was wearing a red-and-white-striped sundress—Mr. Henry's signature colors—and her hair was styled in dreadlocks just like his.

"Do you think they're related?" asked Cha Cha.

"We can ask when we go see him at the library," I said, jotting that down too.

"So to recap, we have half a dozen potential suspects right now," said Calhoun, counting them off on his fingers. "The man in the Grateful Dead T-shirt, the lady in the Red Sox baseball cap, the two teenagers, and the man-who-may-be-related-to-Reverend-Quinn and the woman-who-may-be-related-to-Mr.-Henry."

"My money's still on the guy in the Grateful Dead T-shirt," I told my friends. "But let's keep showing the pictures around town and see if anyone has any more information. You guys will have to do it, though—my dad took my cell phone."

"What about trying to get more information about Dandy Dan?" asked Scooter, who was clearly more interested in pirate treasure than the lost trophy. "How are we going to do that? With you being grounded and all, I mean."

I pondered my dilemma. My grounding came with three

concessions: piano lessons, play rehearsals, and working at Lovejoy's Books. I'd tried to get my father to add swim team to the list of exceptions too, but he'd dug his heels in on that one.

"This is punishment, young lady, not summer camp," he'd snapped when I'd asked.

Maybe there was still a way, though. "I have a piano lesson tomorrow morning, and Ms. Patel's apartment is just around the corner from the library."

"Perfect!" said Jasmine. "We can meet there afterward and talk to Mr. Henry."

Out of the corner of my eye I could see Hatcher shaking his head. "You are going to be in so much trouble if Dad catches you!"

What was the worst that could happen? I'd be grounded for all of eighth grade, instead of just the foreseeable future?

"In for a penny, in for a pound, right?" I told my friends. "I'll see you guys there. Are you in too, Hatcher?"

My brother shook his head. "Can't. Lobster Bob hired me to work at a clambake tomorrow."

With our sisters away at camp and Danny still at work—now that he was home from the wrestling clinic, he'd gone back to his summer job washing dishes at a restaurant in West Hartfield—it was just Hatcher and me and our parents for dinner. Hatcher made the salad while I set the table, stepping carefully over Miss Marple's sleeping form. Mealtimes always found her under the kitchen table, pretending to nap but actually keeping a sharp eye on the proceedings. Miss Marple lived in hopes of food falling to the floor.

"Thank you for helping your aunt close up the shop," said my mother as we all took our seats a few minutes later.

A guilty flush crept over my face. I hoped nobody noticed.

"I went ahead and fed Bilbo, since you were both at rehearsal earlier." She passed a platter of chicken enchiladas to my brother. "How did it go?"

"Great!" he replied. "It's going to be really fun."

I focused on my plate as Hatcher offered a blow-by-blow of our first meeting at the Grange. When he was done, my mother turned to me. "And how about stage crew, honey?"

"Fine."

My father cupped his hand behind his ear and frowned.

"Fine, ma'am," I corrected myself. I told her we'd run into Ella Bellow after the rehearsal—I didn't say where—and that she already knew about Aunt True and Professor Rusty's engagement.

"Of course she does," said my father. "There's no keeping anything from that woman!"

"Now J. T.," said my mother, "Ella is—"

"—a busybody!"

"I was going to say inquisitive," my mother said mildly. She'd gotten into big trouble last winter when Pippa had overheard her call Ella a busybody and then repeated it in public.

My parents smiled at each other across the table. My father reached over and picked up my mother's hand and kissed it gallantly. The two of them had been all moony since their week alone. It was embarrassing.

"Inquisitive it is," he said.

"More like the Inquisition," Hatcher whispered to me, and I choked back a laugh, nearly expelling a bite of enchilada in the process.

"While you two are taking care of the dishes," said my father when we were finished with dinner, "your mother and I are going for a walk."

Hearing the word "walk," Miss Marple sprang to her feet.

"Okay if I head next door afterward?" asked Hatcher. "The Sox are playing the Minnesota Twins tonight and the Mitchells have cable."

My father nodded. "I'll come join you when we get back." He slipped Miss Marple's leash off the peg by the back door, clipped it to her collar, and turned to me. "But you, young lady, are still grounded."

"Yes, sir," I said meekly.

They left, and Hatcher and I cleared the table.

"Do you have time to look around before the game starts?" I asked him. "For Dandy Dan stuff, I mean."

"Sure."

We started in the living room. The two of us stood for

a moment in front of the portrait of our might-be-a-pirate ancestor. Did I detect a glint of mischief in Nathaniel Daniel's eye? He certainly looked the part of a dandy, what with the froths of lace at his collar and cuffs and his fancy gold signet ring with an eagle etched on it. The same ring appeared in Obadiah Lovejoy's portrait, and Jeremiah's, and on down the generations. Gramps wore it now, and someday it would be my father's.

"You sly dog," Hatcher scolded, wagging his finger at the portrait. "Thought you could keep it a secret, didn't you?"

"You don't think there could be something hidden on the back of the frame, do you?"

Hatcher shook his head. "Nah, too obvious."

We decided to check anyway. We carefully lifted the portrait off the wall and placed it facedown on the sofa. But Hatcher was right—there was nothing on the back to see.

"How about Prudence?" I asked.

Again, nothing.

"You'd think there'd be a clue *somewhere* as to Nathaniel Daniel's true identity," I said, disappointed.

My brother shrugged. "Maybe that *is* his true identity. Or maybe he was Dandy Dan, but he didn't want anyone to know and carried his secret to the grave. It's not like it was something he could brag about. It would have been a huge scandal! He probably liked being such a distinguished citizen and didn't want to rock the boat."

Hatcher was right, of course. Still, after he left to go watch the Red Sox game, I poked around a bit more. I started by making a circuit of the room, examining the bookshelves and taking down anything that looked super old. I made a pile on the coffee table, then sat down on the sofa and picked the books up one by one and riffled through their pages. I had no idea what I was looking for, but I figured I'd know it if I saw it.

It suddenly occurred to me that this was the first time I'd ever been in the house alone. My skin prickled. Old houses tended to make a lot of weird noises, and Gramps and Lola's house was no exception. I found myself on high alert with every little creak and groan it produced. Was it my imagination, or did the shadows in the room's corners suddenly seem deeper? As I scuttled around turning on all the lights, I decided I was done snooping for the night. No way was I going up to the attic by myself!

The front hall stairs creaked again. Thoroughly creeped out by now, I jumped up from the sofa and went over to the piano. The pile of Fourth of July sheet music we'd had out for the family reunion was still on the rack.

Sitting down on the bench, I placed my hands on the keys and swung into "The Stars and Stripes Forever," one of my dad's favorite military marches. Nothing like a little John Philip Sousa for chasing away the ghosts of Lovejoys past.

CHAPTER 26

The next morning, on the way to my piano lesson, I stopped by the bookstore to say hi to Aunt True and Belinda. Well, that and to rustle myself up some free mini blueberry donut muffins. I was barely through the door when I spotted a poster propped on the table at the front of the shop. I stopped short and stared at it, horrified.

"What is THAT?!" I screeched.

Aunt True, who was standing by the cash register, looked up in alarm. I pointed wordlessly at the poster.

She frowned. "Um, it's an advertisement for a book signing?"

"I can't believe you invited *her* to do a book signing at our store!"

"Why wouldn't I?" Aunt True looked baffled.

Time to spill the beans, I decided, figuring my friends would understand.

My aunt's eyebrows rose higher and higher as I explained about everything that had happened on Cape Cod. I showed her the passages I'd found in *Saga of a Ship* and told her my theory on Dandy Dan. I told her what had happened at the Brewster Store book signing and about the finders keepers law and how oddly Dr. Appleton had reacted to Mackenzie's question.

Aunt True was quiet when I finished. One of the things I loved best about my aunt was that she always took me seriously. She didn't waste time arguing with me that my theory was improbable or a "stretch," as Hatcher had called it. She read the passages in the book I showed her, then sighed.

"Here's the thing," she said. "I can't uninvite her. That would be rude and unprofessional. Plus, the best way to figure out what she's up to—if she's really up to something—may be to spend time with her and hope she lets something slip. The book signing will give us the perfect opportunity."

I hadn't thought of that. My aunt was not only a marketing whiz, she was also a genius.

"We can talk about strategy later," she added, crossing back to Cup and Chaucer and grabbing a handful of mini blueberry donut muffins. She passed them to me and shoved me out the door. "For now, though, you'd better get going or you'll be late."

I was still so rattled by this development—Amanda Appleton? at Lovejoy's Books?—that my piano lesson was pretty much a disaster. My fingers stumbled all over the keyboard, and everything I tried to play sounded horrible.

"Is everything all right, Truly?" Ms. Patel asked finally.

Her voice was soft and had a slight lilt to it. *Mourning dove,* I thought automatically.

"You seem nervous."

I folded my hands in my lap and nodded. That was as good an excuse as any. "I usually play a lot better."

"So I see." She flipped through the folder of sheet music and piano exercise books I'd brought along to show her. "These are fairly advanced pieces."

I sat there miserably, feeling like a musical failure.

She regarded me for a moment, then smiled. "I'll tell you what—how about we spend the rest of this lesson playing some simple duets—fun ones that are way too easy for us, just to loosen up and get acquainted a bit, musically. When I was your age, it was always a big deal to change piano teachers."

Things went a little better after that, and I was genuinely enjoying myself by the time we finished. I could tell I was going to like Ms. Patel.

ON MY WAY! I texted my friends as I left her apartment. I had my cell phone back, thanks to my mother.

"If you want Truly out at night working on stage crew, she might need it," she'd insisted to my father at breakfast this morning. He'd grumbled, but finally agreed.

My friends were waiting for me on the front steps of the town library. Inside, we found Mr. Henry in his usual spot upstairs in the children's room. For once, though, he wasn't wearing his signature red and white. Or if he was, it was hidden under a pair of painter's coveralls.

"To what do I owe this pleasure?" he asked from where he was perched on a ladder, paintbrush in hand. The walls were empty of bookshelves and books and the Charlotte's Web statue was covered with drop cloths, as was the floor. The old carpet had been ripped up, and rolls of the new carpet were waiting in the hallway, covered in plastic.

Something else was different too. I frowned, trying to put my finger on it.

"How do you like the new skylight?" Mr. Henry asked. "It was installed over the weekend."

I glanced up. That was it! Light streamed in, brightening what was formerly a cozy but somewhat dim room.

"It's going to be brilliant, don't you agree?" He winked. "Literally as well as figuratively."

I smiled. "Mr. Henry, if someone wanted to find out about our town's history—and about some of its early residents—where would they start?"

He climbed down from the ladder and placed his paintbrush on one of its rungs, then wiped his hands with a rag. "Funny you should ask that question. A woman came in just yesterday wanting to know the same thing."

My friends and I looked at each other in dismay. Dr. Appleton had beaten us to it!

We followed Mr. Henry downstairs to the reference room, where he showed us a shelf of books about the history of Pumpkin Falls and a drawer full of old maps.

"If you really want to go way back, I believe the Lovejoy papers are in the archives over at the college," he told us. "They would most certainly contain information about the town's early history."

My ears perked up at that. "Papers? Like newspapers?"

"The term usually refers to a broad range of items," Mr. Henry explained. "For an author, it might mean manuscripts and research material and correspondence with an editor or publisher, that sort of thing. In this case, it may mean letters, diaries, account books, deeds, and more. And yes, newspaper clippings as well."

He looked over at Calhoun. "You'll have to get special permission to visit the archives. Perhaps your father can get you access, R. J." He turned to me. "Or you might try asking Professor Rusty. The fact that you're a Lovejoy should work in your favor."

This sounded promising. Dr. Appleton wasn't a Lovejoy, and she didn't have a father who was the college president or a soon-to-be uncle in the history department. Maybe we could still stay a few steps ahead of her.

"By the way, how's the case of the missing trophy going?" Mr. Henry looked at us expectantly.

"Um, slowly," I replied.

Scooter pulled out his cell phone and scrolled to the picture of the woman at the finish line in the red-and-white-striped sundress. "We were wondering if you knew this person."

Mr. Henry took one look and burst out laughing. "My sister Sarah? Yes, in fact I do know her."

My friends and I exchanged sheepish glances.

"The thing is," I continued, "we had to ask. Just because we recognize somebody or know them doesn't mean we can automatically eliminate them as a suspect."

Mr. Henry nodded soberly. "Just doing your due diligence," he said. "I understand." He placed his right hand over his heart—or where his heart would be under his painter's coveralls. "What is it your father always says, Truly? Cross my heart and hope to fly, my sister did not take the trophy."

I made a show of pulling my notepad out of my backpack and crossing her off our list.

"I suppose you heard about the special town meeting that Ella Bellow called while you girls were away," Mr. Henry told us. "Some folks are fired up to go ahead and have a new trophy made, but most of us voted to wait a bit longer. We're still hoping that the original will turn up." He winked at my friends and me. "Keep up the good work! Everyone in Pumpkin Falls is counting on you. Well, everyone except, perhaps, Officer Tanglewood. I for one hope you solve this before he does."

Mr. Henry went back upstairs. I looked at my friends. "Divide and conquer?"

Each of us took a stack of books from the shelf and started flipping through the pages, looking for information about Nathaniel Daniel, aka Dandy Dan, any mention of pirates, or anything else that might prove useful.

After half an hour, though, we came up empty-handed. Well, except for the fun facts that my ancestor won the town's very first Halloween pumpkin toss in 1769, the same year he founded the town, and that his wife Prudence was "possessed of a greene thumbe and civick spirit," as one newspaper of the era put it.

If we'd been hoping to discover a long-lost treasure map, that didn't happen either. The drawer that Mr. Henry had pointed out proved almost as much of a dead end, yielding only a topographical map of the Lake Lovejoy area that included MacPherson's Island, aka Cherry Island. Scooter took a picture of it with his cell phone for future reference.

"I have to get back to the bookstore," I told my friends, glancing up at the clock. "My father will notice if I'm gone much longer."

"We'll stop by the bookstore if we hear anything about the other suspects," Calhoun told me. "Otherwise, see you tonight at the Grange."

I nodded. I was stuffing my notebook into my backpack when I heard a sharp intake of breath from Jasmine. I looked up to see Amanda Appleton standing in the doorway of the reference room.

"Hello, kids." She cocked her head, a puzzled expression on her face. "Wait a minute—I recognize you girls! You were at the book signing on the Cape!"

Cha Cha and Jasmine and I nodded cautiously.

"Nice to see you again." Glancing at the open map drawer behind us, she pursed her lips. "What brings you all here?"

Her question caught me off guard. "Research," I blurted, and instantly could have bitten my tongue off. "For the play we're all in, I mean," I added quickly.

"Really? What play is that?"

"The Pirates of Penzance."

She arched an eyebrow. "Pirates? How interesting." A smile flitted across her lips. "Well, happy hunting!" She walked briskly back across the lobby toward the bank of computers by the front desk.

"What was that all about?" Calhoun whispered.

"That was Amanda Appleton," I whispered back. "I shouldn't have told her anything."

"Do you think she suspects?" asked Cha Cha.

I lifted a shoulder. "I don't know. I hope not."

I was still wondering when I turned onto Main Street a couple of minutes later. Glancing across the street at the Starlite Dance Studio, I read the sign in the window: WINNER OF THIS YEAR'S PUMPKIN FALLS FOUR ON THE FOURTH ROAD

RACE! But the pedestal in the middle of the display was empty.

Between the missing trophy and Dr. Appleton, the Pumpkin Falls Private Eyes certainly had their hands full. If there was one thing I knew for sure, we weren't giving up just yet on either account.

CHAPTER 27

The afternoon passed agonizingly slowly. I was keyed up about Amanda Appleton and eager to talk to Hatcher. He was still with Lobster Bob, though. I channeled my nervous energy into vacuuming the entire store, helping Belinda unpack the latest shipment of books, and taking turns with Aunt True at the Cup and Chaucer counter.

Later, back home after my shift was over, I slam-dunked a quick dinner, then gathered the cleaning supplies that Dr. Calhoun had asked us to bring to the Grange. My mother was backing the minivan out of the barn when Lobster Bob's truck finally appeared and Hatcher hopped out.

"You're late," I told him, wrinkling my nose. "Plus, you smell like fish."

He grinned and tipped his new baseball cap at me. It was red, with a white lobster on the front. "You were expecting roses?"

"I was expecting maybe you'd take a shower before rehearsal!"

"Hey, all we're doing tonight is cleaning. I'm just going to get all sweaty and dirty anyway. Chill, Drooly."

The Grange was already abuzz with activity by the time our mother dropped us off. Elmer Farnsworth, Belinda, and Augustus, who must have finished the draft of his new book, because his laptop was nowhere in sight, were beating the curtains onstage with brooms. Bud Jefferson and Lucas trailed in their wake with a pair of vacuum cleaners, attacking the clouds of dust that had been stirred up. A group of actors was mopping the floor, and Mr. Henry and Lucas's mother and the rest of the costume and makeup team were tackling the windows with buckets of water and rags.

"Ah, the cavalry is here!" said Dr. Calhoun, swooping down on my brother and me. He handed us each a long-handled duster. "How does cobweb duty sound?"

We started with the chandeliers. As we swiped at the cobwebs, I filled Hatcher in on what had happened at the library, from our dead ends to Amanda Appleton's surprise appearance.

"So do you think she suspects anything?"

I shrugged. "That's what Cha Cha asked. I honestly don't know."

"Maybe I should get another perspective," he said a few

minutes later, and wandered off to talk to Cha Cha, leaving me on my own to start on the rafters. He'd been talking to Cha Cha a lot lately. I dragged a ladder into place and was halfway up when I heard a voice below.

"Hey!"

I looked down to see Calhoun standing there, smiling at me. I was suddenly acutely aware that I was covered in cobwebs. I smiled back. "Hey yourself."

"Want to take a break and help me?"

"Sure." I followed him out the back door to where a large, rectangular something was waiting, strapped to a dolly and covered with a drop cloth. It looked kind of like a refrigerator.

"You'll see" was all that Calhoun would say when I asked him what it was.

"Set it by the stage," his father called to us as we rolled it inside. "Gather round, people!"

Work around the Grange halted as everyone came over to stare at the drop cloth–covered object.

"What is it?" asked Jasmine.

"Our time machine to the 1950s!" Dr. Calhoun enthused. He reached for the drop cloth and pulled it away. "Behold, a genuine, bona fide midcentury jukebox!"

"Groovy!" said Belinda. "Does it work?"

He nodded. "Elmer was able to get it going for us."

Calhoun plugged it in, and the machine lit up like a

Christmas tree. Belinda punched a couple of the glowing buttons.

"One, two, three o'clock, four o'clock, rock . . ." The song began blasting from the built-in speakers.

"Five, six, seven o'clock, eight o'clock, rock," Belinda sang, her short white curls bobbing in time to the music. Augustus grabbed her around her ample waist, and the two of them started to dance.

"Nine, ten, eleven o'clock, twelve o'clock, rock," Bud Jefferson continued, as he and Mrs. Winslow followed suit.

"WE'RE GONNA ROCK AROUND THE CLOCK TONIGHT!" bellowed Elmer, twirling his broom around the stage.

The music was upbeat and irresistible, and bit by bit everyone joined in. My brother paired off with Cha Cha. Dr. Calhoun danced with his daughter, Juliet, and Jasmine danced with Scooter. Calhoun took my hand, and the two of us began bobbing up and down to the music too. He'd grown since the last time I'd danced with him during cotillion last winter. We were almost eye to eye.

Dr. Calhoun was grinning broadly when we finished in a breathless whirl. "I knew the 1950s was the right era! If we can bring this same kind of bounce and energy to Gilbert and Sullivan, we'll have the audience eating out of our hands."

We all took turns picking songs as we continued with our cleaning. We sang along to the ones we knew and tapped our toes to the ones we didn't. The rest of the evening flew by, and by the end of it the Grange looked as good as it was going to get without a complete renovation. The windows sparkled, the chandeliers and rafters were cobweb free, the floor was mopped clean, all the chairs were wiped free of dust, and the stage was neat and tidy.

"Good work, team!" said Dr. Calhoun. "You've earned a break. Juliet will hand out refreshments while I go over a few housekeeping items and give you a brief outline of my vision for the play."

"Chocolate with chocolate ganache frosting or carrot cake with spiced cream cheese frosting," whispered Juliet as she passed around a tray of cupcakes. "My father made them."

"The operetta usually opens aboard a ship or a beach along the coast of Cornwall," Dr. Calhoun continued. "But in this case, we'll open in a 1950s malt shop."

Lucas's hand flew up. "What's a malt shop?"

"Like a diner," Dr. Calhoun replied. "With lots of ice cream on the menu. A malted is kind of like a milkshake. Anyway, I thought we'd name it the Rockin' Mermaid to give it a nautical flair, as a nod to the traditional setting. As the prelude begins, a pair of pirates will wheel in the counter and stools, and atop the counter will be our own resident mermaid, Miss Truly Lovejoy, the Esther Williams of Pumpkin Falls!"

"Like a float in a parade," whispered Scooter.

More like a fish on a platter, I thought in dismay, feeling my face flame.

"This will bring in another nautical element and help set the scene a bit." Dr. Calhoun outlined his vision in broad strokes, from the pirates dressed in black leather jackets, white T-shirts, and a hairstyle called a ducktail, to the high school prom dance floor where the second act would take place. I tuned out after a while and focused on my chocolate cupcake with chocolate ganache frosting. It was delicious. Dr. Calhoun really knew how to bake.

When he got to the finale, though, I tuned back in again big-time.

"It's here that the pirates are revealed to actually be noblemen, and thus entitled to wed the daughters of the Major-General"—my brother hopped up and took a bow—"and then of course there's the big smooch between Frederick and Mabel at the end."

Dr. Calhoun added this last bit almost as an afterthought.

I sat in shocked silence. Scooter, being Scooter, gave a wolf whistle. Calhoun was expressionless in his seat beside me, staring straight ahead. Farther down the row, Cha Cha had gone beet red. This was clearly a surprise to both of them, too.

"I understand that this can be awkward for actors your age," Dr. Calhoun told his son and Cha Cha, "so fake it for now during rehearsals. We'll save the real thing for the performances."

The real thing?

He couldn't mean it!

But he did.

This was really truly happening! My crush was going to kiss my closest friend in Pumpkin Falls onstage right in front of me, and there wasn't a thing I could do about it!

CHAPTER 28

"It's not fair!" I wailed, flinging myself into Aunt True's arms.

"What's not fair?" she asked, bewildered.

"Calhoun is going to kiss Cha Cha in front of everyone!"

"Oh, honey," she said, patting my back soothingly as I explained what had happened. "It sounds like you need a cup of tea." She drew me inside and shut the door behind us.

Hatcher and I and the others had all left the Grange shortly after Dr. Calhoun dropped the kiss bomb. On the drive home, I'd asked my mother if she could swing by Aunt True's apartment above the bookstore.

"I forgot to show her where I put the shipment of new teas she ordered for Cup and Chaucer," I fibbed. "I'll walk home afterward."

Now, as my aunt poured me a cup of her best Earl Grey, the floodgates opened.

"What if Calhoun *likes* kissing her?" I said, the tears starting up again. "I thought he liked me, but maybe he'll like her better."

"Well—" Aunt true started to reply, but I barreled on.

"And it's not just the kiss—it's everything! Being grounded. Mackenzie living so far away. The stupid mermaid stuff. Even Hatcher—all he wants to do these days is hang out with Cha Cha. My own brother likes her better too!" I was being irrational, but I didn't care. My voice rose and cracked. "Plus, you're getting married and you'll probably have a baby and not even want to work at the bookstore anymore!"

My aunt nearly spat out her tea. She looked over at me, astounded. "Whoa, how did we get from misplaced kiss to baby and quitting the bookstore?"

I shook my head, too miserable to answer.

"Look, things do change, Truly, I won't lie. Life is all about change. People grow up, people grow apart, they move on and move out of our orbit, or we move out of theirs. But not all change is bad, sweetie. There are happy surprises around every corner too. New people move into our orbit while others we thought were gone suddenly reappear. Look at Rusty and me! And new experiences, even the difficult ones, can bring unexpected blessings—just look at how far your father has come."

She handed me a tissue, and I wiped my nose.

"Have you talked to your mother about all this?"

I shook my head again. "She's too busy. Besides," I

added bitterly, "she didn't even want me around this summer, remember?"

"Truly!" My aunt gave me a reproachful look. "Your mother is never too busy for you, and you know it. And as for not wanting you around, don't you think maybe you're being just a little bit unfair? Try and think about things from someone else's perspective for a moment. It wasn't just your father's arm that was shattered in Afghanistan. Many of your parents' hopes and dreams and plans for the future were shattered too. And with your father struggling to recover, your mother had to completely reorient her life to help support him. Now, just like him, she's trying to build a future she didn't expect either."

"I know, but—"

Aunt True held up her hand. "There are no buts," she told me firmly. "This is one time in your life when you have to be completely unselfish. Your parents had the rare opportunity to spend a few short days together this summer all by themselves, and they took it. Can you really blame them?"

I stared at the floor. Memphis was sitting on the carpet, swishing his tail back and forth. Without warning, he coughed up a hairball, then glared at me like it was my fault. *Great,* I thought. Even the cat was judging me.

"It's not like your parents abandoned you by the side of the road!" my aunt continued, grabbing a paper towel and calmly cleaning up the mess. "You got to go to—"

"Mermaid camp?" I gave a short laugh.

"Come on, you know you had fun. I have the pictures to prove it! You were having a blast out there in the pool in that tail thing—at least before the wardrobe malfunction." She started to chuckle. I glared at her, but pretty soon we both were laughing.

"The look on that girl's face when your tail hit the water!" Aunt True gasped, struggling to catch her breath.

That set us off again. When we were finally able to compose ourselves, my aunt gave me another hug. "Better?"

I nodded.

"Good." She chucked me under the chin. "Now get back out there and be the tall timber that you and I both know you are. And as for the fake kiss, that's all it is—fake. Trust me, as a former member of the West Hartfield High School Thespian Club, I know! I've had my fair share of stage kisses, and they're nothing like the real thing."

Easy for her to say, I thought as I started for home. I hadn't had the real thing yet. And at this rate, it was entirely possible that I never would.

CHAPTER 29

Back home, I had just passed the portrait of my namesake on the stairs when my cell phone buzzed. It was Mackenzie.

GOT TIME TO VIDEO CHAT?

I texted back a thumbs-up and sprinted the rest of the way to my bedroom, shutting the door behind me. A moment later, her face appeared on my cell phone screen.

"Hey!" she said.

"Hey yourself! I thought you were on the way to Yellowstone with your parents?"

My cousin shook her head. "We don't leave until tomorrow morning. How's it going?"

I filled her in on everything that had happened since she left. Like me, she let out a screech when she heard about Amanda Appleton's upcoming appearance at Lovejoy Books, and another when I told her about our encounters at the

General Store and the library. She also wanted to know if we'd found the silver pumpkin trophy yet.

"No, but we have five suspects. I still think it's the Grateful Dead guy, but the guys think maybe it was the teenagers." I explained about how our friends had been taking the crowd-sourced photos around town. "They were at Lou's this morning during Romeo hour, and one of the men was almost certain he'd seen the two teenagers before."

In Pumpkin Falls, "Romeo hour" had nothing to do with Calhoun and everything to do with what Reverend Quinn had dubbed the "Retired Old Men Eating Out" club. A couple of times a week, the Romeos arrived early at Lou's and lingered over coffee and breakfast.

When I told Mackenzie about the kiss at the end of *The Pirates of Penzance*, I had a hard time not bursting into tears again.

She was quiet for a moment. "Ouch," she said. "I get how tough that is. But you know, Truly, there's a simple solution to your problem."

I looked at her in surprise. "There is?"

"Sure. You kiss Calhoun first!"

My mouth dropped open. "But—"

"But what? Why not?" She gave me a sly smile. "That's what I did with Cameron, you know."

"Mr. Perfect?"

"Don't call him that."

"You never told me that's what happened!"

"You never asked! I could tell he was working up the courage, and I beat him to the punch, that's all. Maybe it's the same with Calhoun."

Was it possible she was right?

We chatted for a while longer, then I told her I hoped she'd have fun at Yellowstone and we said good night. As I was getting ready for bed, my cell phone buzzed again. This time it was Jasmine.

YOU GUYS WANT TO EXPLORE CHERRY ISLAND TOMORROW?

My cell phone buzzed like crazy as her question brought a series of enthusiastic texts from the other Pumpkin Falls Private Eyes.

DON'T KNOW IF I CAN SNEAK AWAY, I replied cautiously. I'LL TRY.

I gave it my best shot the following morning at the bookstore.

"Um, the books that Mom ordered for Lauren and Pippa just came in," I told my father a few minutes after I showed up for my shift. "Is it okay if I ride my bike out to camp and deliver them?" I quickly added, "Sir?"

"Nice try," he said calmly, not even looking up from his computer. "You're grounded, remember?"

Aunt True came to my rescue. "And you're being unreasonable, J. T.! It saves us time and money if she's willing to be our delivery girl—plus, Artie Olsen liked your Terminator hot sauce, and he put in an order for half a dozen bottles for the Parents' Weekend barbecue. Truly can take those with her."

Silence. Then: "Fine, but no dawdling. I expect you to come right back here."

Coming right back to the bookstore wouldn't leave me enough time to check out Cherry Island. I wondered what white lie I might be able to produce that would help with that. A flat tire on my bike, maybe?

But I didn't need to resort to a lie, white or otherwise.

"Nonsense! For Pete's sake, J. T., it's July!" said Aunt True sternly. My father looked up, opened his mouth to say something, then closed it again. Resistance was pointless when my aunt was in full big-sister mode. "The girl has been working her socks off for us this year—without pay, may I remind you—and it's a long ride out to the lake. She's earned a little R and R. You can ground her again afterward."

My father crossed his arms over his chest and frowned. "I'm clearly outflanked," he said, dismissing me with a flap of his hand.

Aunt True shooed me toward the door. "Take your towel and bathing suit with you and go for a swim if you get the opportunity," she whispered. "Just make sure you're back in time to help me set up for the book signing."

I wasn't looking forward to that.

. . .

"How are we going to get out to the island?" asked Jasmine when we all met up a little while later on the road to the lake.

"We'll figure it out when we get there," I said. "Swim if we have to. The island isn't that far from the public beach. Lauren says that kids from Camp Lovejoy swim to it all the time."

Luck was with us, though, in the form of Artie Olsen.

"You kids are going to do what?" he said, when he overheard us talking as I delivered his order of hot sauce. "Absolutely no way. Not a good idea to swim that far without supervision. We always send a canoe out with the campers when they do the Cherry Island swim. Why do you want to go, anyway?"

I thought quickly. "There's a bald eagle's nest out there," I replied, which was true. "My grandfather has taken me to see it a few times. I'm a birder." Which was also true.

Mr. Olsen smiled. "A birder! As am I." He eyed us thoughtfully. "How about if I lend you our war canoe?"

"War canoe?" Lucas's eyes widened in alarm. I could tell he was thinking that his mother wouldn't like the sound of that.

"Just another name for a big canoe, son. It can seat up to fifteen, but six can man it nicely."

"Wow—thanks, Mr. Olsen!" I said.

"No problem. It's the least I can do for a fellow birder—

and the daughter of the man who makes my new favorite hot sauce." He put a finger to his lips. "Don't tell a soul, though, or I'll have the whole town down here wanting to use our equipment." He made us promise to wear life preservers and, after glancing at the clock, said he'd go ask the kitchen staff to pack us a lunch. "Can't have you starving to death on camp property."

I asked at the front office about Lauren, who I learned was away on an overnight hike, so I left her new book in her cabin.

"Ooo, a mermaid book," said Cha Cha as I set it on my sister's bunk. "*The Tail of Emily Windsnap*—she'll love it."

My mother definitely had mermaids on the brain. She'd bought a copy of a picture book called *The Mermaid* for Pippa, who we found doing something with glitter in the arts and crafts studio.

"Truly!" she squealed, running over to give me a big hug. She turned to her cabin-mates and announced proudly, "She's my SISTER!"

"Is she a giant?" whispered one of them, and Scooter started to laugh.

"Don't," I warned him, but it was too late. He couldn't resist.

"Truly gigantic," he teased.

"Shut up, Scooter," said Calhoun, but he was smiling too.

Actually, to my surprise, so was I. *Maybe Aunt True was right*, I thought. Maybe people did grow and change—even me.

It was an easy paddle out to the island, thanks to Jasmine and Scooter, who knew their way around a canoe and told us exactly what to do. When we reached the shore, which was mostly rocky, Jasmine hopped out and guided the boat to a small sandy stretch that sloped up toward a tangle of bushes lining the shore. The canoe was heavy, and it took all six of us to pull it high enough out of the water that it wouldn't float away.

Calhoun shucked off his backpack and took a seat on a fallen log. "Eat first, then explore."

No one protested that idea. I sat down beside him. For one wild moment I wondered what he'd do if I grabbed him and kissed him. Not that I was actually planning to, of course.

He glanced over at me. "What are you laughing about?"

"Nothing."

I'd only had a couple of mini blueberry muffins since breakfast, and I was starving. Thelma Farnsworth and her sister Ethel, who worked in the camp kitchen during the summer, had packed substantial lunches for us, I was happy to see. Turkey sandwiches, potato chips, apples, peanut butter cookies, and bottles of water to wash it all down. I ate happily, enjoying the slight breeze that rustled the leaves in the trees above. I tipped my head back and closed my eyes, feeling the warmth of the sun on my face. A shadow fell over me, and I looked up.

"Check it out! It's an eagle!" I'd been hoping we'd see one.

My friends all shaded their eyes and looked up too.

"Wow, it's huge!" said Scooter.

"Right? They're amazing."

We watched as the large bird circled overhead, then landed in a dark mass of branches high up in one of the trees.

"That's its nest," I explained. "Did you know that a bald eagle's nest can weigh up to a ton and measure up to eight feet across?"

"Ooo, 'Fun Facts with Truly'!" Cha Cha sounded like Mackenzie, who loved to tease me about what she called my obsession with birds. She quickly added, "But that's a really cool fun fact."

After lunch, it was time to explore. Scooter pulled out his cell phone and scrolled to the picture of the topographical map we'd found at the library.

"How about we start with the trail that circles the island," suggested Calhoun, squinting at it.

"What are we looking for?" asked Jasmine.

I shrugged. "I have a feeling we'll know it when we see it."

Our loop around the small island revealed exactly nothing, though.

"Guess we're going to have to bushwhack in toward the center," said Calhoun.

The island's tangled interior was not an inviting prospect. But Calhoun was right—there really wasn't an alternative.

"Let's head for that big tree with the eagle's nest in it," I suggested. "We want to look for something that might have been around when Nathaniel Daniel was here. A tree like that one, a big rock—some landmark that would have been easy for him to find again."

"Good thinking," said Cha Cha, but after another half hour we still had nothing, unless you counted the scratches on our arms and legs from pushing through the undergrowth.

"Too bad we don't have a treasure map." Jasmine leaned back against a tree trunk and pulled out her water bottle. The rest of us pulled ours out too. It was hot, even in the shade.

We were quiet for a while, listening to the lapping of the water on the shore nearby. It was disappointing to have come so far and not find anything that looked remotely like a pirate's hideout.

"If you were going to stash a treasure someplace," I mused aloud, "where would you put it?"

"Inside a hollow tree?" Cha Cha suggested.

I shook my head. "Lightning could strike, the tree could fall down in a storm—not safe enough."

"It's not like there's a bank vault out here," said Scooter.

"Not a vault, but someplace secure," I told him. "Dandy Dan had a lot of pirate gold to stash away, and he'd have wanted to keep it safe."

Calhoun dumped the rest of the contents of his water bottle over his head. "Let's take one more look, then call it a day. I want to go for a swim."

We spread out this time, and for a while there was nothing but the sound of branches snapping underfoot and people slapping at mosquitoes. Then Scooter gave a yelp that brought the rest of us thrashing toward him through the underbrush.

"It's probably nothing," he said, pointing to what looked like a dark crevice beside a boulder. "It's so overgrown I almost missed it."

The six of us tugged on the vines and branches that covered the crevice, and a few minutes later were rewarded with what was clearly a genuine opening. My skin prickled in excitement. "This could be it, guys!"

"What if it's a bear's den?" asked Lucas.

My excitement fizzled. Jasmine took a step back in alarm. It did kind of look like it could be a bear's den.

Calhoun shook his head. "No scat."

"No what?" Scooter's forehead puckered.

"Scat," I told him. "Animal droppings—poop. Calhoun is right. I don't think anything or anyone lives here."

We turned on the flashlight apps on our cell phones and shined them inside. The opening led to a narrow passageway—too narrow for most of us—and blackness beyond.

I looked over at my friends. "Lucas, you and Cha Cha are the only ones small enough to fit."

Cha Cha scowled. "No way am I going in there!"

Lucas turned even paler than his usual shade of pale. "My mother would kill me."

"So don't tell her, duh!" scoffed Scooter.

"Shut up, Scooter," said his sister.

"Maybe we should come back tomorrow with better flashlights," said Cha Cha,

As we turned to go, Calhoun shrugged off his backpack again. "No time like the present," he said, and we paused to watch as he pulled out a length of rope, a bike helmet, a headlamp, and some duct tape. Noticing us staring at him, he straightened. "What? You can't go spelunking without the proper equipment."

Scooter's forehead pleated again. "Spe-what?"

"Spelunking—you know, cave exploring. I figured a cave might be one possibility that Dandy Dan would consider, and I thought I might as well come prepared in case we found one."

I stared at him, wondering if he would ever cease to amaze me.

"You can do this," Calhoun said, turning to Lucas and cinching the rope around his waist.

Swim team had been good for Lucas. He was still skinny, but he'd added muscle over the past months. He still looked anxious, though.

"You can't breathe a word about this to your mother!" I told him.

"Are you crazy?" He shook his head vigorously. "Not a chance."

Calhoun settled the bike helmet on Lucas's head and strapped it firmly in place. Then he reached over and flipped on the headlamp he'd attached with duct tape. "Okay, buddy, in you go. Just take it slow and steady, inch by inch. There's no rush."

Squaring his narrow shoulders, Lucas nodded, then crouched down and squeezed into the opening. "Yuck," he said. "It's kind of damp in here." There was silence for a bit. We could hear him scrabbling around. "The tunnel gets bigger!" His voice echoed. He sounded nervous, but a little excited, too. And then there was silence again.

"Lucas?" Calhoun called.

There was no response.

"Lucas!" This time, Calhoun's question was answered by a squeak and more scrabbling as Lucas came backing swiftly out of the opening. He was covered with dirt and leaves and pine needles.

"Is it a bear?" asked Jasmine, her eyes wide.

Lucas shook his head. "Worse. There's a big hole in the ground, and I almost fell in!"

CHAPTER 30

It took some convincing, but we finally got Lucas to go back into the cave again.

"Take your cell phone this time," I told him. "See if you can get some pictures."

He reappeared a few minutes later, and we all gathered around. There wasn't much to see in his photos, mostly just the dim outline of rocks on the ground and roots sticking out overhead.

"There," said Lucas, pointing. "There's the hole."

It was difficult to make it out, but he was right. There was a hole in the ground.

I peered at a faint glimmer of light in the corner. "What's that?"

Lucas shrugged. "I'm not sure. I held my cell phone out over the edge, but I was afraid I might drop it, and I didn't want to lean over very far myself in case I fell in. I think maybe there's water down at the bottom, though. I could hear sloshing."

"I'm going in," I told my friends.

"You won't fit," warned Calhoun.

"Truly gigantic," Scooter added again helpfully.

I gave him a look. "I've got to try, at least. If you guys hold really tight to the rope, maybe I can lean down over the edge and get a better view. I'm a lot taller than Lucas." I looked over at Scooter. "Just don't."

He didn't. But he grinned.

"Okay, then," said Calhoun briskly. He transferred the bike helmet from Lucas's head to mine and fastened the rope securely around my waist. "One tug means yes, two means no. Three tugs from you means you're ready for us to pull you out."

Crouching down, I sucked in my breath—and the rest of me—and somehow managed to squeeze myself through the narrow gap beside the boulder. Lucas was right, the passage smelled like wet leaves and dirt. I winced as I scraped my head against the low roof.

"See anything?" called Cha Cha.

"Not yet."

"The hole sneaks up on you!" Lucas warned. "Be careful!"

Inching cautiously forward, I soon reached the edge of the hole. I knelt down on all fours, turning my head slowly as I shined the headlamp around its circumference. It was larger than I thought, probably at least as wide as I was tall. If I was expecting to see a big sign that said THIS WAY TO PIRATE TREASURE! though, I was disappointed.

There wasn't much to see anywhere else, either. Just dirt and roots and rocks. Nothing to indicate that this was anything but an ordinary cave.

"Doing okay in there?" I heard Calhoun's muffled voice in the distance and gave the rope one sharp tug in reply. Flattening myself onto my stomach, I crawled forward and peeked over the edge of the hole.

It was deep. Very deep. Lucas had been right about the sloshing sound—I could hear it too. I groped around for a rock and dropped it in. It seemed a long time before I heard a plunk as it hit the water below. I inched forward again until my entire head and shoulders were extended out over the edge, then aimed the headlamp directly downward. I peered into the darkness. Light from my headlamp reflected on the water, but I could also see light reflecting up *through* the water. It had to be coming from outside! There was another entrance to the cave!

I tugged on the rope three times and my friends started to haul me back.

"Ouch," I called in protest as my chest scraped against a sharp rock. I heard my T-shirt tear. "Slowly!" Flinging out an arm to steady myself, I grabbed on to what I thought was a root. It pulled away from the dirt, and I was still clutching it when I emerged into the sunlight.

"There's another entrance," I panted, dropping the root and swiping at my dirt-encrusted clothes. "I could see daylight in the water down at the bottom of the hole. The underwater opening must be somewhere along the shore."

"Which direction?" Calhoun asked.

I looked around, disoriented. "I have no idea."

"What's that?" Cha Cha pointed at the ground.

"A root." I prodded it with my toe.

She bent down and picked it up. "I don't think so, Truly."

We all leaned in to examine it more closely.

"I looks kind of familiar," said Jasmine. "I think it's a piece of rope, like the kind we saw at the pirate museum on Cape Cod."

My friends and I stared at each other in awe.

"She's right!" I whispered. "I think we found Dandy Dan's cave!"

CHAPTER 31

We hid the opening to the cave as best we could, piling up branches and leaves until it was nearly invisible again. Covering our tracks back to the main path was almost impossible, though. We'd broken a lot of branches in our initial rush to get to Scooter. We could only hope that if anyone else came out to the island they wouldn't notice.

I really, really wanted to hunt for the underwater entrance, but it was getting late, and I was due back at the bookstore for Amanda Appleton's signing. "We can come back again tomorrow, maybe," I told my friends, tucking the length of tarred rope safely into my backpack.

Cha Cha looked Lucas and me up and down, smiling. "You guys had better wash off before we go back."

I glanced over at Lucas. If I looked anything like he did, she was right. He was streaked with dirt, there were wet leaves tangled in his hair, and as for his clothes—well, he was going to have a hard time explaining them to his mother.

I waded out into the water and dove in. Lucas followed, and so did the rest of our friends. We swam around for a few minutes, splashing each other and whooping with excitement over our discovery.

After we paddled back to the camp and returned the war canoe to Artie Olsen, we got on our bikes and headed for home. We were halfway to Pumpkin Falls when a red sports car with a kayak strapped to its roof passed us going in the opposite direction.

Cha Cha's head swiveled around. "Hey!" she called over her shoulder. "Wasn't that—"

"Yeah," I replied, steering my bike to the edge of the road. "Amanda Appleton."

My friends pulled over to join me, and we exchanged worried glances.

"She's headed toward the lake," said Lucas. "What if she goes out to the island?"

Calhoun shook his head. "She won't have time. The book signing starts in an hour."

Hopping back on my bike, I picked up my pace, arriving at the bookstore just as Aunt True and Belinda finished setting up the chairs. "Sorry I'm late!"

"No worries." Aunt True's eyebrows flew up when she looked at me. "You might want to freshen up before the customers start arriving, though. You can borrow something of mine."

I ran upstairs to her apartment. When I saw myself in her bathroom mirror, I almost burst out laughing. The swim in the lake had cleaned most of the dirt off, but my hair was sticking up every which way, and my T-shirt was torn in three places.

I washed my face and brushed my hair, then rummaged through my aunt's closet for something suitable to wear. Aunt True and I had totally opposite tastes in clothing. My aunt was a parrot, never happier than when she was parading around in bright colors and wild fabrics. I was—what was I, anyway? A partridge, maybe? I glanced in the mirror again. Yeah, a partridge. Mainly brown plumage, with just a few understated stripes in my feathers.

I settled on a pair of jeans, a T-shirt in a not-too-bright shade of teal, and a pair of sandals that weren't my usual style, but whose teal beads matched the color of the shirt I'd chosen. On a whim, I added a pair of dangly turquoise earrings. *Stripes in my feathers,* I thought, smiling to myself.

"Very nice!" said Aunt True approvingly when she saw me. "You should borrow my clothes more often."

"Guess what?" I started to tell her. "We—"

"You can tell me later," she said, twirling me around by the shoulders and giving me a little shove. "Right now, see if you can help Belinda at Cup and Chaucer. Things are hopping over there."

They certainly were. I barely had a moment to catch my breath for the next few minutes as we waited on the crush of customers eager to buy a beverage before the book talk started.

"I'll take a chai tea latte, please."

I looked up to see Dr. Appleton standing in front of me. She was dressed in the same outfit she'd worn for the book signing on Cape Cod—the one that screamed *I may have been a pirate in a previous life*. I blinked. "Uh, sure. Coming right up."

"Did you have a fruitful day yesterday?"

"Fruitful?" I tried not to sound panicked. *Why was she asking? Did she know about Cherry Island and the cave?*

"Successful. With your research. *The Pirates of Penzance*, was it?"

"Oh that!" I nodded, then busied myself with her drink order to cover my relief.

She smiled. "Wonderful. That's what I love about research—the thrill of the hunt."

I gave her a thin smile in return as I handed over her cup. *Definitely a pirate*, I thought, watching as she walked away. And not just in a previous life. In this one too.

"If everyone could take a seat, we'll get started," Aunt True announced.

"Go sit down with your friends," Belinda whispered to me. "I can handle things from here."

I made my way around the edge of the crowd to the back, where I took a seat between Lucas and Cha Cha. Farther down the row of seats, Calhoun leaned forward and waved. I waved back.

"We have a real treat for you today, folks," my aunt continued, holding up a copy of *Saga of a Ship: The Lost Treasure of the Windborne*. "Author Amanda Appleton will be sharing with us the story behind her new book. It's a stirring tale of piracy on the high seas, of skullduggery under the back flag, and of a mysterious missing treasure. Please join me in welcoming her to Lovejoy's Books!"

The crowd clapped enthusiastically as Dr. Appleton crossed to the podium. Before she could say anything, though, the bell over the door jangled, and Ella Bellow came in. Bud Jefferson and Lucas's mother were right behind her, holding hands. Beside me, Lucas's face flushed pink.

"Plenty of seats down front," Dr. Appleton told the late-comers. "You haven't missed a thing—we're just getting started."

As they made their way to the front row, Amelia Winthrop scanned the crowd for Lucas. She spotted him with us and blew him a kiss.

"Ooo, Lukey-pookey!" whispered Scooter. "Mommy loves you!"

"Could you please find another hobby, Scooter?" I whispered back, as Lucas's face went from pink to fire-engine red.

"I'm just teasing!"

"Nobody thinks it's funny but you."

I felt something brush past my ankles and looked down to see Memphis stalk by. My aunt's cat loathed book signings.

Too many people. He crouched under my chair, glaring balefully out at the crowd. Miss Marple, on the other hand, was in her element, making her way up and down the rows of chairs collecting pats. My aunt shooed her onto her dog bed by the cash register as Dr. Appleton began to speak.

Her talk was almost identical to the one we'd heard on Cape Cod. She told the audience about herself and her background, explained her research and writing process, and then shared the story of how she got hooked on hunting for pirate treasure, showing off the silver coin on her necklace. This time, though, when she described the *Windborne*'s final tragic voyage, she zeroed in on Dandy Dan.

"I've recently learned that the *Windborne*'s sole survivor may have a Pumpkin Falls connection," she told the audience. "It's an exciting new development that I'm here in town to explore, in fact."

Ella Bellow's hand shot into the air.

"Yes?"

"If there is indeed a connection, can we expect an influx of visitors and treasure hunters once the news is out?"

Ella loved tourists. They were good for business, she said, which was true.

The author pursed her lips, considering. "It's entirely possible. Quite likely, in fact."

This caused a ripple of interest, particularly among the local business owners.

"How do you feel about that?" asked Bud Jefferson. "More treasure hunters means more competition, right?"

Dr. Appleton shrugged. "My motto has always been, 'May the best man—or woman, as the case may be—win.'"

Was it my imagination, or was she looking directly at me when she said that?

CHAPTER 32

The thing about Lovejoys? We were competitive.

Really competitive.

And unlike Four on the Fourth, this was one race I was determined not just to finish, but to win. Especially now that we'd had a taste of victory with the discovery of what was very likely Dandy Dan's cave. I didn't want Amanda Appleton unraveling my family secret before I did. This was my mystery to solve, not hers.

I said as much to my friends as we all crowded into the big booth at the back of Lou's Diner with my aunt after the book signing. My father didn't like my being there one bit, but he could hardly argue with the fact that I'd just worked another two-hour shift—for free—and that I needed to eat before rehearsal.

"I'll buy her dinner and then drop her off at the Grange," my aunt had told him. "No detours, I promise."

After we placed our order, we finally had a chance to show my aunt what we'd discovered on Cherry Island.

"This is astonishing!" she said, running a finger along the length of rope. "I mean, it's got to be, what, nearly three hundred years old?" She shook her head in amazement. "The tar must have helped preserve it from rotting. Rusty will be beside himself." Seeing the looks on our faces she added hastily, "But don't worry—I won't breathe a word to him until you give me the okay."

She made us promise we wouldn't go back to Cherry Island alone, though. "Caves are notoriously dangerous," she warned. "I don't want anyone getting hurt."

As for Dr. Appleton, Aunt True had come up with a brilliant plan for finding out what she was up to. She'd sicced Ella Bellow on her.

"It hit me the minute Ella walked in the bookshop," she told us. "If you have a secret weapon, you might as well use it, right?"

As everyone had lined up to get their books signed, Aunt True had pulled Ella aside and hinted that she thought something about the author was a little fishy. That instantly caught Ella's attention, and she'd spent the rest of the evening plying Dr. Appleton with questions. She'd managed to extract a fair amount of information, too.

Aunt True ticked the details off on her fingers. "She's staying at the Pumpkin Falls Bed and Breakfast; her plans are 'indefinite'—which means she probably won't be leaving anytime soon—and she's been fishing in the college archives."

My friends and I looked at each other in dismay. Once again, Dr. Appleton was one step ahead of us!

"Has she made the connection between Dandy Dan and Nathaniel Daniel?" I asked.

My aunt shrugged. "Maybe? She mentioned to Ella that she was looking into all the early settlers who arrived here in Pumpkin Falls soon after the wreck of the *Windborne*."

It wouldn't be long before she zeroed in on Nathaniel Daniel Lovejoy in that case, I thought glumly, if she hadn't already.

After dinner, Mrs. Abramowitz was waiting outside to drive us to the Grange. She'd volunteered to help with the choreography for the show.

"*The Pirates of Penzance* is one of my favorites!" she said as we piled into Cha Cha's SUV. "And the fifties setting is so fabulous—I'll have you all doing the bunny hop and the jitterbug in no time. You kids are going to have a blast!"

This did not sound like a blast to me. I stared down at my feet, which didn't always cooperate in the dancing department, grateful for once that they'd be safely encased in the shimmertail.

So far, stage crew had been less boring than I'd expected. Lucas was good company, despite his standoffishness with Bud Jefferson, who was clearly determined to make this the bonding experience that Mrs. Winthrop was hoping for. Plus, my knack for the window displays at the bookshop seemed to have carried over to stage design, as I'd come up with several good ideas that nobody had thought of, including the addition of an ice cream–themed mural on the back wall of the Rockin' Mermaid Malt Shop.

Tonight, while my brother and friends rotated between costume fittings, their first few scene run-throughs, and vocal and dance practice, the members of the stage crew were brainstorming details for props and set decorations. We figured that the second act, which would take place in a high school gymnasium during prom, was a no brainer.

"All we need is a disco ball, a bunch of streamers and banners, and boom we're done," Belinda said, and we all agreed.

The set for the first act, though, was more challenging. Recreating a 1950s malt shop was going to take a lot of work.

"I'm hanging up my hat after this production, and I want to go out on a high note," Belinda told us, hoisting her kitten-du-jour, a little orange tiger, into the air for emphasis. "This has to be a real showstopper."

"CORN POPPER?" said Elmer Farnsworth.

"SHOWSTOPPER!" Belinda repeated.

"I HAVE A CORN POPPER IN MY TRUCK!" he assured her, springing to his feet. "OTHER STUFF TOO."

Belinda heaved a sigh as Elmer darted off. "Come on, team. We might as well go take a look."

She passed her kitten to Augustus, who reached for it automatically and put it in his backpack. We all followed them out back to where Elmer's truck was parked. It looked to be nearly as old as he was, and it was loaded to the gills. The junk pile in Elmer's barn was legendary around Pumpkin Falls, and he appeared to have brought half of it with him.

"All right, folks, dig in!" said Belinda. "We're looking for anything that might remotely work as a prop for a 1950s malt shop."

Before we knew it, we were wrestling a vintage red Coca-Cola machine, a couple of old diner booths, a set of heavy chrome stools, and assorted kitchenware into the Grange.

"These will make swell props, Elmer—thanks!" Belinda enthused. She looked over to where I was setting a toaster down on the floor of the stage. "Think you could handle an art project, Truly?"

I shrugged. "I could try, I guess."

A little while later, Hatcher wandered over and looked at the big piece of plywood propped up against the stage in front of me. "Not bad, Drooly," he said, watching over my shoulder as I sketched a mermaid onto it for the Rockin' Mermaid sign that Dr. Calhoun envisioned.

"Don't call me that," I said automatically. I frowned, concentrating on getting the sweep of her tail just right. "You didn't sound too bad just now either."

"Thanks. My solo is really hard, though. Do you think

you might have time to help me practice at home?"

I looked at him, surprised and pleased that he wanted to hang out with me. "Sure!"

Over on the other side of the Grange, Ms. Patel struck a chord on the piano, and Cha Cha started to sing. Hatcher and I both turned to watch. For someone so small, Cha Cha sure was loud. And if her speaking voice was low, her singing voice was just the opposite. She didn't sound like a kazoo at all. She could really hit the high notes, and most of them were even on pitch.

"Gather around, people!" Dr. Calhoun said when Cha Cha finished. "Parents' Weekend is coming up at Camp Lovejoy. Gwen and Artie Olsen, the directors, got wind of our production, and they've invited us to perform a sneak preview as entertainment for their big barbecue this weekend. I realize that's not much notice, but I told them yes. We'll do just a few songs—the first one featuring our pirates, of course. Then Mabel's 'Poor Wand'ring One,' which we just heard from Cha Cha and which is coming along nicely, and"—he looked over at my brother—"if you're feeling ready by the weekend, Hatcher, I thought we'd end with your solo. 'I Am the Very Model of a Modern Major-General' always brings down the house."

My brother gave a crisp salute. "Reporting for duty, sir!"

Dr. Calhoun scanned the cast and crew, his gaze settling on me. "While we won't be bothering with much in the way of sets or costumes," he continued, "I thought that since we'll be performing lakeside, it would be fun to wow everyone with our resident mermaid. I'd like you to open for us, Truly, since there's actual water for you to swim in. You'll be a big hit with the campers!"

My face turned the same shade as the vintage Coca-Cola machine. I was going to have to perform in public *again*? "Um, fine, I guess." At least I wouldn't have to worry about a wardrobe malfunction this time around.

"I'll leave the actual choreography up to you," Dr. Calhoun told me. "Just be sure to make a splash!"

That I could definitely do, especially in a shimmertail.

As I headed back to my art project, I passed Bud and Lucas.

"You'll love fishing!" I heard Bud assure my friend. "There's nothing better than being out on the water before dawn when the world is quiet."

Lucas looked like he could think of a lot of things that sounded better than that.

"You just name the time, and I'll take you," said Bud. "I don't even need advance warning. Canoe's always on my truck this time of year."

Later, while my brother and friends and I all waited for Mrs. Abramowitz, we told Hatcher about our trip to Cherry Island.

"That's awesome!" he said, inspecting the piece of rope I'd found. "I wish I could have been there with you. What's next?"

"The cave is off-limits for now," I told him. "Aunt True doesn't want us going back out there alone." I told him about Amanda Appleton and the information that Ella Bellow had extracted at the book signing. "Dr. Appleton has been fishing in the college archives, and she may have made the connection between Nathaniel Daniel and Dandy Dan. We need to find out what fish she's caught, if we want to get to the treasure first."

CHAPTER 33

The following morning, Lucas stopped by the bookstore after swim practice. "Ready to go?" he whispered, helping himself to a trio of blueberry donut muffins.

I glanced toward the office, where my father was frowning at his computer. "Um, not yet," I whispered back. "My dad hasn't left for physical therapy."

I continued tidying up Cup and Chaucer while Lucas killed time showing customers the crowdsourced photos of our suspects in the missing trophy case. It had been nearly two weeks now since the race, and it was hard not to get discouraged. We'd managed to narrow down our list of suspects a bit more—Reverend Quinn had vouched for his cousin in the baggy shorts—but we still hadn't had any luck figuring out who was behind the theft.

The bell over the door jangled, and Officer Tanglewood strolled in. "How about a cappuccino, Nancy Drew?" He snagged a handful of muffins while I prepared his beverage. Taking a bite of one he asked, "Mmmmph mmmmph?" which I was pretty sure translated to "Did you kids solve the case yet?"

I shook my head. "We're close, though," which wasn't necessarily true, but I wanted to wipe the smirk off his face, which it did.

My father left shortly after Officer Tanglewood did. I waited until Belinda arrived and Aunt True was busy with a sales rep, then slipped out.

"What happens if your father finds out?" Lucas asked as we jogged down Main Street toward Lovejoy College.

"He won't," I told him with more confidence than I felt. I was skating on thin ice these days, as Grandma G would say, and I knew it. My luck had held this far, though, and we really needed to get a look at the Lovejoy papers.

As we passed through the iron gates that marked the entrance to the college, I heard someone call my name. I turned to see Erastus Peckinpaugh coming toward us on one of the paths crisscrossing the campus.

Uh-oh, I thought in dismay. If Professor Rusty let it slip that he'd seen me here, my name would be mud.

"I thought you were grounded, Truly."

I nodded and crossed my fingers behind my back. "I'm just running a quick errand for the bookstore."

"Well, when you see your aunt, would you please tell her

not to forget we have an appointment with Reverend Quinn this afternoon at the church?"

Lucas looked surprised. "I thought my mom said the wedding wasn't until this fall."

My future uncle laughed. "We're not getting *married* today, Lucas. It's just some counseling that's required for engaged couples." He checked his watch. "Oops, duty calls—in this case my summer session class on American westward movement."

He loped off again. Lucas and I continued on to the college library, where we found our friends waiting for us on the broad granite steps.

"Where have you guys been?" rasped Cha Cha, rising to her feet. "We've been here forever!"

"Sorry," I told her. "We had to wait until my dad left."

Calhoun texted his father to let him know we were all here, then led us inside past the security guard. While we were waiting for Dr. Calhoun, I crossed the spacious lobby to the famous statue of my possibly pirate ancestor, who was also the college's founder.

"Time to give up your secrets, Nathaniel-Daniel-looks-like-a-spaniel," I whispered. Just like in his portrait at home, his nose was the most prominent feature on his face—and the shiniest, thanks to generations of college students who rubbed it for luck before exams. I reached out and rubbed it too. We could use all the luck we could get right about now.

"I think it's admirable that you want to learn more about our town's history," Dr. Calhoun told us a few minutes later as he steered us toward the stairs. "I'm impressed."

We followed him into the basement and down a long hallway to a door marked ARCHIVES. Inside, we had to surrender our backpacks and sign an official-looking form that basically said we promised not to steal or damage anything, or quote anything or take pictures of anything without permission.

Lucas glanced around the room. "It's kind of dark in here, isn't it?"

"Natural light isn't good for old documents and antiquarian books," Calhoun's father explained. "This area is climate-controlled. We have to keep it at just the right temperature and humidity levels to best preserve our college's treasures."

At the word "treasures," my friends and I exchanged glances. Calhoun's lips quirked up in a half smile. I knew exactly what he was thinking, because I was thinking the same thing—if his dad only knew what we were up to!

I recognized the archivist from the bookshop. She was a regular at our author events. She'd been at Amanda Appleton's, and she often hung out at Cup and Chaucer after work and on the weekends.

"You're the bookstore girl!" she blurted when he saw me.

"I see you're acquainted with our archivist, Peregrine Butler," said Calhoun's father.

I looked at her with interest. Peregrine falcons were my second favorite bird, next to owls. I'd never met anyone named after one, though. The archivist didn't look much older than most of the college students on campus. Her short, spiky hair sported a broad green streak, and she also had a nose ring and a tattoo that spelled out *Dewey Decimal* circling her left wrist like a bracelet. I liked her immediately.

"I'll leave you in Dr. Butler's capable hands, then," Dr. Calhoun said. "I'll be upstairs in my office if you need me."

The archivist gave us a cheerful smile as he left. "Call me Peregrine, please. All this flurry of interest in Nathaniel Lovejoy! First Dr. Appleton, and now you kids. Of course, now that we know about a possible connection between Pumpkin Falls and the missing pirate treasure, it makes sense that people are looking into our town's early settlers. Is that what triggered your interest as well?"

"Partly," I replied. "That and the fact that he's my ancestor, and I've always wanted to know more about him."

Which was true, or at least true-ish.

"Well, let's see if we can satisfy your curiosity." Peregrine led us to a table at the back of the room, where she'd arranged an assortment of things for us to look at. Before we could touch any of them, though, we had to put on white cotton gloves.

"It's just like cotillion," said Scooter, waggling his fingers at me.

I groaned. "Don't remind me."

There was a lot of stuff to examine. The selection of Nathaniel Daniel's "papers" that had been set out for us included letters, account ledgers, deeds to his property, and his last will and testament.

"How are we supposed to read these?" Scooter complained, picking up one of the letters and squinting at the spidery script.

"I'm actually pretty good at deciphering old handwriting," said Calhoun, who apparently had no end of hidden talents. "My dad has a bunch of letters that my great-grandparents wrote to each other during World War Two. They're really interesting."

"Great," I told him. "You're in charge of the letters."

"I'll take the account ledgers," said Scooter quickly. "The numbers look easy to read."

His sister agreed to help him, while Cha Cha and Lucas zeroed in on the deeds. That left me with Nathaniel Daniel's last will and testament. I picked it up gingerly. It was old and fragile and looked like it would tear easily.

"That's been transcribed." Peregrine passed me two type-written pages. "You'll find this easier to decipher."

"No fair!" said Scooter.

"You chose the ledgers, you stick with the ledgers," I told him loftily. And settling into a chair, I started to read.

I, Nathaniel Daniel Lovejoy, being of sound mind, do hereby declare this document to be my last will and testament, the transcript began. Everything seemed pretty normal. He left his house—the one my family and I lived in now—and "all his worldly goods" to his wife, Prudence, except for a few bequests. There was money to help with the upkeep of the church, and some for the college, and even some to help with repairs on the covered bridge.

You wily fox! I thought. Nathaniel Daniel had covered his tracks well. Nobody in a million years would believe this public-spirited citizen was a pirate, which was likely just the way he'd wanted it.

There were also bequests of a few personal items. He left his gold pocket watch to his son, Obadiah, whose portrait I passed every day in the stairwell at home—and a harpsichord to his daughter, Abigail, whose portrait hung right beside her brother's. My eyes drifted down the page. A copper teakettle to a cousin, a horse to his friend and neighbor John Wainwright, blah blah blah, the list went on. I was just about to hand the pages back to the archivist when my gaze landed on the last item. It was tossed in almost like an afterthought, only it wasn't an afterthought.

It was the pot of gold at the end of the rainbow.

I sat up straight in my chair, every hair on the back of my neck at attention. *And finally, to my beloved wife, Prudence, I leave a parting gift—my signet ring engraved with an eagle in flight.*

That was the ring that Nathaniel Daniel was wearing in

his portrait at home! The one that had been passed down to my grandfather and would someday belong to my dad!

I continued reading. *May it serve to remind her of our courting days in the sunrise of our youth. Always remember, my love: Where the eagle flies, there lies the prize. Where the eaglet sleeps, harken to the deep.*

Where the eagle flies. Gramps had told me once that eagles had nested on Cherry Island for as long as anyone could remember. Had they nested there in Nathaniel Daniel's day too?

The clue fell into place as neatly as the final number in a sudoku puzzle.

To most readers, those words would seem just what they appeared to be—a sentimental gift from a loving husband to his wife. But they were likely much more than that. "The prize" had to be the pirate treasure, and Nathaniel Daniel was telling Prudence where she could find it! *Where the eaglet sleeps.* The eagle's nest in the tallest tree on the island was the key.

"May I take a picture of this?" I asked Peregrine, trying to keep the excitement out of my voice.

She glanced up from her desk. "Of the will? Sure."

I slipped my cell phone out of my pocket and snapped photos of the transcript. Then I kicked Cha Cha under the table and cut my eyes urgently toward the door.

She got the message.

"Hey, you guys," she said, setting a faded document back on the table. "I'm getting hungry. Can we break for lunch?"

The archivist looked surprised. "I told Dr. Calhoun I'd be happy to stay open as long as you need."

"Thank you, but we're starving," I said, handing her back the transcript. "This is really cool, though. Maybe we can come back again another day?"

I practically bolted out the door. I grabbed my backpack from the security guard and ran up the stairs two at a time. My friends were right behind me.

"What's your hurry?" asked Scooter.

"Look what I found!" I exclaimed, pulling out my cell phone and holding it up.

"'Where the eagle flies, there lies the prize,'" Calhoun read aloud, and I explained my theory about the nest.

"It can't possibly be the same tree," scoffed Scooter. "Nathaniel Daniel wrote that will back before the Revolutionary War!"

"There are plenty of trees around Pumpkin Falls that have been here for hundreds of years," I retorted. "My grandfather is always pointing them out. There's even one in our yard. Why not one on Cherry Island, too?"

"I guess it's possible," said Calhoun, but he sounded doubtful too.

"I just *know* this is it," I insisted. "This has to be the key to finding the treasure."

Jasmine frowned. "Do you think Dr. Appleton figured it out too? She's pretty smart."

"She may have figured out the connection to Cherry Island, and she may have figured out the part about the tree, but she still doesn't know about the cave."

"At least we hope she doesn't," said Lucas.

"So what do we do now?" asked Scooter.

"We 'harken to the deep.' We have to go back to the island. We have to find the underwater entrance and get to the treasure before Dr. Appleton does."

Cha Cha looked at me. "But we promised your aunt we wouldn't go alone!"

"We'll figure something out!" I called over my shoulder as I ran out the front door of the library—and smack-dab into my father.

CHAPTER 34

The thing about skating on thin ice is that you almost always fall in.

I should have known that my run of luck wouldn't last. My father was bound to find out about my escapades sooner or later, and now, thanks to a last-minute cancellation of his physical therapy session, he had. And he wasn't happy about it at all. In fact, I hadn't seen him this mad since I'd gotten an F-plus in math last winter.

Lieutenant Colonel Jericho T. Lovejoy did not like being lied to. Not one bit. He marched me home on the double.

"This is a breach of trust, young lady!" he stormed. "You knew the agreement—bookstore, piano lessons, stage crew." He ticked them off on the fingers of his good hand. "That's it! And now I find you've been sneaking around the whole time—"

"Not the whole time."

"Don't you talk back to me!"

"No, sir," I said meekly.

"I *knew* I was being too lenient! I never should have listened to your aunt."

When the dust finally settled, I was banned from the bookshop until further notice. The only reason I was still allowed to take piano lessons was because my parents had prepaid for the summer, and the only reason I was still allowed to be part of the stage crew was because my father considered it community service.

I was basically under house arrest.

"It's awful, Mackenzie!" I was sitting in my bedroom closet, video chatting with my cousin, who was at a lodge in Yellowstone. My father had taken away my cell phone again, but thanks to the fact that I'd kept my laptop hidden in my dresser drawer, he'd overlooked it. I kept my voice to a whisper since he was right downstairs. He'd set up a satellite office in the dining room now that I'd been deemed untrustworthy. "I can't even go out in the yard!"

"Hang in there," Mackenzie whispered back. "Your dad blows his top sometimes, but he'll calm down eventually. He always does."

I snorted. "Maybe by the time I'm twenty." My laptop dinged just then, and I glanced at the incoming request. "It's the PFPEs—gotta go."

"Say hi to everyone for me!"

I promised I would, and we hung up. I clicked on the icon to answer the other call. "Hey!" I whispered.

My friends' faces appeared onscreen. "Sorry you're grounded again!" they chorused.

I gave them a wan smile. "I thought you'd be at Cherry Island by now."

Cha Cha shook her head. "Not without you."

"We're going to head over to the Pumpkin Falls Farmer's Market instead," Jasmine explained. "We figured that would be a good place to show the photos of our suspects from the Four on the Fourth."

"Somebody out there has got to recognize one of our suspects," said Lucas. "I can't believe we keep coming up empty-handed!"

Our suspects had dwindled to four people: the woman in the Red Sox baseball cap, the two teenage boys who locals thought might be from West Hartfield, and the older man in the Grateful Dead T-shirt and aviator sunglasses.

"Good luck," I told my friends. "Keep me updated." I told them to keep their eyes—and ears—out for any developments with Amanda Appleton, too, and then I hung up.

Bird-watching from my bedroom window killed some time, and I spent an hour practicing the piano. Miss Marple was at my heels as usual as I went back upstairs after that. She wasn't at the bookstore today because she'd been to the groomer this morning.

"At least I have you for company," I told her as the two of us settled onto my bed. Technically Miss Marple wasn't allowed up there, but I needed at least one friend by my side. I put my arm around her and buried my face in her fur. She smelled good, like coconuts. The bookstore's loss was my gain—Miss Marple was always fluffy and soft when she came back from the groomer.

I did a few sudoku puzzles and read another chapter in the book about eagles that I'd picked up at the library, but mostly I was bored. It was going to be a long summer if I had to spend it indoors.

By the following afternoon, I was still grounded and still bored.

The only bright spot was that between the rest of yesterday and most of today, I'd had plenty of time to help Hatcher practice his solo. We'd spent so much time at it, in fact, that our entire family knew the melody and words by heart. It was pretty catchy—more like a rap than a song. I'd overheard my mother singing it while she was washing the dishes last night, my father humming the tune at breakfast, and I'd even caught Danny, who between his summer job and hanging out with his girlfriend was hardly ever home except to sleep, whistling it to himself as he left on his late morning run.

Now I found myself whistling it, too, as I paced my bedroom. Miss Marple watched me anxiously, then clambered down from the bed and paced with me, whining. I had to find a way to be allowed out of the house! The chances of that happening, though, were slim to none. Not unless I could get my mother on my side, but that wouldn't be easy. My parents liked to present what they called a "united front" when it came to discipline.

I had one thing going for me, though. My mother felt my father was being too harsh. I knew this because I'd overheard them talking in the kitchen last night, after they finished the dishes. I'd gone downstairs to get a snack—I was still allowed to eat, as far as I knew—and paused on the stairs when I heard their voices.

"First no swim team and now no bookstore? Seriously, J. T.?"

"It's the principle of the thing!" my father replied stubbornly. My father was big on the principle of things.

"What's True going to do without her? She really depends on Truly, you know."

I could practically hear my father's jaw clenching. "That girl needs to learn a lesson. No means no."

Later, my mother had come upstairs to my room. "Hey," she said, poking her head in my door.

"Hey," I replied without enthusiasm.

She sat down on the end of my bed. "I've been so busy with summer school and work at the Starlite"—my mother had a part-time job at Cha Cha's parents' dance studio to help make ends meet—"that I feel like I haven't had time to spend with you, Little O."

Little O was her special nickname for me, short for Little Owl.

I lifted a shoulder.

"I'm sorry our plans got postponed by mermaid camp."

"Mermaid academy," I said automatically, and she laughed.

"You know what I mean. Anyway, I didn't want you to think I'd forgotten about you. I promise we'll squirrel away some mother-daughter time before you go back to school, okay?"

I nodded, and she leaned down and kissed the top of my head. "That's my girl."

She went back downstairs, leaving me to think about what she'd said. I recalled what my aunt had told me earlier, too, about my parents needing some time together. I felt a stab of guilt as I thought about how hard they were both working, my mother at her college classes and her part-time receptionist job at the Starlite, and my father at the bookstore. I knew money was tight these days, and it hadn't even occurred to me that I might be giving them more to worry about. I'd only been thinking about myself. Why was it so difficult to be unselfish and look at things from somebody else's perspective?

I took my binoculars out and watched idly as the postman made his rounds along Maple Street. Miss Marple, who had serious postman radar, knew he was on his way even without binoculars. She woofed and ran downstairs to sit by the door as he came up the front path. Another woof announced that our mail had whooshed through the slot and landed on the entry hall rug.

"Truly!" my mother called a few moments later. "You've got mail!"

I never got mail, unless it was my birthday, which it wasn't. Puzzled, I went downstairs where I found a postcard and a letter waiting for me. The postcard was from Glacier National Park, where Zadie had somehow gotten wind of *The Pirates of Penzance*. "Break a leg—or a tail!" she'd written on the back, which I knew from the fountain of knowledge that was Calhoun was theater-speak for "good luck."

The letter was from Delphine.

Dear Grania,

I did it! I signed a lease on a restaurant space and will be opening a café in Brewster this fall! I'm calling it Mermaid Crossing. My mother is trying to get Carson Dawson to feature me on Hello, Boston! *Fingers and flukes crossed! I hope you're having a great summer, and that you come visit next time you're on the Cape. I'll make Mermaid Chip Cookies just for you.*

Love,

Delphine

PS How is the shimmertail doing?

I tossed the letter onto my bed. *Hanging in the back of my closet*, I thought. I wasn't looking forward to wearing the tail—or the clamshell bra—again in public.

Later, at dinner, I stared glumly at the red-circled dates on our kitchen calendar. We had our next-to-last rehearsal tonight before the sneak preview of *The Pirates of Penzance* at Camp Lovejoy. After that, it was just ten days until opening night, when I'd have to watch Calhoun kiss Cha Cha Abramowitz.

Hatcher was working for Lobster Bob again, and Danny was at the movies with his girlfriend, so it was just my parents and me at the table. My father basically pretended I wasn't there. He read the newspaper while he ate, and my mother's few attempts at conversation fizzled.

"Are you going to drive her to rehearsal tonight, J. T., or should I?" she asked finally.

My father grunted.

"How about we both take her?" my mother suggested. "We'll drop her off, then swing by the General Store for ice cream. It seems to me you could use some cheering up."

My father grunted again, but it was an "okay, fine" kind of grunt. I slanted him a glance. Was it possible there was a thaw in the ice?

"We'll be back promptly at nine to pick you up," my father told me as they dropped me off at the Grange. "No dawdling."

"Yes, sir."

Inside, I discovered that Elmer and Belinda had been busy. The set was nearly done! The two of them had stopped by for a couple of hours earlier in the day to finish painting the black-and-white-checkerboard pattern on the floor covering. It was almost dry.

"What do you think?" asked Belinda.

"I think it looks awesome!"

She looked pleased.

The ROCKIN' MERMAID sign was done too, so I turned my attention to putting the finishing touches on the mural. I still had a trio of larger-than-life sundaes to complete. As I painted, I hummed along with the cast, who were hard at work practicing the songs that they were scheduled to sing at tomorrow's sneak preview performance.

During the snack break—lemonade and Dr. Calhoun's homemade cowboy cookies—I had a few minutes to catch up with my friends. There'd been no new developments in the missing trophy case. The photos they'd been circulating around town had brought nothing but blank stares.

"And there's more bad news," said Cha Cha. "We saw Amanda Appleton heading out of town toward the lake again this morning with her kayak."

If Dr. Appleton found the treasure before we did, I'd never forgive myself! It was my own dumb fault that she had such a big head start on us, though. If it hadn't been for my pigheadedness in disobeying my father, I might have been free to rejoin the Pumpkin Falls Private Eyes by now.

I returned to my stage crew chores feeling discouraged.

An hour later, Belinda declared the paint on the floor dry enough to finish putting the set together. While Bud and Lucas nailed my ROCKIN' MERMAID sign over the fake door at the back of the stage, Belinda corralled Augustus into helping Elmer move the diner booths and jukebox and red Coca-Cola machine into place.

"Now this," said Belinda when we were done, "is what I call a showstopper!"

"Indeed," Augustus agreed, slipping an arm around her waist.

"All we need are some smaller props on the shelves and counters," she continued. "Plates, glasses, sundae dishes, that kind of thing. Maybe an old-fashioned milkshake mixer. Elmer!"

Elmer cupped his hand behind his ear.

"Do you have anything that could go on the shelves?"

"WHAT'S THAT ABOUT ELVES?"

"*SHELVES,* ELMER, *SHELVES!*" Belinda repeated. "WE NEED STUFF TO DISPLAY ON THE SHELVES!"

"YOU DON'T HAVE TO YELL! I'LL CHECK MY BARN WHEN I GET HOME."

"Gather round, people!" Calhoun's father called a few minutes later. "Our sneak preview performance is tomorrow. Since it's a Saturday, we'll be able to squeeze in a run-through first thing in the morning. Let's plan to meet back here at the Grange at nine a.m. sharp, okay?" He turned around and waved an arm grandly at the stage. "And how about a big round of applause for the stage crew for bringing our marvelous malt shop to life!"

The hall burst into cheers, and Belinda and Bud and Elmer and Lucas and I all took a bow.

Belinda crossed to the jukebox and punched a couple of buttons. "La Bamba" was one of my uncle Rooster's favorites, and as its familiar strains poured from the speakers, I joined in as everyone started jumping around to its infectious beat. It felt good to let off some steam.

"This looks amazing!" Surprised, I turned to see my mother gazing at the stage. My father was beside her. "You helped build this, Truly?"

I nodded. "I didn't do all that much. Just the 'Rockin' Mermaid' sign and that fake tile stuff behind the counter, and the mural."

"Well, I think it looks spectacular," said my mother. "Don't you agree, J. T.?"

My father gave a short nod. "Hard work always pays off."

Just five words, but they gave me hope. I knew it was pushing my luck, but I had to at least try. "Am I still grounded?"

My father snorted. "Of course you are!"

I looked over at my mother, who gave me a regretful look but didn't say anything. The united front was clearly still in full force.

I couldn't help myself. "Please, Dad! I'm really, really sorry I disobeyed you!"

"As you should be." He turned on his heel and stalked out.

I might as well just hand Dandy Dan's treasure over to Amanda Appleton, I thought bitterly as I followed him to the car. At this rate, the Pumpkin Falls Private Eyes would never be back in business.

CHAPTER 35

Dress rehearsal was a disaster in every possible way.

"People, people!" wailed Dr. Calhoun, clapping his hands over his ears. "Have you forgotten everything we've practiced? Listen to the piano and stay on pitch!" He shook his head wearily. "And you sounded so good last night!"

"It's okay," Belinda whispered, handing me a kitten for comfort. A tiny black one with a white splotch on its nose. "Dress rehearsals are traditionally terrible."

Lucas and I exchanged a worried glance. This terrible? Hatcher seemed to have forgotten all the words to his song, Cha Cha's high notes were in danger of shattering the glass on the chandeliers, and Calhoun and the other pirates were bumbling through their dance steps like—well, like Scooter and me at cotillion practice last winter.

We were going to be a laughingstock!

Bud Jefferson came up behind us and clapped a paw on

Lucas's shoulder. "Looking forward to our expedition tomorrow?" He'd finally worn Lucas down and, after promising Lucas's mother that he'd make him wear a life preserver, sunscreen with at least SPF 50, a hat, and wraparound sunglasses, they were scheduled to go fishing.

"Yeah, about that," Lucas replied, squirming away. "I don't think I'm going to be able to go after all."

Bud's smile wavered. "Oh, okay. Well, another time then?"

I stroked the kitten as I watched Bud droop over to join Elmer and Augustus.

"You know, Lucas," I said, thinking about my aunt's earlier advice, "not all change is bad."

He gave me a puzzled look.

"Bud's a really nice guy. Maybe you could give him a chance?"

"Maybe you could mind your own beeswax, *Drooly!*" Lucas snapped, my nickname shooting up an octave as his voice cracked.

I stared at him in shock as he stalked off. I'd never seen Lucas lose his temper before. When we broke for a midmorning snack a little later, he kept a wary distance as we gathered with our friends.

"We're down to just one suspect," Scooter said, helping himself to one of the donuts from Lou's that Mrs. Winthrop had brought for the cast and crew.

"Whoa!" said Cha Cha. "What happened?"

"It turns out that the woman in the Red Sox baseball cap is a client of my father's. I spotted her outside his office this morning, and, well, I guess I—"

"What my brother means to say is that he got hollered at for accusing her of stealing the trophy," said Jasmine.

"She took my question all wrong!" Scooter protested.

"And it gets worse," Jasmine continued smugly. "It turns out that the teenage boys are her kids. They were all at the race to cheer on their dad. My father hit the roof when he overheard Scooter questioning her."

At least I wasn't the only one whose father overreacted sometimes. "But this is good news, right?" I said. "This means the guy in the Grateful Dead T-shirt and aviator sunglasses has to be the thief!"

Scooter pulled out his cell phone, and we all stared at the picture of the older gentleman again. "How are we ever going to find him, though, since nobody knows who he is?"

"Who *who* is?" asked Augustus, who had wandered over to snag a donut. He peered over Scooter's shoulder and frowned. "Why do you have a picture of Frank on your phone?"

I looked up at him, startled. "Wait, you know him?"

"Sure. That's Frank Peabody, my agent. I've been his client for years. I invited him up to Pumpkin Falls to experience a real New England Fourth of July."

With all the people we'd shown the photo to, I couldn't

believe that we'd forgotten to show it to Augustus Wilde!

"So he didn't steal the pumpkin trophy?"

Augustus's eyebrows flew somewhere north of his hairline. "You kids didn't seriously think—*Frank*? Steal the silver pumpkin?"

"NAPKIN?" bellowed Elmer, who had spotted the donuts too.

"PUMPKIN!" Augustus bellowed back.

"I HAVE NAPKINS IN THE TRUCK!"

Augustus did a face-palm as Elmer trotted off.

My friends and I looked at each other in dismay. This was more than discouraging; this was disastrous for the Pumpkin Falls Private Eyes. Our final suspect had just gone down in flames. How were we ever going to face Officer Tanglewood now? We'd never hear the end of it.

One good thing came out of the rehearsal, though. We finally came up with a plan for getting back to Cherry Island. Or at least my friends did.

"You know," said Calhoun, taking a bite of donut, "since we're going to be at the lake later this afternoon anyway for our performance, it's the perfect opportunity to go back and look for the underwater cave."

"There'll be a ton of people around, though," Cha Cha pointed out. "How are we going to slip away?"

"Could we get our parents to drop us there early?" asked

Jasmine. "Maybe tell them we want to spend the afternoon at the beach to relax before the show or something?"

"No way I can do that," I told them. "I'm still grounded. *Really truly* grounded this time."

"Okay, then, we wait until the barbecue to make our move," said Scooter. "People will be so busy eating and talking, they won't notice we're gone."

"What part of 'grounded' don't you understand?"

He looked at me and smiled. "C'mon, Truly! You found a way out of it before—you can find a way out of it again."

It was tempting.

Especially since a pirate treasure might hang in the balance.

But then I thought of my parents, and how hard they'd both been working this summer. They didn't need me adding to their worries. I was tall timber, I reminded myself. I could stand my ground and do the right thing for once.

"Nope," I told my friends. "You'll have to go without me this time."

CHAPTER 36

"'The play's the thing / Wherein I'll catch the conscience of the king,'" quoted Dr. Calhoun. We were in Camp Lovejoy's Lower Lodge, getting ready for our performance. It was stuffy inside, despite a whisper of breeze that drifted through the screened windows, and the large room smelled faintly of past fires in the giant stone fireplace. "That's the Bard, of course, from *Hamlet*. Not that our goal is to catch anyone's conscience! But if we can catch the *interest* of the audience, now that's a noble goal. With any luck, this sneak preview will whet their appetites and spur ticket sales."

We'd all been worried after this morning's dress rehearsal. Really worried. But Dr. Calhoun had tried to calm our fears. "Dress rehearsals are often less than perfect, to say the least," he'd said on the ride over in the camp bus that Artie Olsen had sent to pick us up. "Sure, you were a little rough this morning, but I've heard you practicing all week, and I have full confidence that you'll pull this off without a hitch."

Now he clapped his hands and beamed at us. "I have two surprises for you, people! First, we have been given special permission by Camp Lovejoy to use a very special stage for our performance—*Dreamboat*, the camp's floating cabin!"

There was a gasp of excitement at this announcement. Pippa and Lauren had told me about *Dreamboat*. One of the high points of camp was when each cabin got a turn to have a sleepover on it.

"And second," Dr. Calhoun continued, "Mrs. Winthrop stayed up late the last few nights, and she finished the costumes!"

A whoop went up as the cast crowded eagerly around Lucas's mother. She handed each actor his or her costume, and everyone scattered to the four corners of the room, which had been curtained off with bedsheets, to try them on.

Everyone except me. My costume was stuffed into the enormous duffel bag at my feet, and I wasn't planning on putting it on again until the very last minute.

"Check it out!" crowed Scooter, strutting across the lodge toward me a few minutes later. He was wearing jeans, a white T-shirt, and a fake black leather jacket with a skull-and-crossbones patch sewn on its breast pocket.

Calhoun was right behind him, dressed in an identical costume.

"Looking good, boys!" said Cha Cha, who resembled a

pint-size ball of fluff in her pink poodle skirt and matching pink cardigan.

"Thanks," said Calhoun, smiling at her. "You, too."

I'd been trying really hard not to think about their onstage kiss. At least the real thing was still over a week away. For this sneak preview performance, we were just doing a trio of numbers from the first act.

Hatcher emerged next in his Modern Major-General costume, which featured a ton of gold braid, rhinestone buttons, and big, flashy fake medals. Bling! Definitely nothing Lieutenant Colonel Jericho T. Lovejoy would ever be caught dead wearing, but it was going to look great onstage.

We all retreated to a quiet spot by one of the windows to go over the plan one more time. I glanced outside to see if I could spot my family and was dismayed to spot Amanda Appleton's familiar red sports car pulling into the parking lot. "What's she doing here?"

"My dad invited her," Calhoun replied sheepishly. "I totally forgot to tell you. He ran into her at the library again today after dress rehearsal and, well, I guess he thought that with her interest in pirates, she'd get a kick out of the show."

"Great." I heaved a sigh. "You guys will have to be extra careful when you head to the island, or she might try and follow you."

I scanned the crowd on the grassy lawn that led to the water-ski beach. My parents were here, of course—all of our parents were here. And so were Aunt True and Professor Rusty and both of my sisters. The wheelbarrow races were just finishing up, and there was a lot of shouting and cheering going on.

"After the show, when the barbecue starts, Hatcher will create a diversion," Scooter began. "On my signal, we'll peel off one by one and head for the kayaks."

"Wait, you're just going to take Camp Lovejoy's kayaks?" I said. "Without permission? This is your plan?"

"You've got a better one?"

I flapped my hand. "I'm sitting this one out, remember?"

"Like I was saying," Scooter continued, clearly enjoying the role of team leader for a change, "we head for the kayaks. Once we paddle out to the island, we'll find the eagle's nest tree, and Lucas will do the rest."

I looked over at Lucas, who had been avoiding me all day and still wouldn't look me in the eye. "Are you sure he's up to it?"

Calhoun shrugged. "He's the best swimmer we've got besides you."

Was it my imagination, or was Lucas looking paler than usual? I was guessing he didn't like this idea any more than I did, but he wasn't going to admit it. I chewed my lip. This whole thing had disaster written all over it. But what could I do to help? Nothing, that's what.

"Truly! I've been looking for you!" I turned to see Dr.

Calhoun crossing the room toward us. "Now that we're going to be using *Dreamboat* as our stage instead of the H dock, perhaps we should rethink your opening number."

We'd planned to have me embedded with the crowd of actors making their way toward the H dock—our original stage—before the performance. While they acted as a sort of human shield, I'd pull on the shimmertail and slip into the water unnoticed.

"*Dreamboat* is anchored in the cove on the other side of camp," Calhoun's father explained. "We're going to have Artie tow it around the point and surprise the audience after your opening number."

I saw the dilemma. With the cast aboard *Dreamboat*, how was I going to get into the water without the audience seeing me? Six-foot-tall mermaids were pretty hard to miss.

Suddenly I had a brainstorm. "Hey, Mr. Jefferson!" I called to Bud. He was standing over by Mrs. Winthrop as she helped make a few last-minute alterations to the Pirate King's costume. Hearing me call, he came right over.

"What's up, Truly?"

"Do you have your canoe with you?"

He nodded. "I always have my canoe with me."

That's what I'd been counting on.

"Would you be willing to be my camouflage? To help get me into place for the opening number, I mean. We could drive over to the public beach, and while you paddle I could hitch a ride back to camp along the far side of your canoe, where the audience won't see me."

"Brilliant!" said Dr. Calhoun. "What do you say, Bud?"

"Sure, no problem."

Five minutes later, Bud and I took off for his car as the pirates and maidens headed down to the cove where *Dream-boat* was waiting.

"I just have to put this thing on," I told Bud, patting my duffel bag as we pulled into a parking spot at the beach.

"No rush," he said. "It'll take me a few minutes to get the canoe into the water."

As I wiggled and squirmed my way into the shimmertail, the sensation was both familiar and strange. Sirena's Sea Siren Academy felt like a million years ago.

"Say, that thing looks real!" said Bud when I was done.

"Yeah, it's pretty cool." I scooted forward on the sand into the water, then propelled myself over to the far side of the canoe. Holding on to the gunwale while Bud paddled, I let myself be towed along the shoreline toward Camp Lovejoy. It was only a short distance from the public beach, and soon Bud was cutting over toward the center of the H dock. He drew up beside the leg closest to the water-ski beach. The waiting audience paid us no attention—to them, he was just another boat in the water.

"How's this?"

"Perfect," I said. "Thanks!"

As he paddled away, I held my breath and slipped below the surface of the water, emerging a moment later under the dock, where I clung to one of its supports and waited for my cue. I had a good view of the beach from here. People were spreading out towels and setting up folding chairs for the performance, including my parents, who were talking to Cha Cha's family. Bud had paddled his canoe to shore and joined Mrs. Winthrop; Ella Bellow was sitting with Belinda and Augustus. I spotted Amanda Appleton talking to Aunt True, who had a pleasantly bland expression on her face. I also spotted the tall red-haired girl from the road race—Cassidy something?—and Felicia Grunewald, Professor Rusty's assistant. They were both surrounded by their campers.

As the loudspeakers crackled and the first notes of the overture floated out over the water, Dr. Calhoun gave me a thumbs-up.

"Showtime," I whispered, determined to make Esther Williams—and Zadie and Lenore—proud.

Taking a deep breath, I dove down and dolphin-kicked my way underwater out to what I guessed was about the center of the area in front of the beach. Swishing the shimmertail back and forth mightily, I breached the surface like a rocket, then arced forward and dove down again, smacking my flukes against the water hard. Dr. Calhoun had asked me to "make a splash," and that was exactly what I planned to do.

The rest of my opening routine was made up of moves

pieced together from the revue at Sirena's. After a few more dolphin dives, I flipped over onto my back and, sculling the water with my arms, held my legs up in the ballet leg position, waving my flukes back and forth.

"THAT'S MY SISTER!" I heard Pippa shriek, and I smiled wide and blew her a kiss.

Swim pretty, I reminded myself, and I did my best, smiling and waving just like I'd been taught at mermaid academy. The audience ate it up. As the overture neared its finish, I criss-crossed the water in front of the beach in a series of butterfly strokes, ending with one final dive and powerful splash of my flukes. As the onlookers clapped and cheered, I swam over to the H dock and pulled myself up onto it, perching on the edge to watch the rest of the performance.

Hearing the low thrum of the water-ski boat, we all craned to watch as it came into view around the edge of the point.

"*Dreamboat*!" someone called, and the audience hooted and shouted "aaargh!" at the sight of the flag bearing the skull and crossbones that fluttered from a pole on the roof. When the floating cabin was in position directly in front of the beach, Artie hopped aboard, dropped an anchor, then hopped back into the ski boat and putt-putted away.

The music swelled, the front door and windows of *Dreamboat* flew open, and pirates came flooding out. The crowd roared as they launched into the rousing opening number.

Dr. Calhoun stepped forward when the pirates were done

singing and sketched in the plot for the audience. It was lame but funny. Today was Frederic's—Calhoun's—twenty-first birthday, and he'd finally completed his years of servitude to the Pirate King. Now he'd decided to become an upstanding citizen. This wasn't going to be a smooth road, of course.

The maidens were up next, and after their opening chorus, Cha Cha—as Mabel—took center stage and belted out "Poor Wand'ring One" to Frederic, who had fallen in love at first sight.

Another synopsis from Dr. Calhoun followed. He explained that the girls were all the high-born daughters of the Major-General, and thus not marriage material for lowly pirates. Then it was Hatcher's turn. I held my breath as he began:

I am the very model of a modern Major-General,
I've information vegetable, animal, and mineral . . .

The lyrics to his rap-style song were complicated and silly. "Patter" was the term for it, Dr. Calhoun had explained to us, and it was one of the hallmarks of Gilbert and Sullivan. I sang along under my breath as the tempo increased. Had we practiced enough? Would Hatcher mess up? Faster and faster the music and lyrics went as the song neared its end, until Hatcher was flying along so fast I was sure he'd stumble.

But he didn't!

When he finished, the audience leaped to its feet.

"Bravo!" shouted Aunt True, and my brother took a bow, smiling his Gifford sunflower smile and looking enormously pleased with himself. I saw him shoot a glance at Cha Cha, who smiled back at him.

"There you have it, folks," said Dr. Calhoun, "a sneak preview of our upcoming performance at the Pumpkin Falls Grange, where we hope you'll join us for an evening of musical fun and fantasy! Tickets are available now at the General Store!"

While Artie returned with the water-ski boat to tow *Dreamboat* back to the cove, my little sister and a gaggle of her cabin-mates came rushing over to ooh and aah at the shimmertail. My parents trailed along behind them.

"Is it real?" asked one of the little girls shyly, reaching out a finger to touch it. I was pretty sure her name was Meri.

I shook my head. "No, but wouldn't it be cool if it were?"

Pippa gave me a hug, and so did my mother.

"Your daughter is doing a splendid job!" Dr. Calhoun told my parents. "Both as a mermaid and on our stage crew. She's proved herself an invaluable member of our team this summer and you should be proud of her."

My father leveled a gaze at me. "Should we now."

My mother elbowed him. "J. T.! For heaven's sake lighten up!"

He sighed, then leaned down and gave me an awkward

one-armed hug. "Sentence completed with honor, Truly-in-the-Middle," he said gruffly. "But fair warning—the punishment will be worse next time if you lie to us again."

"I won't, I promise," I told him. "Thanks, Dad."

I couldn't believe my ears—I wasn't grounded anymore! I could hardly wait to get out of my shimmertail and join the Pumpkin Falls Private Eyes again.

CHAPTER 37

"Now *that* was awesome!" said Scooter, basking in the afterglow of a successful performance.

Jasmine nodded. "It's so different with a real audience."

My brother and friends were clustered around me, chattering gleefully as they waited to make their move. *Our* move now, since I was free to join them.

"Hey, guys, I've been thinking," said Lucas. "When we get to the island, I think one of us should take some rope and go to the tunnel by the boulder, just in case—"

Scooter's hand shot out, muffling him.

"Scooter!" I protested.

He jerked his chin toward something behind me. I whipped around to see Amanda Appleton standing there.

"Just in case what?" she said. Her eyes were hidden behind her sunglasses, but I knew they were focused on us with hawk-like intensity.

"Nothing," I told her, smiling sweetly. "We were just talking about the play."

"Of course." She smiled back equally sweetly and walked away.

I looked around wildly for my brother. "Hatcher! Diversion! Now! I think she overheard us."

"One diversion, coming right up," he said, pulling a bottle of Terminator hot sauce from his pocket. He grinned and waggled it at me.

I frowned. "What are you planning to do with that?"

"Spike the lemonade."

"*That's* your diversion? Hot sauce in the lemonade? Hatcher, what are you *thinking*? You can't do that! Remember Uncle Rooster's reaction? These are little kids we're talking about! Somebody could get hurt!"

My brother's face fell.

"You'll have to think of something else—and fast."

In the end, though, he didn't have to. Whether inspired by Frederic and Mabel's romance onstage, or by the sunset over the lake, or by something else entirely, Bud Jefferson chose that moment to drop to one knee and ask Lucas's mother to marry him.

Beside me, Lucas went rigid.

We couldn't hear Mrs. Winthrop's response from where we were, but it was obvious from the whopper of a kiss that Bud planted on her that she'd said yes.

As everyone rushed to congratulate the happy couple, I scanned the crowd for Amanda Appleton, then turned to my brother and friends. "She's going for her kayak! Grab that wheelbarrow and stick me in it—there's not a moment to lose!"

They manhandled me in, shimmertail and all, and thirty seconds later I was jouncing down the beach as Calhoun trundled me off in hot pursuit.

Cha Cha trotted alongside me. "Where are we going?"

"Bud's canoe," I said. "He left it on the far side of the H dock."

When we reached Mr. Jefferson's boat, my brother and our friends ran over and started dragging it toward the water.

"Paddle as fast as you can for Cherry Island," I told them. "I don't know how the finders keepers law works, but my guess is whoever stakes their claim first wins. And she is not going to win!"

"What about you?" called Hatcher as he jumped in and grabbed a paddle.

I glanced back down the beach. Dr. Appleton was headed for the lake, kayak in tow. That gave me an idea. "As soon as I take this shimmertail off, I'll borrow one of Camp Lovejoy's kayaks," I called back. "You guys go on ahead."

"I'll stay behind with you, Truly," said Calhoun.

Giving the canoe a strong push, he launched my brother

and our friends into the water, then came over to where I was struggling to get out of the wheelbarrow.

"Help me out of this thing," I told him. "I've changed my mind—I don't have time to take this tail off. I'm going to have to swim for it."

He nodded. "I'll grab a kayak and follow you."

"Wait! Before you do, could you go tell my aunt True? We're going to need backup, and she'll know what to do."

"Sure." He leaned over to heft me out of the wheelbarrow. "Oof! Dude, you weigh a ton!"

"I'm wearing thirty pounds of shimmertail!"

"Really? I hadn't noticed," he gasped, staggering across the sand toward the lake, but he winked to show me he was only teasing.

Out on the lake, my brother and our friends were paddling furiously, as instructed, but Dr. Appleton was already rounding the H dock in pursuit.

"She's moving fast," I fretted. "They're never going to beat her to the island!"

"They might not, but you will," Calhoun told me. "You're the best swimmer I know, Truly."

He smiled at me, and I smiled back at him.

Now, I thought, remembering Mackenzie's advice.

Maybe Calhoun was thinking the same thing, because a moment later our noses bumped together.

"Ouch!" I protested, rubbing mine.

"Sorry," he said. "I was just—"

"Yeah, me too."

We smiled at each other again, and then he dumped me into the lake.

CHAPTER 38

I was flying.

And it wasn't just the shimmertail. Calhoun had tried to kiss me!

I am Grania—hear me roar! I thought, slicing through the water. It was half a mile to Cherry Island from shore, roughly eight hundred meters. That was farther than I'd ever swum the butterfly stroke. Usually I swam butterfly as part of a relay, but it was my best stroke, and my fastest, and I needed every ounce of speed if I was going to reach shore first. I fell into the rhythm of it easily, grateful for the shimmertail, which propelled me faster with each thwack of its flukes than my own size-ten-and-a-half feet ever could.

Too bad Coach Maynard isn't here to clock my time, I thought, as I passed Bud Jefferson's canoe. Hatcher waved his paddle and gave a Texas-size whoop.

"Go, Truly!" shouted Scooter.

I pushed on, sucking down air with each forward arc of my body. Thanks to countless hours spent in countless pools at countless swim team practices, my legs and arms knew exactly what to do. As the shimmertail propelled me up and out of the water again, I glanced quickly over my shoulder. Dr. Appleton's kayak was closing in fast. I couldn't see Calhoun. Had he alerted Aunt True? I hoped so.

Amanda Appleton and I were almost neck and neck by the time we reached the shore. I gave one last flying dolphin leap and flung myself onto the sand. "I claim this island and any treasure it may contain!" I managed to gasp.

If Dr. Appleton heard me, she didn't give any sign of it. She threw her paddle aside, scrambled out of her kayak, and crashed away through the undergrowth without a word to me.

What just happened? I thought as I lay there in the shallows like a beached whale, struggling to catch my breath. I pondered my next move. I desperately needed witnesses to my claim. Otherwise it would be her word against mine, and who would believe a kid like me over someone with a PhD?

I could see the canoe moving steadily toward the island, and I heard the thrum of Camp Lovejoy's ski boat in the distance. Calhoun had come through—help was on the way.

But I couldn't just sit here and wait.

It wouldn't be long before Amanda Appleton found the boulder, and with it, the entrance to the cave. I, however, had one last card to play: The underwater entrance. Dr. Appleton may have overheard us talking about the tunnel, but she didn't know about the underwater entrance yet. If I could find it first and get to the treasure, surely that would be all I needed to stake my claim?

When my heart had stopped racing and my breathing had returned mostly to normal, I pushed out into the water again and dove down, making a slow pass along the shore. I wished that I had my swim goggles. The sun was sinking lower in the sky, and the water was murky. Still, it was obvious there wasn't an opening anywhere.

I surfaced again, feeling frustrated. What was it that Nathaniel Daniel's last will and testament had said? *Where the eagle flies, there lies the prize. Where the eaglet sleeps, harken to the deep.* There was something else, too, though. Something I was forgetting. I racked my brain, trying to remember. Something about courting days, and—wait, that was it!—*the sunrise of our youth.*

I glanced behind me, where the sun was slowly sinking toward the horizon.

I was on the wrong side of the island! I was on the *west* side, and the entrance was on the *east*—the side where the sun rose!

The canoe bearing Hatcher and Scooter and Cha Cha and Jasmine was in clear view now. I waved my arms overhead to attract their attention, then thrust a finger in the air and motioned going over the island, hoping they'd get the message that I was heading to the opposite side.

Without waiting for a response, I slipped beneath the surface and circled the island as quietly as I could. There was no point alerting Dr. Appleton to my plans. When I reached the other side, I looked for the tallest tree, the one with the eagles' nest in it. It wasn't difficult to spot—one of the enormous birds was perched on its edge, watching me. Hopefully he didn't think I was dinner. I did not want to tangle with those talons.

I did another surface dive and this time almost immediately found a spot where the shore fell away into a sharp drop-off. *Bingo!* I thought, swimming down to the tangle of roots and vines at its base. Grabbing a handful, I peered into the murk. If there was an underwater entrance, it was horribly overgrown.

I surfaced again and swished my tail back and forth, sculling my arms and treading water like a mermaid the way Zadie had taught me. I was trying to decide what to do when I heard a loud shriek from the interior of the island: "GOTCHA!"

Dr. Appleton had found the tunnel that led to the cave!

That did it. My Lovejoy competitive genes kicked in with a vengeance. I took a deep breath and dove down again. When I reached the tangle of roots and vines this time, I grabbed them and pulled with all my might. At first they didn't budge, but as I kept pulling and tugging, bit by bit they shifted. Not much, but enough for me to at least poke my head through. I could see that this was definitely the entrance to the cave.

But I could also see that this was definitely too dangerous for me to try and explore by myself.

Unlike last time, I didn't have a headlamp, I didn't have a rope, and, most importantly, I didn't have backup. *Never swim alone*, Sirena had said, and deep down I knew she was right. Thinking about entering the cave on my own reminded me of how I felt about hot sauce—it just wasn't worth the risk.

Still, I consoled myself as I swam to the surface again for more air, Dr. Appleton would be finding the tunnel by the boulder a tight squeeze. And it wasn't like she was going to be able to lower herself into the hole in the ground without help.

That meant the score was even for now. We'd both hit a roadblock, and the deciding factor for who got to explore further was the finders keepers law. My best bet was to wait for the witnesses to arrive and stake my claim again in front of them.

There was still no sign of the boats, though. Had my signal not been clear? Was everyone still on the other side of the island looking for me? I weighed my options. While I was waiting I could at least explore a little more around the *outside* of the cave's entrance, couldn't I? There was no harm in that.

Slipping underwater again, I dove back down to the bottom, then swam back and forth in front of the opening, patting the sand beneath me with both hands. Nothing. All I managed to do was dislodge a layer of leaves and debris.

I decided it was probably okay to poke my head through and take another look, which I did. There wasn't much light to see by, but what there was revealed a whole lot more nothing. Certainly nothing remotely resembling a treasure chest.

This time when I went to pull my head back out, though, my hair caught on one of the roots. I tugged at it impatiently. Still stuck. I twisted and turned, scratching my face in the process, but I couldn't break free.

Stronger measures were called for. Drawing my knees to my chest, I positioned my body as if preparing for a kick turn in the pool. Steeling myself for what I knew was coming, I thrust out with the shimmertail as hard as I could.

The pain was sharp. I'd yanked out what felt like a fistful of hair. I had to press my lips together hard not to cry out, which would only result in me gulping down water.

But my head was free!

Unfortunately, though, now my tail was not.

My flukes were wedged firmly into the tangle of roots. Taking off the shimmertail was out of the question. I didn't have time for that. And I was starting to grow short of air. Sirena had said that she used to be able to hold her breath for almost two minutes, back when she was a professional mermaid. But I was just an amateur, and a slightly panicked one at that.

I flailed around, grabbing for something—anything!—to help me escape. My fingers closed on an object lying nearby in the sand. It was round and flat and heavy. A rock. Clutching it, I hammered away at the roots and at my tail, but to no avail. I was really truly stuck.

I floated there for a moment, exhausted, feeling the downward drag of the heavy shimmertail. I wasn't sure that I had the strength to make it to the surface.

And then a hand appeared in front of me—a pale, skinny hand.

Lucas!

I grabbed him and held on for all I was worth. As he pulled, I mustered all of my remaining strength and yanked, too. Together we finally managed to free my flukes, although not without nearly shredding them.

And then the two of us floated up toward the air and the light and the sun.

EPILOGUE

The water-ski boat was waiting for us when we surfaced. The canoe was tied up behind it. As Artie Olsen and my father pulled me aboard, Bud Jefferson leaned over and plucked Lucas from the water as easily as if he were a fish.

"You had us worried went you went overboard there, son," Bud said, wrapping him up in a big towel and an even bigger bear hug. Lucas didn't resist, I noticed.

"Lucas saved my life!" I blurted, and everyone turned and looked at me.

"What on earth were you thinking, going down there alone?" my father thundered.

"Hatcher and R. J. told us everything," said my mother.

I could tell by the expressions on my parents' faces that I had given them a fright. I could imagine I was a sight to behold, as Grandma G would say, from the scratches on my face and the bald spot on my poor scalp, which was bleeding profusely, to the rips in the flukes on my shimmertail.

I knew they wanted explanations.

But first I had something I needed to say. "I claim this island and any treasure it may contain under the finders keepers law."

"What?" My father stared at me, puzzled.

"The finders keepers law," said Aunt True, throwing a towel around me. "It's a treasure hunter thing."

As if on cue, Amanda Appleton came crashing through the undergrowth just then, emerging breathless but triumphant. Cupping her hands around her mouth, she shouted, "I claim this island and any treasure it may contain under the finders keepers law!"

"Too late," Aunt True called back. "May the best man—or in this case, woman"—she pointed to me—"win, remember? She already claimed it! In front of"—she did a quick head count—"ten witnesses!"

We left Dr. Appleton standing there, open-mouthed, and headed back to shore.

"Hey, what's that?" asked Cha Cha. She pointed to my white-knuckled fist, pressed tight against my clamshell bra.

I was still clutching the rock I'd found at the bottom of the lake. "Just a rock," I told her, unclenching my fingers to reveal—something that wasn't a rock at all!

Everyone on the boat turned and looked at my outstretched palm. On it, a big, heavy coin caught the last rays of the setting sun, glinting a warm gold.

. . .

Later, while my parents took me to get my scalp stitched up, Aunt True and Professor Rusty and Bud Jefferson took the coin back to Bud's shop, where Bud did a little research. It turned out I'd found not just any gold coin, but the unicorn of gold coins: an incredibly rare 1703 Queen Anne "Vigo" five guinea piece. Only twenty of them had been minted from gold the British seized in 1702 from treasure ships in Vigo Bay off northern Spain, and of those twenty, only fifteen had been known to survive—sixteen now—and only six had come up for sale in the last half a century.

"I don't want to get your hopes up," Bud told my parents. "But the last one that was auctioned sold for—well, a lot."

Our ancestor's shady past quickly became big news in Pumpkin Falls—and far beyond. DANDY DAN, THE PIRATE MAN! blared the *Pumpkin Falls Patriot-Bugle*'s lame front-page headline. Janet's article accompanying it was good, though, and so were her photos of the coin and of Nathaniel Daniel's portrait. The Pumpkin Falls Private Eyes got star treatment too, with a whole sidebar of our own. We were rapidly becoming hometown celebrities.

The Lovejoy College history department mounted an official exploration of the cave, hiring professional divers and an underwater camera crew. It turned out the coin I'd found was the last of the treasure. There was little else left, just a coil of rope and a few pieces of wood that proved something had been there. Still, it was enough to create plenty of excitement for historians, including Professor Rusty, who had plans to write a book about Nathaniel Daniel. He already had the title for it—*Dandy Dan: The Pirate of Pumpkin Falls.*

After the exploration crew finished, a metal gate was placed across both the underwater entrance to the cave and the one by the boulder, and there were NO TRESPASSING signs on Cherry Island now. The sheriff didn't want anyone else getting hurt.

It was Professor Rusty who solved the mystery of the vanished treasure. The clue was in Prudence Lovejoy's last will and testament, which none of us had thought to look at. She'd left her husband's gold eagle ring to their son, Obadiah, but there was nothing about "the sunrise of our youth" or "where the eagle flies, there lies the prize." It was just a bequest, plain and simple.

A little more digging revealed that Prudence had been just as civic-minded as her buccaneer husband. With the money that he'd left her, she'd helped found the town's hospital, the library, the first school, and even the Grange. She did it quietly, though, and didn't paste her name all over everything.

"It was like she wanted to give it all away," Rusty told us all at dinner one night.

"She probably did," said Aunt True. "They were ill-gotten gains, after all, and she must have known it. And I hope whatever was left when she was done funded a comfortable retirement."

"Except she missed one coin," I added.

Marketing genius that she was, my aunt made hay with that single gold coin, putting it on display at the bookshop "FOR ONE NIGHT ONLY!" She hired Officer Tanglewood to work security for us after his daytime shift, and she rented a pirate costume for my father to wear. He was used to her schemes by now, and gamely put on an eye patch and a bandana and his Captain Hook prosthetic arm and stood around saying "aaargh!" a lot and scowling at anyone who got too close to the glass case with my five guinea piece in it.

The customers loved it. They couldn't get enough of the fake gold coins that Aunt True had specially made for the event, and they scooped up the Terminator hot sauce with its skull and crossbones label, and all the pirate and mermaid books we put out on display.

Miss Marple got to wear a bandana and an eye patch too, and Aunt True had her "conduct" an interview with me for our online newsletter, which proved hugely popular and got picked up by news media around the world. So did Carson Dawson's segment with me on *Hello, Boston!*

Yes, I was on TV again, only this time not in my shimmertail. Bud and Elmer had managed to repair most of the tears in it, but I politely declined Mr. Dawson's request that I show it off. I did, however, recount my adventure as vividly as I could, and I squeezed in mentions of both our bookshop and *The Pirates of Penzance*. Aunt True—and Augustus Wilde—had taught me well.

All the publicity helped sell out our performances at the Grange and brought a flood of tourists to Pumpkin Falls, which made Ella Bellow and all the other businesses in town happy. Aunt True brainstormed with Bud Jefferson and helped him set up a display of "pirate treasure"—pieces of eight, and a gold doubloon, and whatever else he had that looked vaguely piratical. His sales were brisk too.

Bud and Lucas's mother still hadn't set a date yet, but odds on the General Store porch were running in favor of a Christmas wedding. Lucas wasn't exactly enthusiastic about the prospect, but he was spending more time with Bud these days, and the two of them had even gone fishing.

And there was a third proposal that summer too—right in our bookshop! Augustus Wilde swanned in on a scorcher of a day in August—"my namesake month!" he announced to no one in particular—practically hidden behind an armload of purple roses. Getting down on one creaky knee wasn't easy for him, but he managed. His proposal was appropriately flowery, and he even worked in the title of his latest book, *Forever Mine*, the one he'd been working on during our play rehearsals. Belinda nodded shyly, took his flowers, and gave him a kitten in return. Augustus quietly slipped it into his backpack when she wasn't looking.

"We're planning to elope," Belinda confided later to Aunt True and me. "Too old for all that wedding stuff."

Thanks to a literal boatload of witnesses, my claim to the treasure held up in court under the finders keepers law. We were worried that maybe Amanda Appleton would try to contest it, but she didn't.

"Wisely so," my aunt said. "You don't mess with tall timber."

What Dr. Appleton did do was cash in on the publicity gold. She gave interviews that painted her own role in discovering Dandy Dan's secret as much larger than it actually had been, which sent *Saga of a Ship* skyrocketing to the top of the best-seller list.

I didn't mind, though. After all, without her book, I would never have heard of Dandy Dan. And her media blitz ended up benefiting us, too. The auction house estimated that my coin could fetch a sale price of more than a million dollars, thanks to all the hoopla in the press.

Which it did.

Even more boggling was the fact that the money was technically mine.

"You found it, Truly," my father told me. "It's yours. The best woman won, fair and square."

That was nonsense, of course. It was Lovejoy gold to begin with, and it would remain Lovejoy gold. My family would never have to worry about money again. Inspired by

Prudence Lovejoy's generosity—and Nathaniel-Daniel-looks-like-a-spaniel's, too—I did have a few requests, though. I talked it over with my parents, and they agreed that Cha Cha and Jasmine and Calhoun and Scooter and Lucas should each get a share for their help in unraveling the mystery. It would go into their college funds, which thrilled their parents. And I insisted on sending a check to Delphine as a thank-you for the shimmertail, and to Sirena as a thank-you for teaching me how to swim in it. They were both surprised and delighted by this gesture.

Finally, I also secretly funded the restoration of the Pumpkin Falls Grange. I knew Prudence would be pleased, since she'd founded it, and I wanted to do something "civick-minded" to honor her. Our town's history was important, and it was worth preserving. Ella Bellow could be a pain, but she was right about that. She probably guessed who was behind the donation, as I noticed that she was being nicer than usual to my family and me, but for once she didn't say anything.

As for *The Pirates of Penzance*, it was a big success. There was one final surprise on opening night, though. When the curtain went up and the overture started, the audience applauded at the sight of the Rockin' Mermaid Malt Shop, which the stage crew had stayed up late the night before finishing. My family and friends cheered as I was rolled onstage on top of the diner's counter. I hammed it up, leaning back on my elbows and waving my flukes in the air the way Zadie and

Lenore had taught me and smiling a big Esther Williams smile. I knew the set looked great, from the black and white floor and fake tile to the shiny red vinyl on the stools and booths to the jukebox, vintage Coca Cola machine, and shelves filled with sundae dishes, milkshake glasses, and—

"Hey!" blurted Lucas. "Isn't that the missing trophy?"

Elmer Farnsworth had had it all along! He'd picked up the paper bag containing the silver pumpkin on race day, thinking it was junk, and stuck it in his truck, then got distracted and forgot about it. The bag wound up in one of the bins in his barn, and he'd gathered it up along with a bunch of other stuff while looking for props for our set. It was after midnight when he'd put it on the shelf next to the vintage toaster, and he was tired and hadn't been paying attention.

Thelma Farnsworth's face had flushed with embarrassment. "Can't you tell the difference between trash and treasure, Elmer? And don't tell me you didn't hear all the fuss about the trophy being missing!"

"ALL THE FUSS ABOUT KISSING?" shouted Elmer, looking perplexed.

Calhoun and I exchanged a smile at that. We still hadn't had the opportunity for our first kiss. We would, though. I was pretty sure of that.

Things were a whole lot quieter on the porch of the General Store after Thelma insisted that Elmer get hearing aids. Meanwhile, the trophy was delivered to the window of the Starlite Dance Studio, where it would stay on display until next Fourth of July.

My mother followed through on her promise of a mother-daughter day all to ourselves. Shortly before summer camp ended and my sisters were due to return home, she whisked me away on a surprise overnight trip to Boston. We stayed in a hotel overlooking the Public Garden, and we took a ride on the swan boats and went to tea at the Boston Public Library in Copley Square and got manicures and pedicures and facials—which I didn't think I'd like, but which I did, a lot—and we saw a movie and ordered room service and went shopping for new clothes.

"A girl can't start eighth grade without a new wardrobe, Little O," she told me.

Eighth grade! I still couldn't believe it. Only one more year until high school!

There was so much change ahead.

The biggest change of all was the wedding that our family had to look forward to. Aunt True asked me to be her chief bridesmaid, "because tall timber sticks together." Lauren was going to be a bridesmaid too, and Pippa couldn't wait to be the flower girl. My mother would be the matron of honor, and Miss Marple was going to be the ring bearer. Gramps and Lola would be coming home for the wedding too.

The date had been set for October, when all of New Hampshire's hills would be covered in a blaze of glory, as my aunt described it. Autumn was her favorite time of year.

And just like the seasons kept changing in Pumpkin Falls, things would keep changing for me, too. I understood that now. Because life was about change, just like Aunt True had said. There were surprises around every corner.

And that was really truly fine with me.

BLUEBERRY DONUT MUFFINS

1/3 c. vegetable oil

1/2 c. sugar

1 egg

1/2 c. milk

1-1/2 c. flour

2 tsp. baking powder

1/2 tsp. salt

1/4 tsp. nutmeg

1 c. fresh blueberries

Topping:

1/2 c. butter, melted

1/2 c. sugar

1-1/2 tsp. cinnamon

- Preheat oven to 400 degrees. Grease a muffin tin or line with paper cups.
- Cream oil, sugar, and egg. Mix dry ingredients together and add to creamed mixture alternately with milk. Gently fold in blueberries.
- Spoon batter into greased muffin tin and bake 20-25 minutes. Remove muffins immediately from pan, roll in melted butter, then in cinnamon-sugar mixture. Enjoy!

MISS MARPLE'S PICKS

Eloise by Kay Thompson and Hilary Knight
The Little Mermaid by Hans Christian Andersen
The Mermaid by Jan Brett
The Mermaid Handbook by Carolyn Turgeon
The Pirate Queen by Emily Arnold McCully
The Pirates of Penzance by W. S. Gilbert and Arthur Sullivan
The Tail of Emily Windsnap by Liz Kessler
Understood Betsy by Dorothy Canfield Fisher